00 Classics Arrange

o

The Most-Beloved Masterpieces from Piano, Orchestral and Operatic Literature

About This Collection

The 100 pieces in this piano collection have been favorites of music lovers throughout the years. Chosen from the four stylistic periods of piano, orchestral, and operatic literature, each selection has been carefully arranged for intermediate-level pianists. For performance ease, editorial markings such as phrasing, expression marks, and dynamics have been added. Within the collection, the pieces appear in alphabetical order according to the composer's last name. The music will provide hours of enjoyment for pianists of all ages.

Alfred Music Publishing Co., Inc.
P.O. Box 10003
Van Nuys, CA 91410-0003
alfred.com

ISBN-10: 0-7390-6945-4
ISBN-13: 978-0-7390-6945-5

Cover Photos
Piano: © Shutterstock.com / dionis • Rug: © Planet Art

2

Contents by Composer

Bach, Johann Sebastian

Air on the G String 6

Ave Maria. 130

Brandenburg Concerto No. 3 12

Brandenburg Concerto No. 4 14

Cello Suite No. 1 16

Jesu, Joy of Man's Desiring 20

Sheep May Safely Graze 22

Toccata in D Minor 25

Beethoven, Ludwig van

"Moonlight" Sonata 30

Ode to Joy 34

Egmont Overture 38

"Emperor" Concerto 41

"Pathétique" Sonata 42

Rage over a Lost Penny 46

Symphony No. 5 48

Turkish March 52

Bizet, Georges

Habañera 56

L'Arlésienne Suite No. 1 59

March of the Toreadors 62

Toreador Song 64

Borodin, Alexander

Polovetsian Dance 69

Brahms, Johannes

Hungarian Dance No. 5 72

Waltz, Op. 39, No. 15 74

Chopin, Frédéric

Ballade No. 1 in G Minor 77

Etude, Op. 10, No. 3 80

Fantaisie-Impromptu 82

Nocturne, Op. 55, No. 1 86

"Revolutionary" Etude 90

Funeral March. 93

"Raindrop" Prelude 96

Prelude, Op. 28, No. 4 98

"Military" Polonaise. 100

"Minute" Waltz 103

Clarke, Jeremiah

Prince of Denmark's March. 110

Debussy, Claude

Clair de lune 112

Granados, Enrique

Andaluza No. 5 115

Delibes, Léo

Flower Duet. 118

Dukas, Paul

The Sorcerer's Apprentice. 122

Dvořak, Antonín

"New World" Symphony 124

Elgar, Edward

Pomp and Circumstance. 126

Fauré, Gabriel

Pavane 128

Gounod, Charles

Ave Maria. 130

Funeral March of a Marionette. 134

Grieg, Edvard

In the Hall of the Mountain King. . . . 137

Morning Mood 140

Handel, George Frideric

Hallelujah Chorus 143

Hornpipe 146

Joplin, Scott

Solace. 149

The Easy Winners 154

The Entertainer 160

Maple Leaf Rag. 166

Haydn, Franz Joseph

"Surprise" Symphony 172

Lehár, Franz

"Merry Widow" Waltz. 174

Mascagni, Pietro
Intermezzo (Cavalleria rusticana) . . . 176

Massenet, Jules
Meditation (Thaïs) 180

Mendelssohn, Felix
Wedding March
(A Midsummer Night's Dream) . . . 184

Mouret, Jean-Joseph
Rondeau (Suite de symphonies) 186

Mozart, Wolfgang Amadeus
Eine kleine Nachtmusik 189
Variations on
"Ah, vous dirai-je, Maman" 194
The Birdcatcher's Song 198
"Elvira Madigan" Concerto 200
Là ci darem la mano 204
Laudate Dominum 207
Overture from
"The Marriage of Figaro" 210
Queen of the Night Aria 213
Rondo alla Turca 218
Piano Sonata in C Major, K. 545 . . . 224
Symphony No. 40 228
Voi, che sapete 234
Piano Sonata in A Major, K. 331 . . . 238

Offenbach, Jacques
Barcarolle (Tales of Hoffman) 241
Can-Can 246

Pachelbel, Johann
Canon in D 252

Puccini, Giacomo
Doretta's Song 249
Musetta's Waltz 256
O mio babbino caro 260
Un bel dì 264

Schubert, Franz
Ständchen (Serenade) 269
"Unfinished" Symphony 272

Saint-Saëns, Camille
The Swan 274

Strauss, Jr., Johann
The Blue Danube 278

Smetana, Bedřich
The Moldau 282

Tchaikovsky, Peter Ilyich
The Garland Waltz
(Sleeping Beauty) 285
The Nutcracker Suite
Miniature Overture 290
March 294
Dance of the Sugarplum Fairy . . . 298
Russian Dance (Trépak) 302
Arabian Dance 306
Chinese Dance 309
Dance of the Reed Flutes 312
Waltz of the Flowers 316
Piano Concerto No. 1 325
Act I Finale (Swan Lake) 328
1812 Overture 331

Verdi, Giuseppe
Anvil Chorus 334
La donna è mobile 337
Libiamo (La Traviata) 340

Vivaldi, Antonio
Gloria 344
Mandolin Concerto in C Major 348
Spring (The Four Seasons) 352

Wagner, Richard
Bridal Chorus (Lohengrin) 355

Contents by Title (alphabetically)

1812 Overture, Peter Ilyich Tchaikovsky 331

Air on the G String, Johann Sebastian Bach 6

Andaluza No. 5, Enrique Granados 115

Anvil Chorus, Giuseppe Verdi 334

Arabian Dance (from "The Nutcracker")
Peter Ilyich Tchaikovsky 306

Ave Maria, Johann Sebastian Bach—
Charles Gounod 130

Ballade No. 1 in G Minor
Frédéric Chopin 77

Barcarolle (Tales of Hoffman)
Jacques Offenbach 241

Birdcatcher's Song, The
Wolfgang Amadeus Mozart 198

Blue Danube, The, Johann Strauss, Jr. 278

Brandenburg Concerto No. 3
Johann Sebastian Bach 12

Brandenburg Concerto No. 4
Johann Sebastian Bach 14

Bridal Chorus (Lohengrin), Richard Wagner . . . 355

Can-Can, Jacques Offenbach 246

Canon in D, Johann Pachelbel 252

Cello Suite No. 1
Johann Sebastian Bach 16

Chinese Dance (from "The Nutcracker")
Peter Ilyich Tchaikovsky 309

Clair de lune, Claude Debussy 112

Dance of the Reed Flutes (from "The Nutcracker")
Peter Ilyich Tchaikovsky 312

Dance of the Sugarplum Fairy (from "The
Nutcracker"), Peter Ilyich Tchaikovsky 298

Doretta's Song, Giacomo Puccini 249

Easy Winners, The, Scott Joplin 154

Entertainer, The, Scott Joplin 160

Egmont Overture
Ludwig van Beethoven 38

Eine kleine Nachtmusik
Wolfgang Amadeus Mozart 189

"Elvira Madigan"
Wolfgang Amadeus Mozart 200

"Emperor" Concerto
Ludwig van Beethoven 41

Etude, Op. 10, No. 3
Frédéric Chopin 80

Fantaisie-Impromptu
Frédéric Chopin 82

Flower Duet, Léo Delibes 118

Funeral March
Frédéric Chopin 93

Funeral March of a Marionette
Charles Gounod 134

Garland Waltz, The
Peter Ilyich Tchaikovsky 285

Gloria, Antonio Vivaldi 344

Habañera, Georges Bizet 56

Hallelujah Chorus
George Frideric Handel 143

Hornpipe, George Frideric Handel 146

Hungarian Dance No. 5, Johannes Brahms 72

Intermezzo, Pietro Mascagni 176

In the Hall of the Mountain King
Edvard Grieg 137

Jesu, Joy of Man's Desiring
Johann Sebastian Bach 20

L'Arlésienne Suite No. 1
Georges Bizet 59

Là ci darem la mano
Wolfgang Amadeus Mozart 204

La donna è mobile, Giuseppe Verdi 337

Laudate Dominum
Wolfgang Amadeus Mozart 207

Libiamo (La Traviata), Giuseppe Verdi 340

Mandolin Concerto in C Major
Antonio Vivaldi 348

Maple Leaf Rag, Scott Joplin 166

March (from "The Nutcracker")
Peter Ilyich Tchaikovsky 294

March of the Toreadors, Georges Bizet 62

Marriage of Figaro, The (Overture)
Wolfgang Amadeus Mozart 210

Meditation (Thaïs), Jules Massenet 180

"Merry Widow" Waltz, Franz Lehár 174

"Military" Polonaise
Frédéric Chopin 100

Miniature Overture (from "The Nutcracker")
Peter Ilyich Tchaikovsky 290

"Minute" Waltz
Frédéric Chopin 103

Moldau, The, Bedřich Smetana 282

"Moonlight" Sonata, Ludwig van Beethoven 30

Morning Mood, Edvard Grieg 140

Musetta's Waltz, Giacomo Puccini 256

"New World" Symphony, Antonín Dvořak 124

Nocturne, Op. 55, No. 1
Frédéric Chopin 86

Ode to Joy, Ludwig van Beethoven 34

O mio babbino caro, Giacomo Puccini 260

"Pathétique" Sonata
Ludwig van Beethoven. 42

Pavane, Gabriel Fauré 128

Piano Concerto No. 1
Peter Ilyich Tchaikovsky 325

Piano Sonata in A Major, K. 331
Wolfgang Amadeus Mozart 238

Piano Sonata in C Major, K. 545
Wolfgang Amadeus Mozart 224

Polovetsian Dance, Alexander Borodin 69

Pomp and Circumstance, Edward Elgar 126

Prelude, Op. 28, No. 4, Frédéric Chopin 98

Prince of Denmark's March
Jeremiah Clarke 110

Queen of the Night Aria
Wolfgang Amadeus Mozart 213

Rage over a Lost Penny, Ludwig van Beethoven. . 46

"Raindrop" Prelude
Frédéric Chopin 96

"Revolutionary" Etude
Frédéric Chopin 90

Rondeau (Suite de symphonies),
Jean-Joseph Mouret 186

Rondo alla Turca
Wolfgang Amadeus Mozart 218

Russian Dance (Trépak) (from "The Nutcracker")
Peter Ilyich Tchaikovsky 302

Sheep May Safely Graze
Johann Sebastian Bach. 22

Solace, Scott Joplin 149

Sorcerer's Apprentice, The, Paul Dukas 122

Spring (from "The Four Seasons")
Antonio Vivaldi 352

Ständchen (Serenade), Franz Schubert 269

"Surprise" Symphony, Franz Joseph Haydn . . . 172

Swan, The, Camille Saint-Saëns 274

Swan Lake (Act I Finale),
Peter Ilyich Tchaikovsky 328

Symphony No. 5
Ludwig van Beethoven. 48

Symphony No. 40
Wolfgang Amadeus Mozart 228

Toccata in D Minor
Johann Sebastian Bach. 25

Toreador Song, Georges Bizet 64

Turkish March, Ludwig van Beethoven. 52

Un bel dì, Giacomo Puccini 264

"Unfinished" Symphony, Franz Schubert. 272

Variations on "Ah, vous dirai-je, Maman"
Wolfgang Amadeus Mozart 194

Voi, che sapete
Wolfgang Amadeus Mozart 234

Waltz, Op. 39, No. 15, Johannes Brahms. 74

Waltz of the Flowers (from "The Nutcracker")
Peter Ilyich Tchaikovsky 316

Wedding March (A Midsummer Night's Dream),
Felix Mendelssohn 184

Air on the G String

(from *Orchestral Suite No. 3 in D Major*)

Johann Sebastian Bach (1685–1750)
BWV 1068
Arranged by Jerry Ray

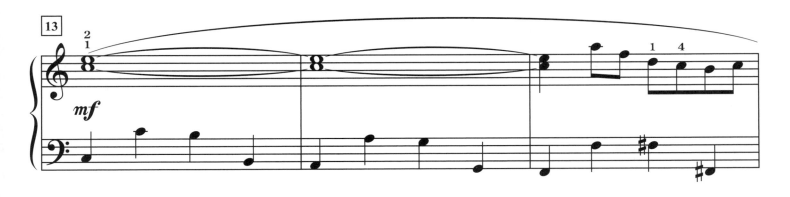

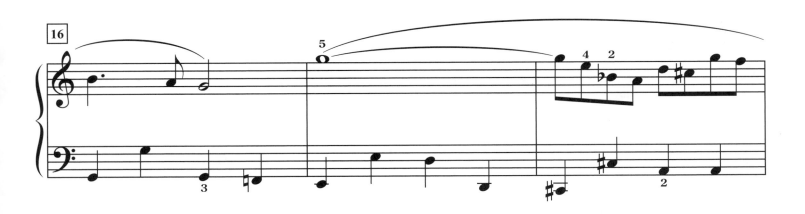

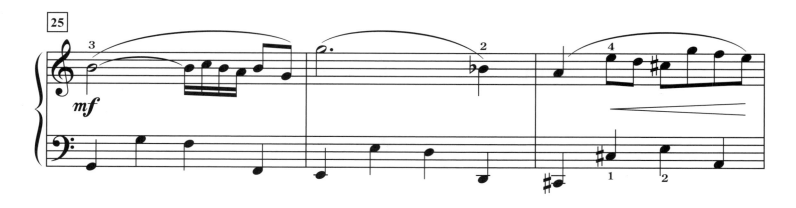

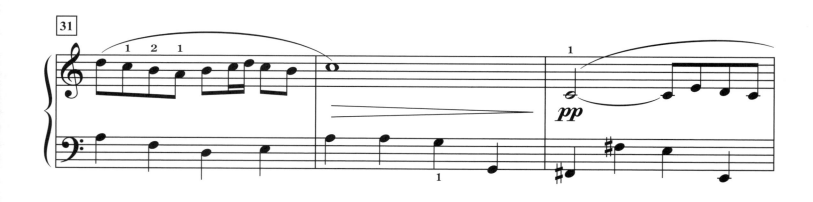

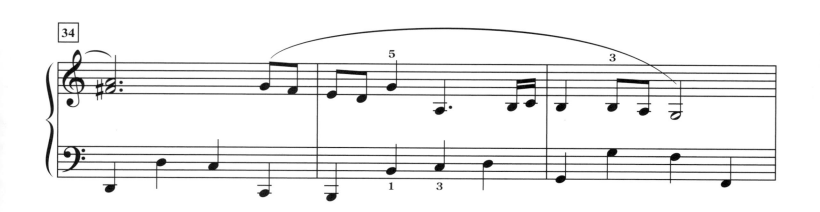

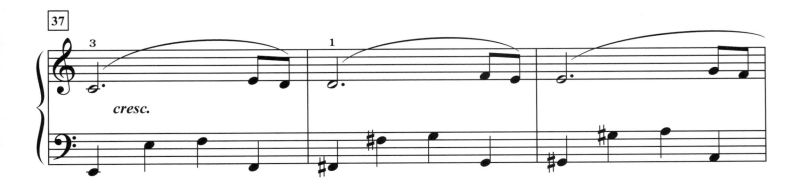

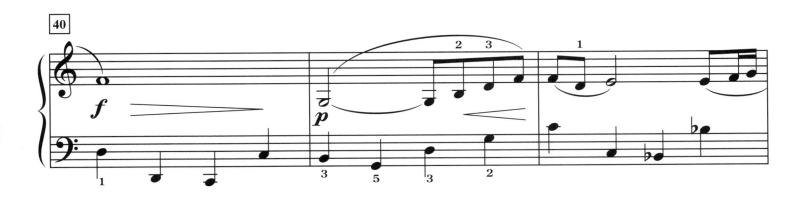

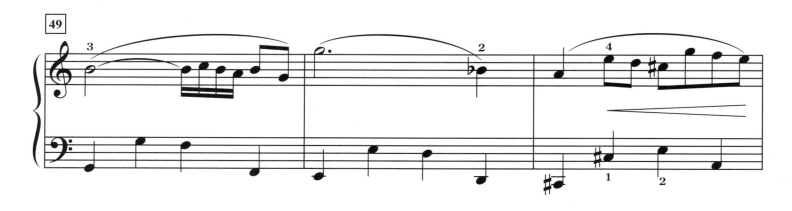

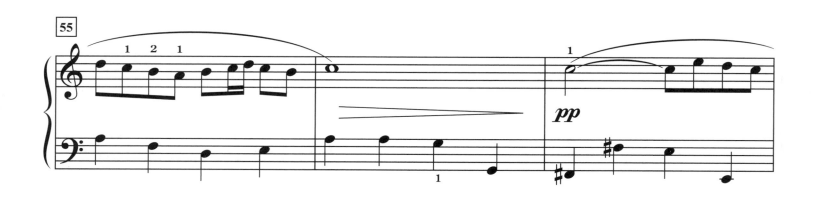

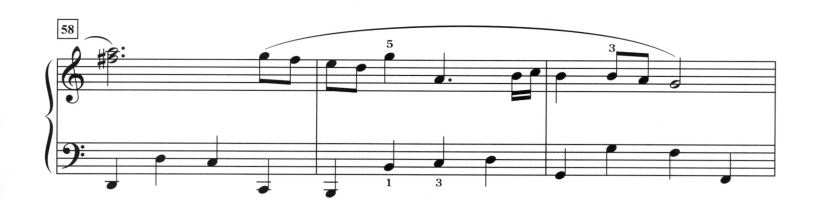

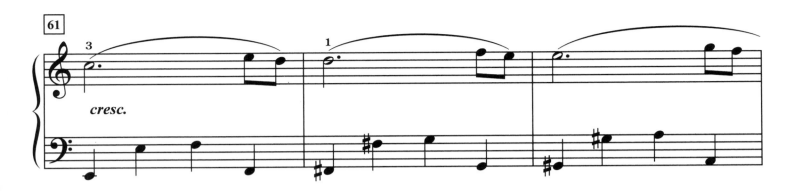

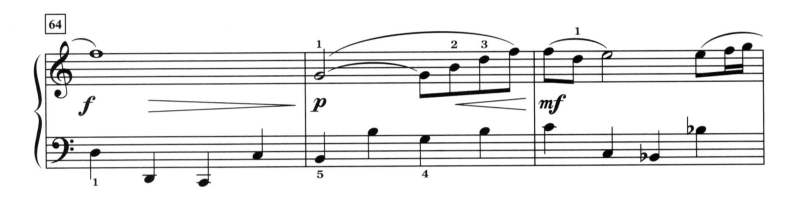

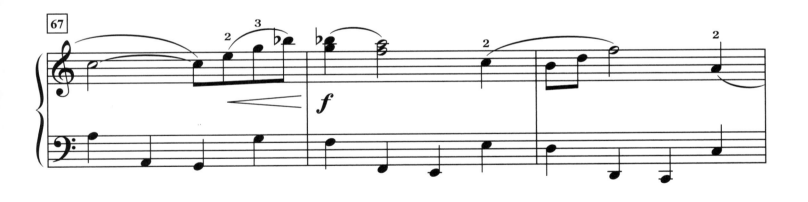

Brandenburg Concerto No. 3 in G Major

(First Movement)

Johann Sebastian Bach (1685–1750)
BWV 1048
Arranged by Bruce Nelson

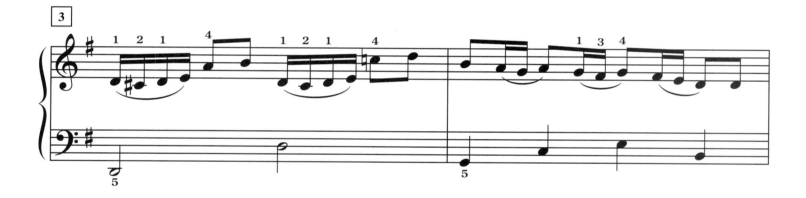

Brandenburg Concerto No. 4 in G Major

(First Movement)

Johann Sebastian Bach (1685–1750)
BWV 1049
Arranged by Jerry Ray

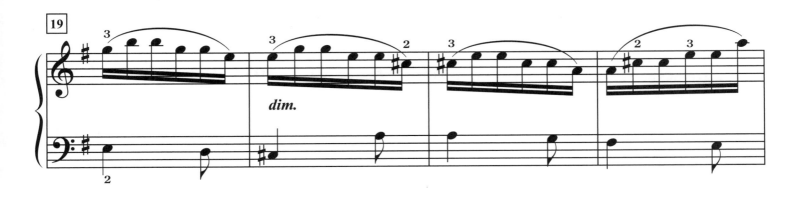

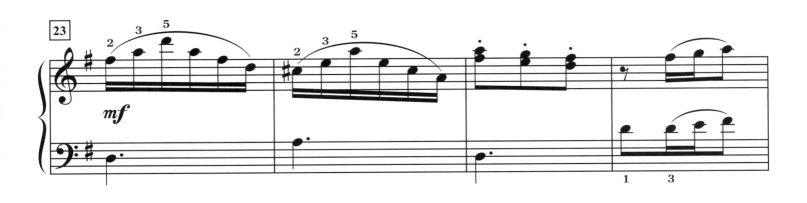

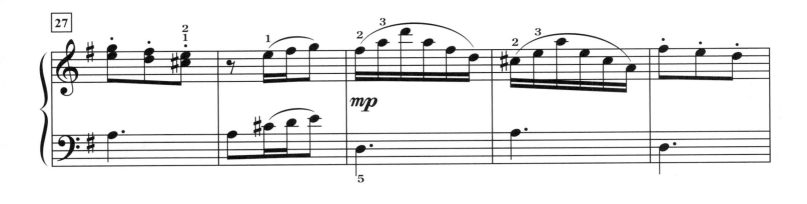

Cello Suite No. 1 in G Major

(Prelude)

Johann Sebastian Bach (1685–1750)
BWV 1007
Arranged by Bruce Nelson

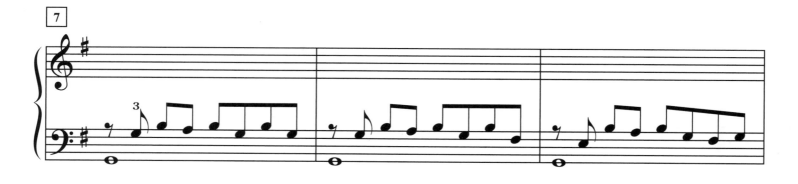

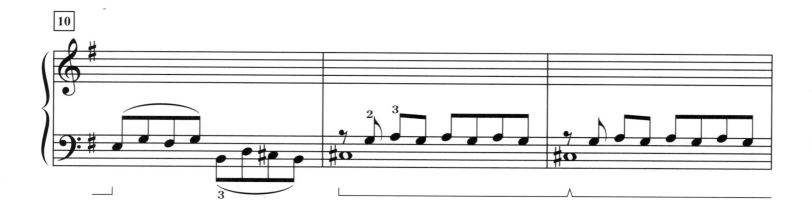

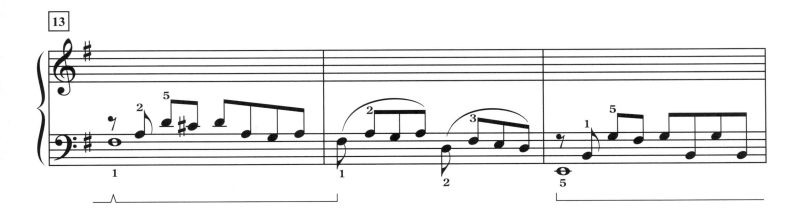

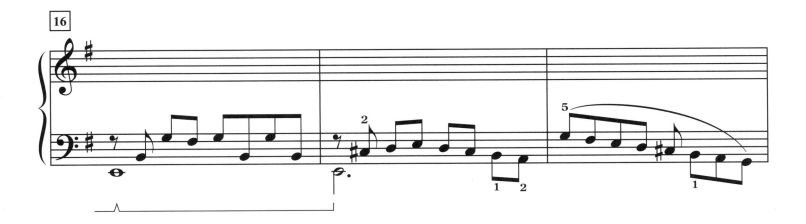

Jesu, Joy of Man's Desiring

Johann Sebastian Bach (1685–1750)
BWV 147
Arranged by Bruce Nelson

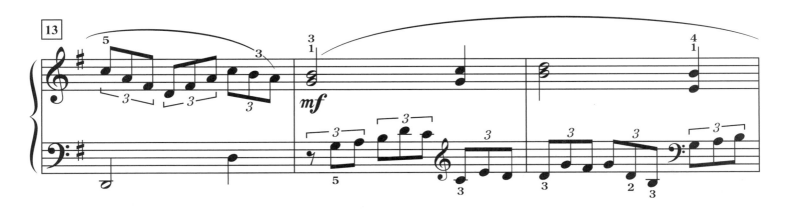

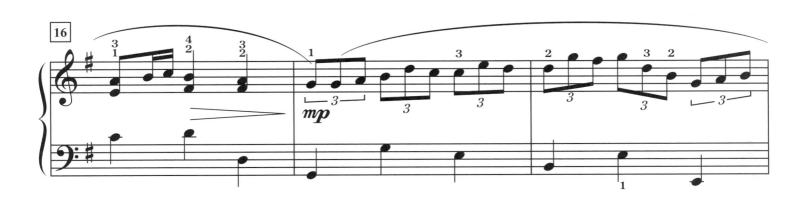

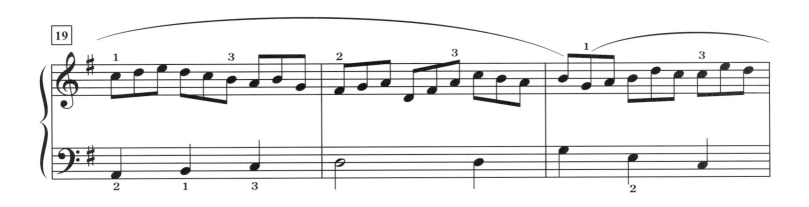

Sheep May Safely Graze

Johann Sebastian Bach (1685–1750)
BWV 208
Arranged by Bruce Nelson

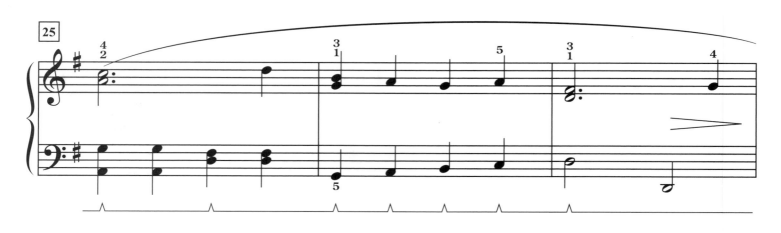

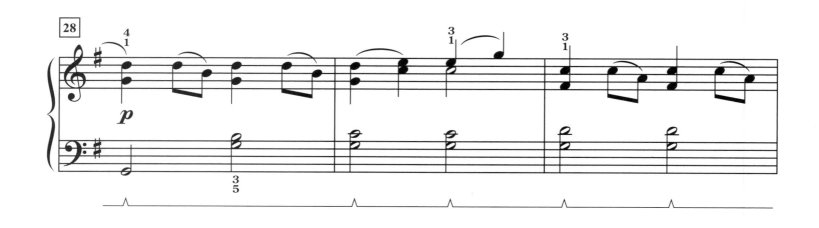

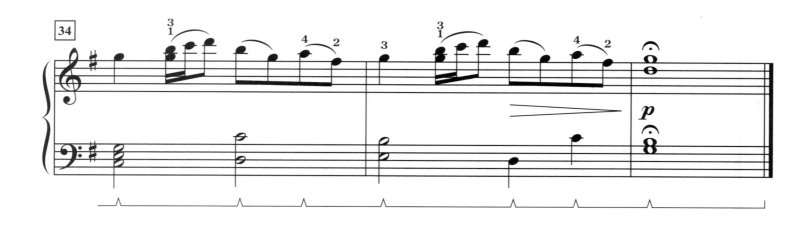

Toccata in D Minor

Johann Sebastian Bach (1685–1750)
BWV 565
Arranged by Bruce Nelson

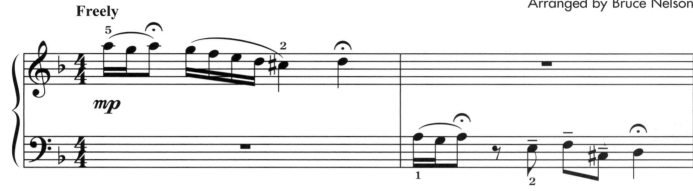

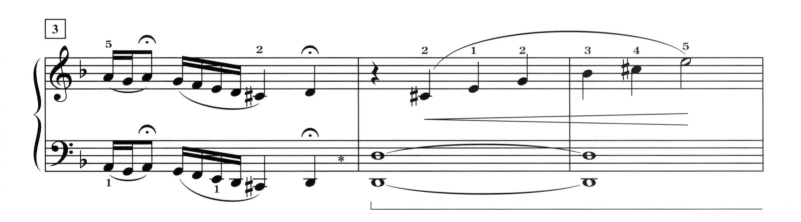

* The octaves in measures 4–7 may be played one octave lower.

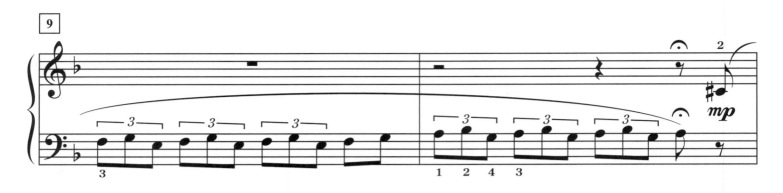

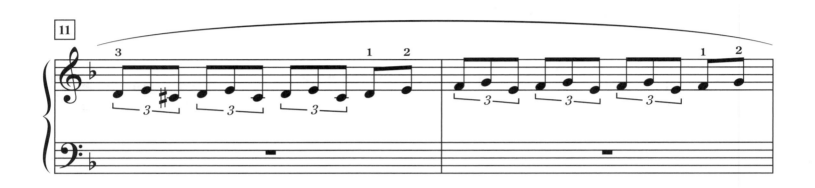

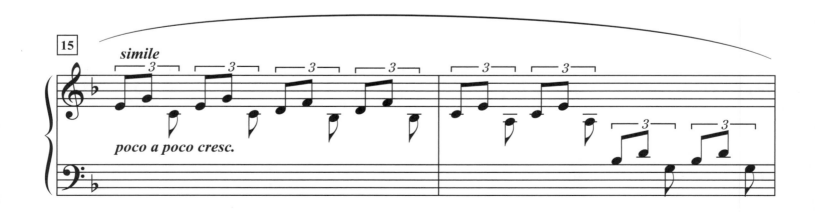

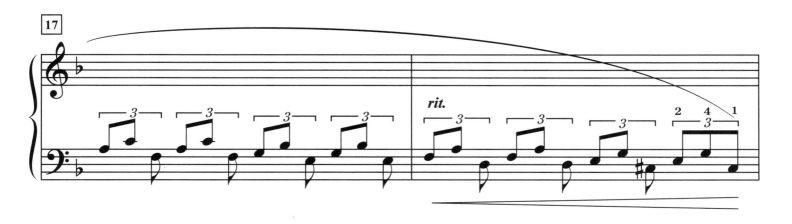

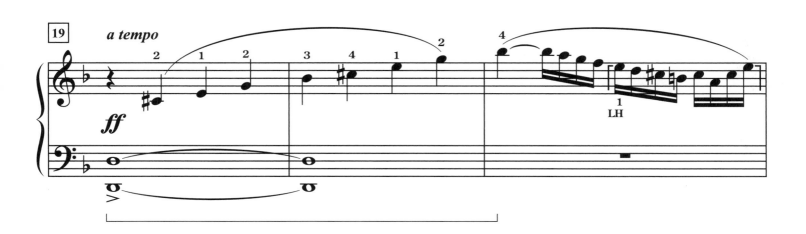

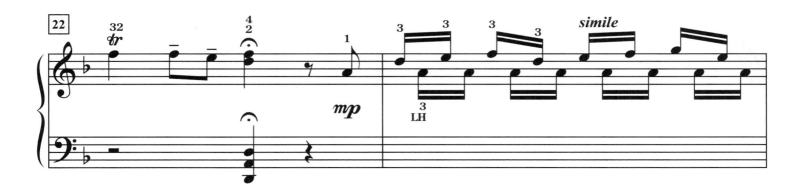

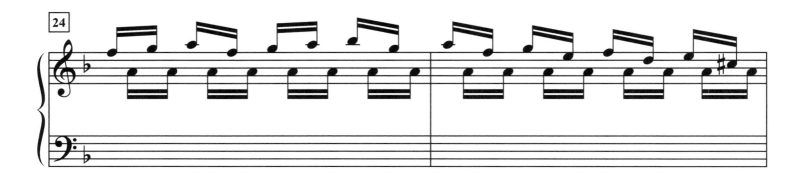

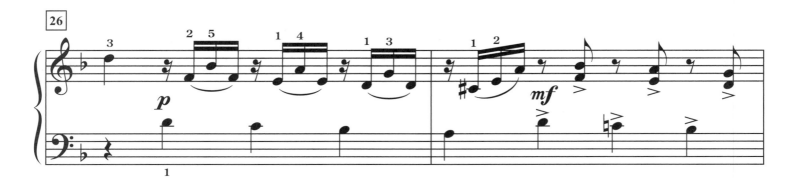

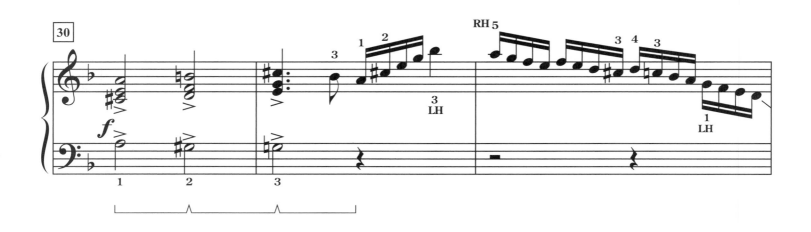

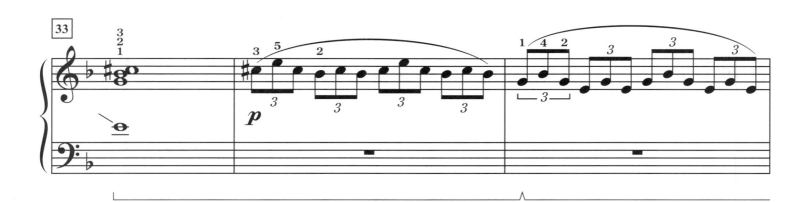

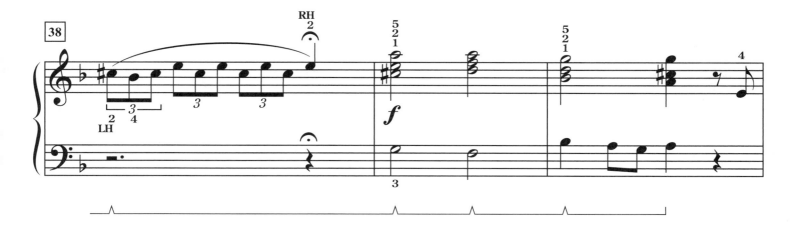

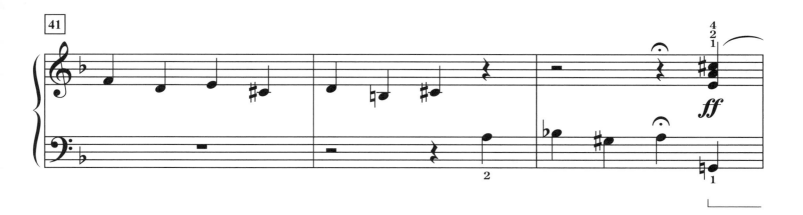

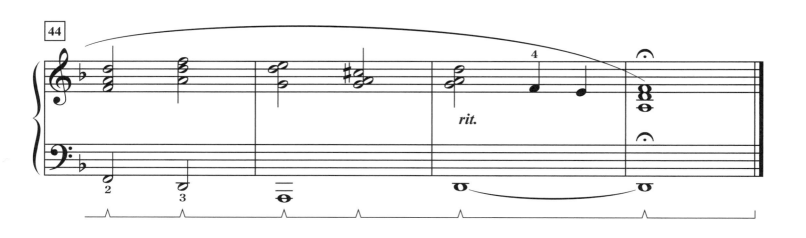

Piano Sonata No. 14 in C-sharp Minor—Moonlight

(First Movement)

Ludwig van Beethoven (1770–1827)
Op. 27, No. 2
Arranged by Mary K. Sallee

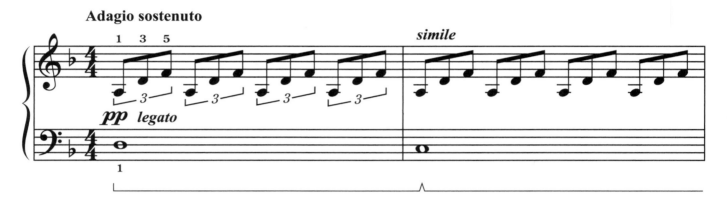

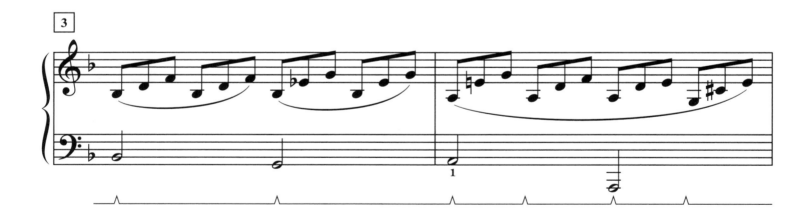

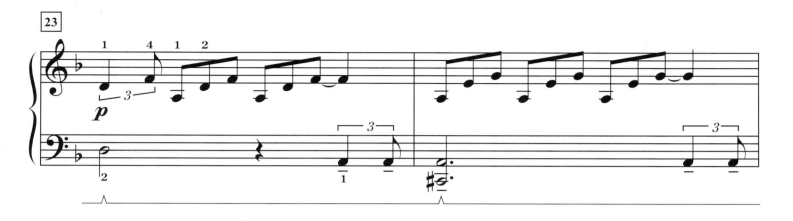

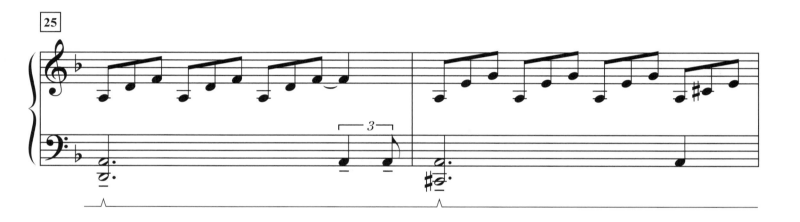

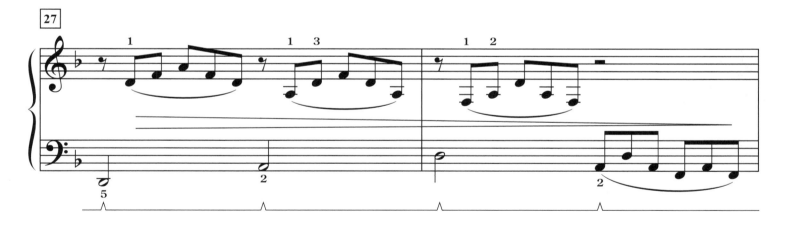

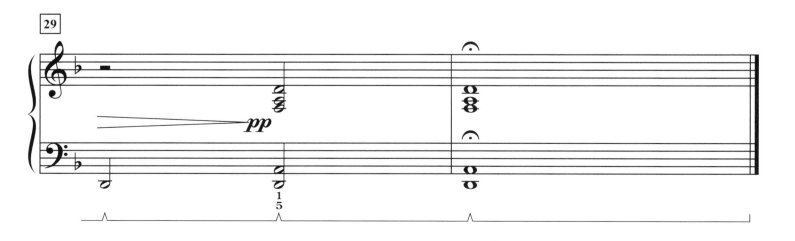

Symphony No. 9 in D Minor—Ode to Joy

(Fourth Movement)

Ludwig van Beethoven (1770–1827)
Op. 125
Arranged by Mary K. Sallee

Allegro

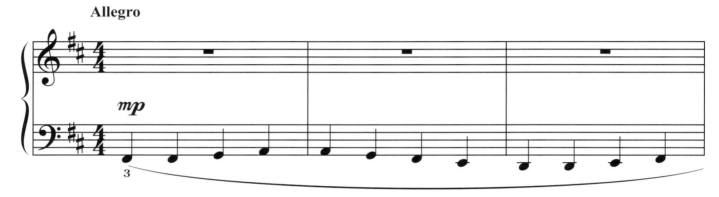

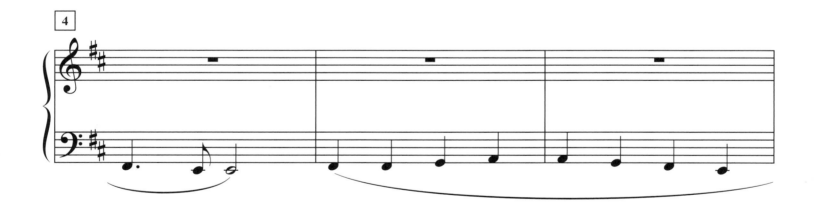

ⓐ The RH in m. 17 (and similarly in mm. 25–27, and 38) may be played:

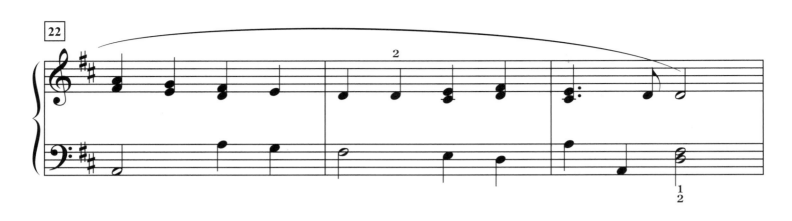

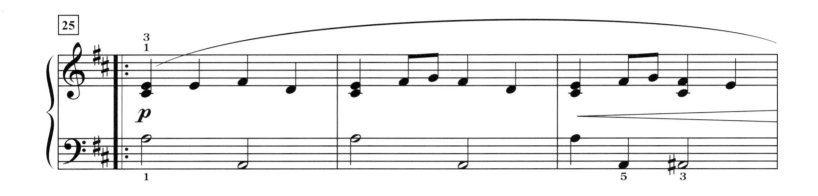

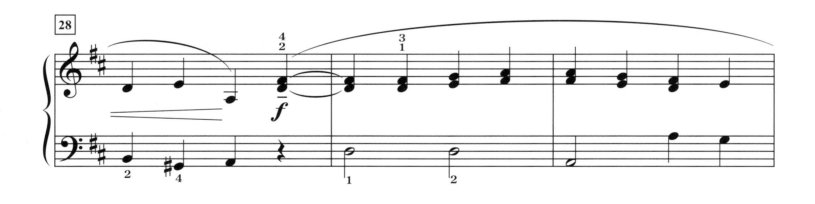

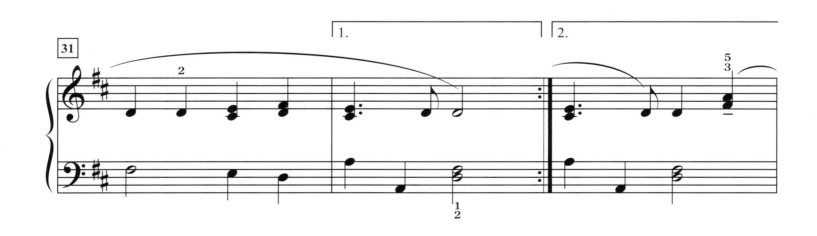

Egmont Overture

Ludwig van Beethoven (1770–1827)
Op. 84
Arranged by Jerry Ray

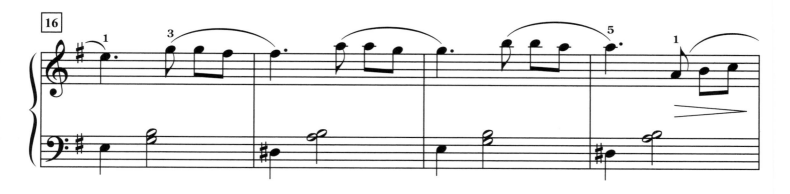

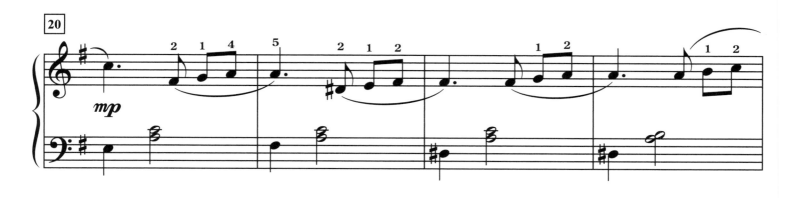

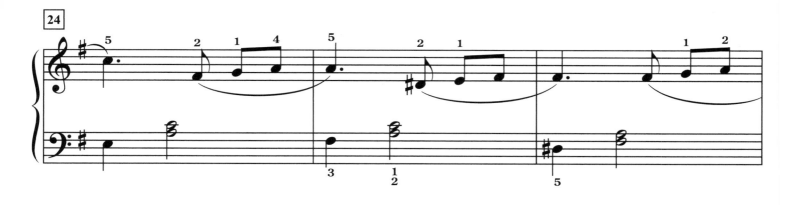

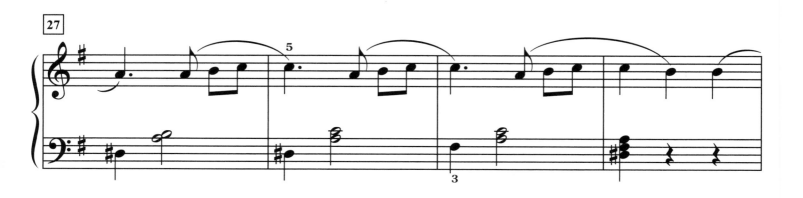

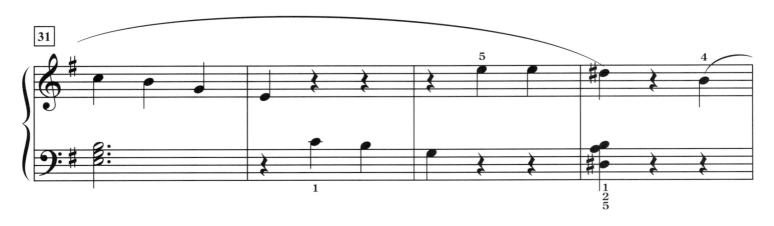

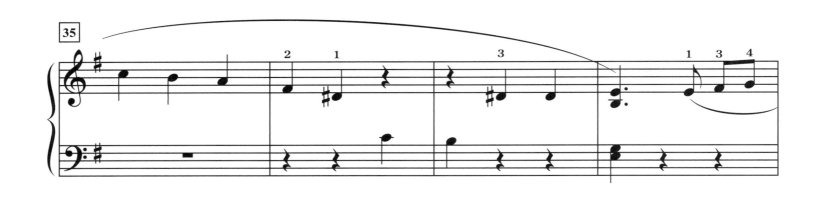

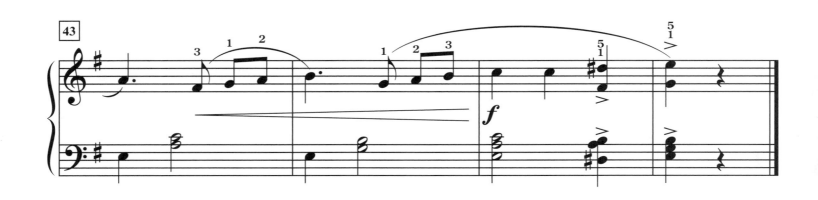

Piano Concerto No. 5 in E-flat Major—Emperor

(Second Movement)

Ludwig van Beethoven (1770–1827)
Op. 73
Arranged by Jerry Ray

Piano Sonata No. 8 in C Minor—Pathétique

(Second Movement)

Ludwig van Beethoven (1770–1827)
Op. 13
Arranged by Jerry Ray

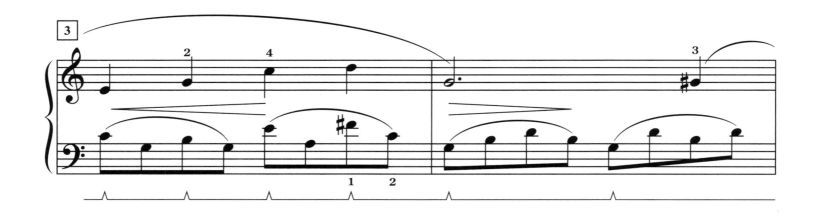

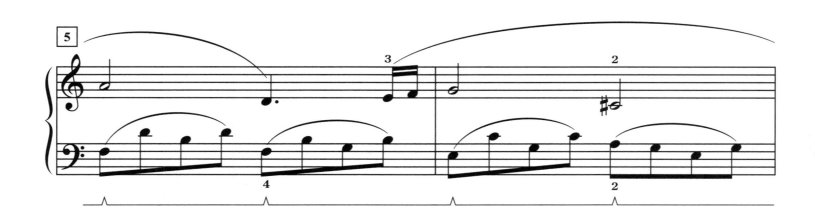

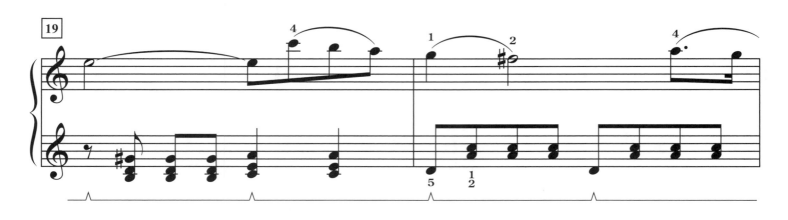

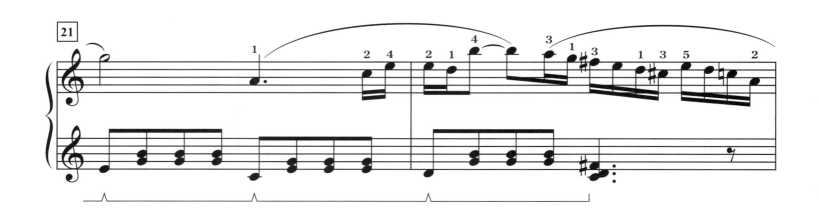

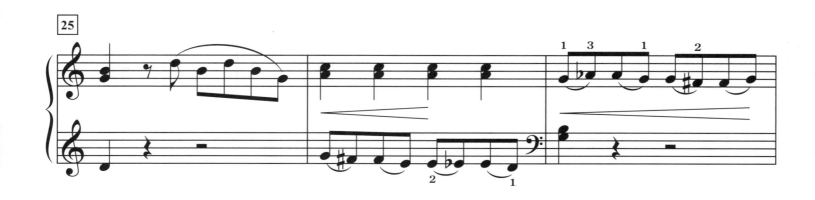

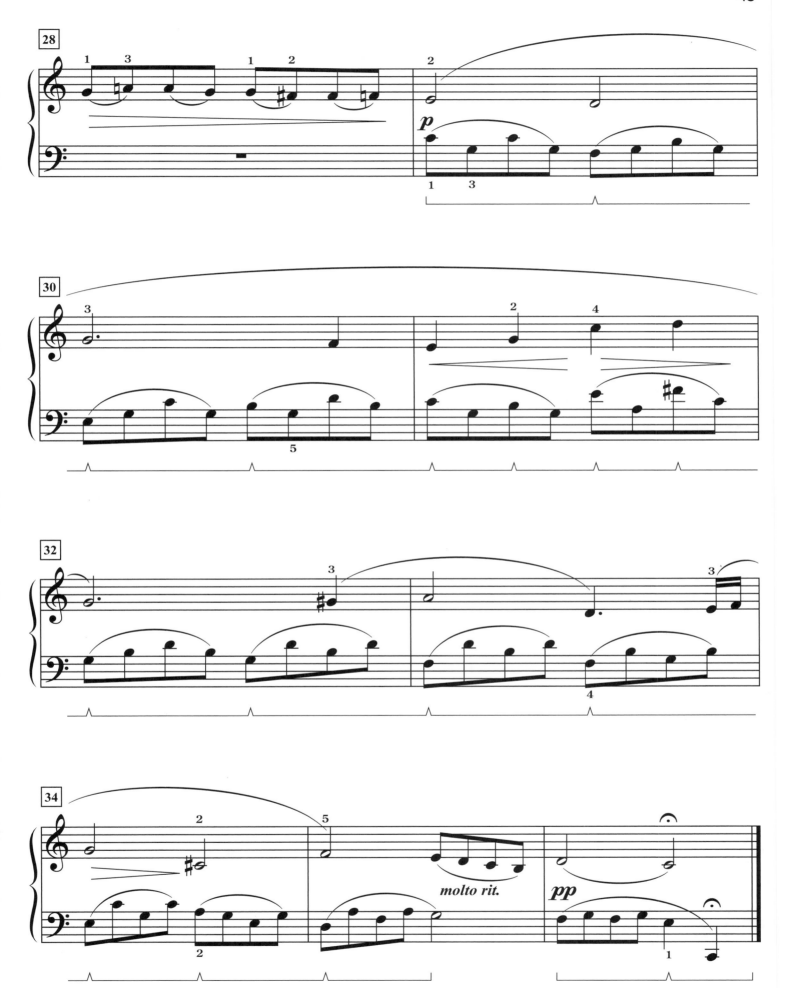

Rondo a capriccio—Rage over a Lost Penny

Ludwig van Beethoven (1770–1827)
Op. 129
Arranged by Mary K. Sallee

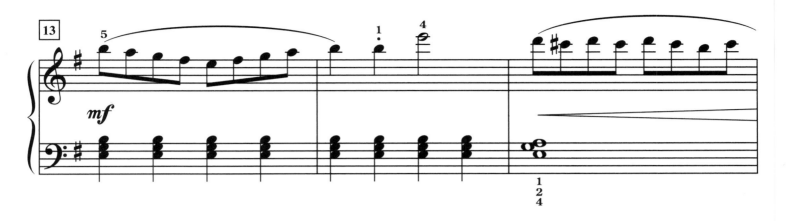

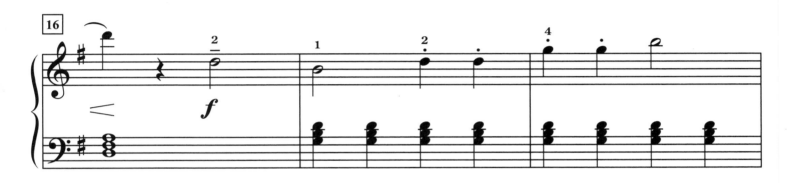

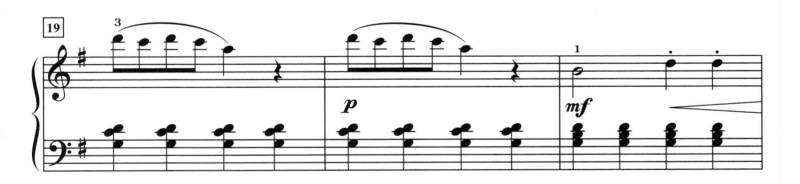

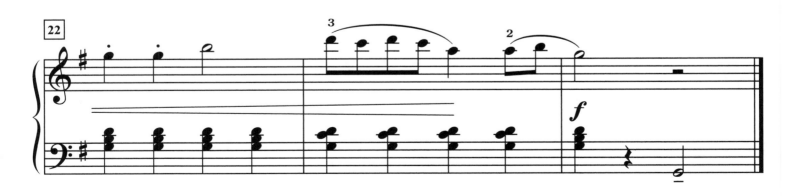

Symphony No. 5 in C Minor

(First Movement)

Ludwig van Beethoven (1770–1827)
Op. 67
Arranged by Robert Schultz

Allegro con brio

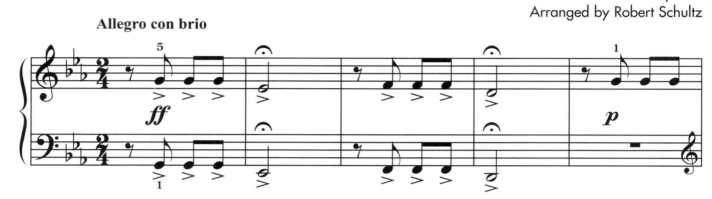

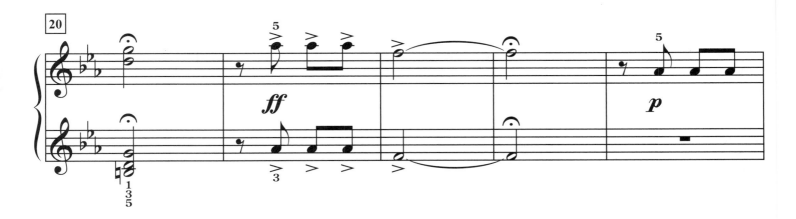

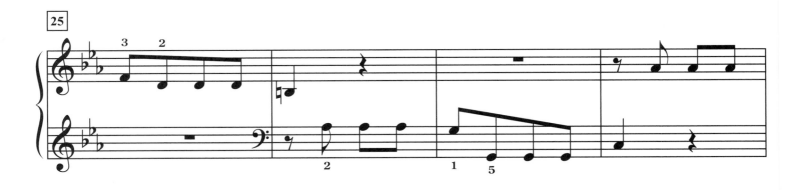

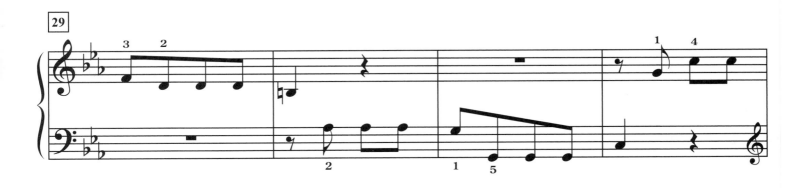

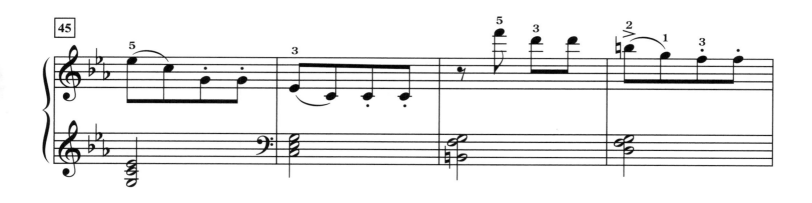

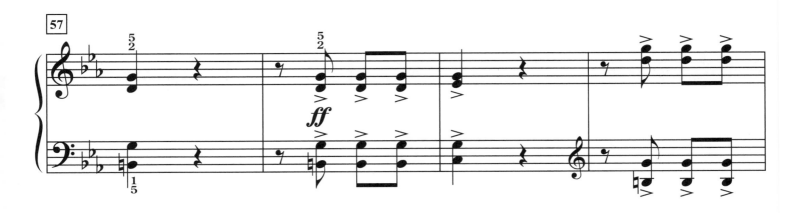

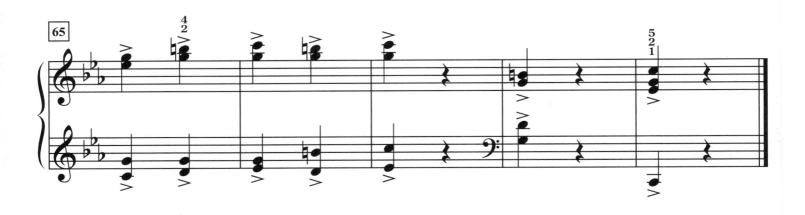

Turkish March

(from *The Ruins of Athens*)

Ludwig van Beethoven (1770–1827)
Op. 113
Arranged by Mary K. Sallee

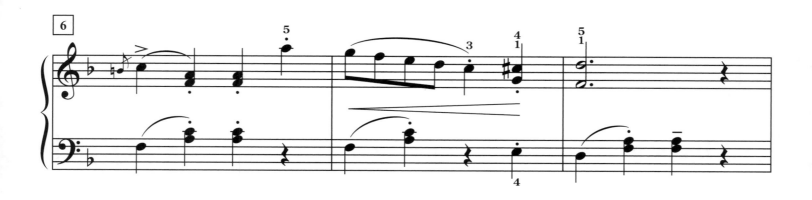

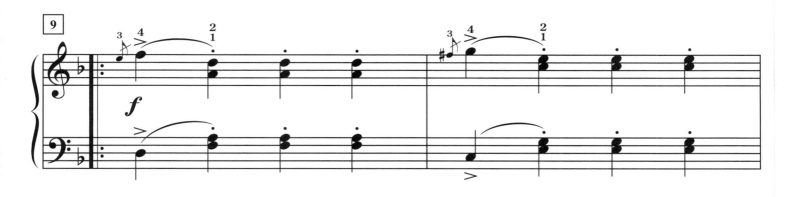

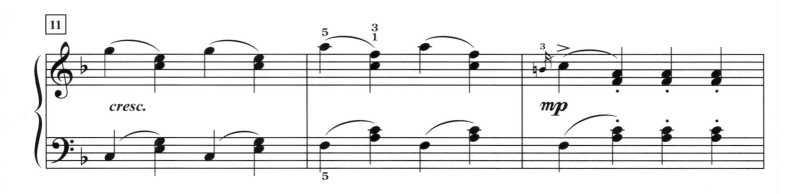

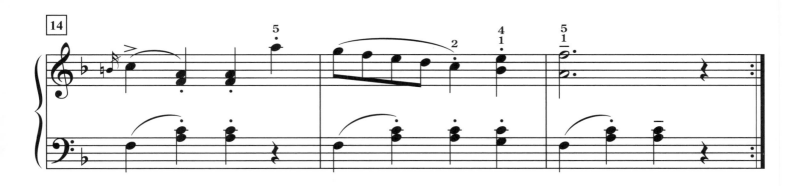

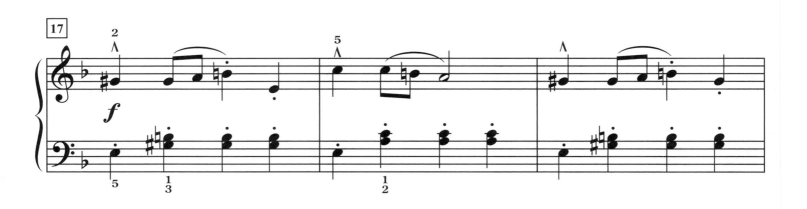

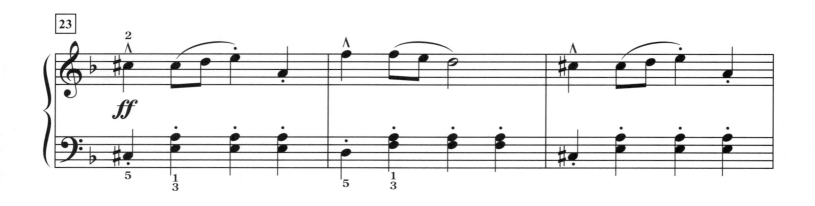

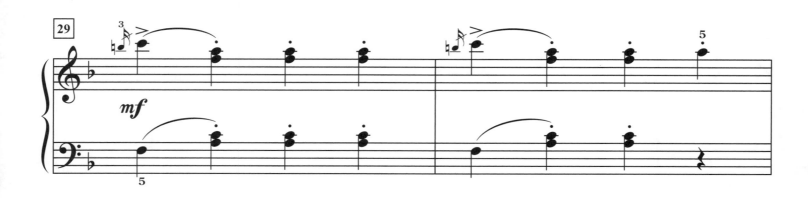

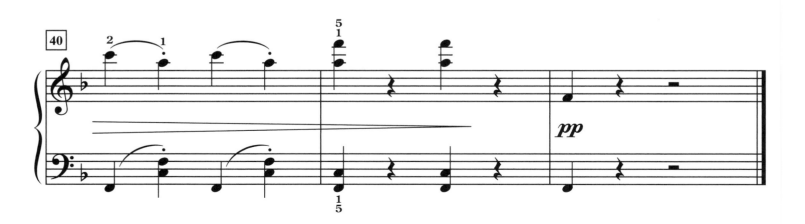

Habañera
(from *Carmen*)

Georges Bizet
(1838–1875)
Arranged by Tom Gerou

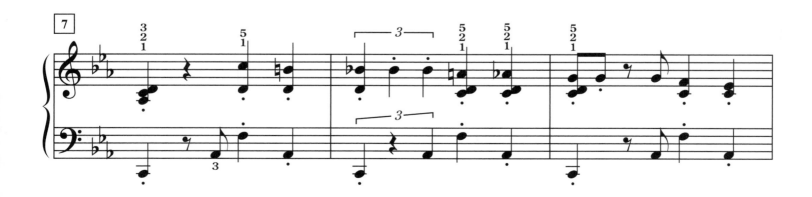

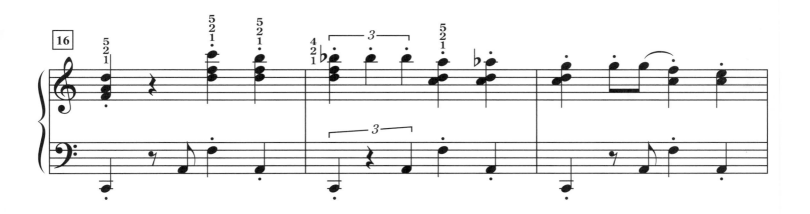

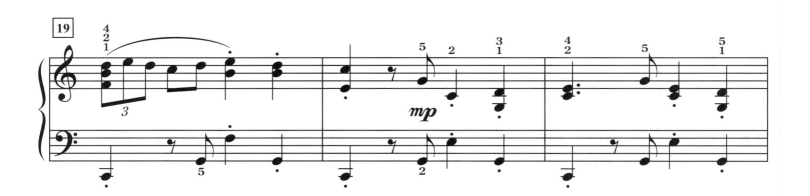

L'Arlésienne, Suite No. 1

(Prelude)

George Bizet
(1838–1875)
Arranged by Robert Schultz

Allegro deciso

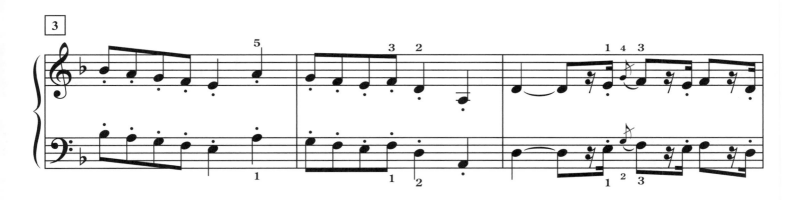

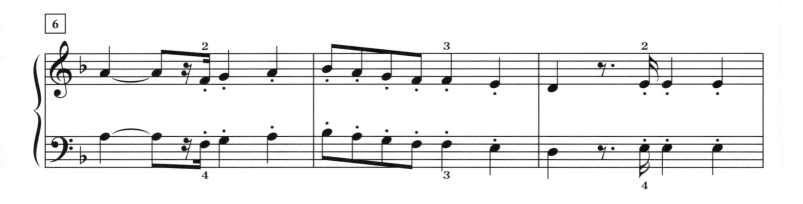

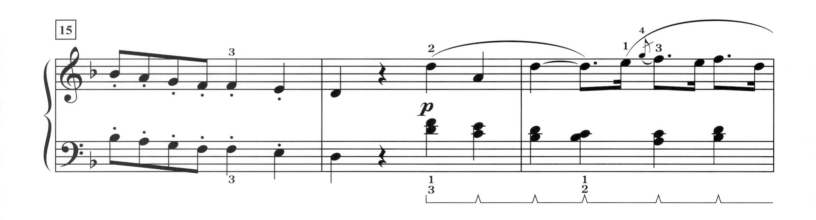

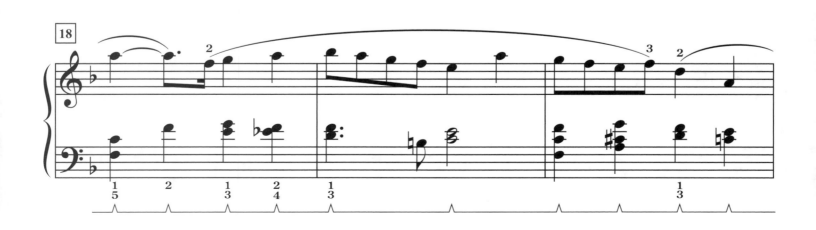

March of the Toreadors

(from *Carmen*)

Georges Bizet
(1838–1875)
Arranged by Robert Schultz

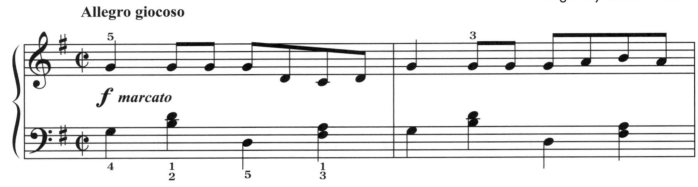

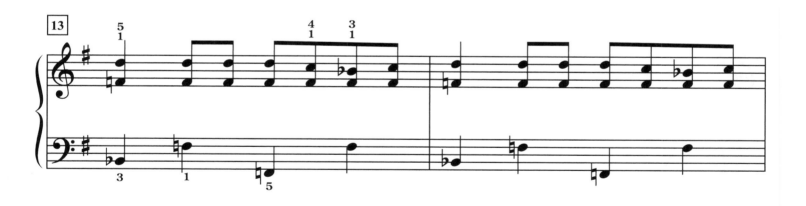

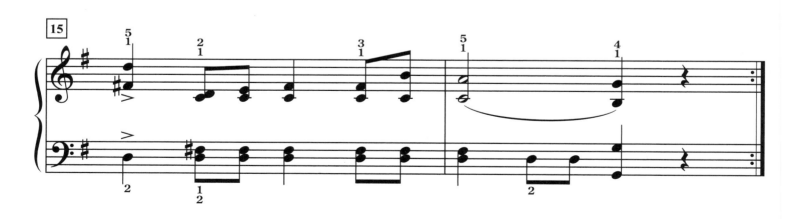

Toreador Song

(from *Carmen*)

Georges Bizet
(1838–1875)
Arranged by Tom Gerou

Allegro moderato

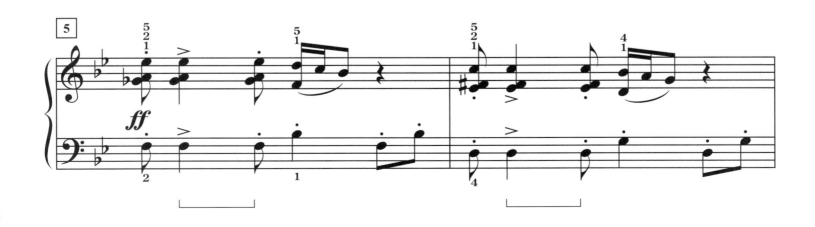

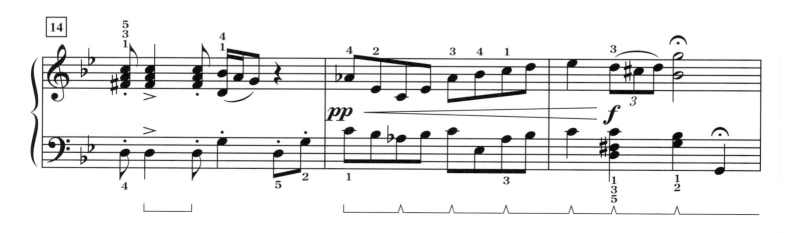

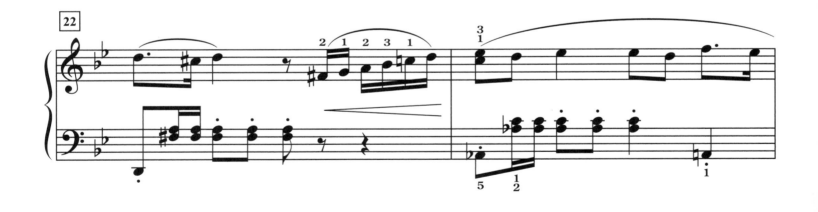

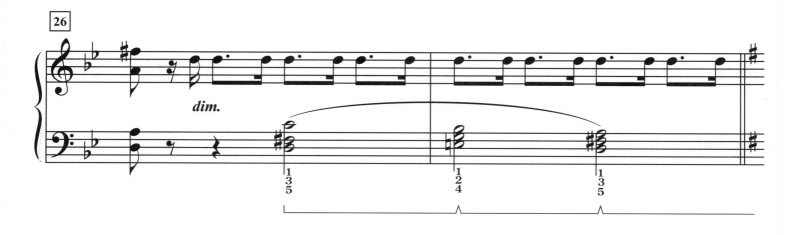

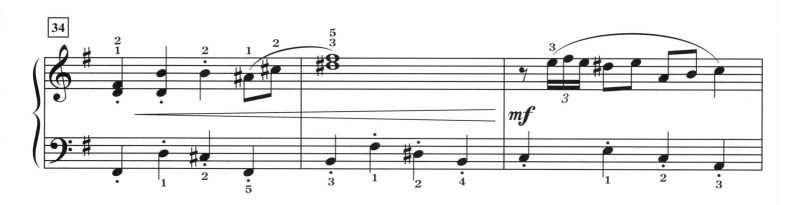

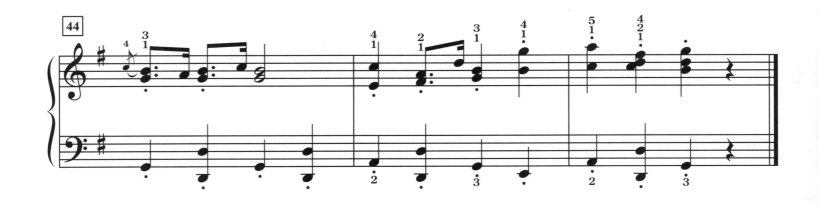

Polovetsian Dance

(from *Prince Igor*)

Alexander Borodin
(1833–1887)
Arranged by Robert Schultz

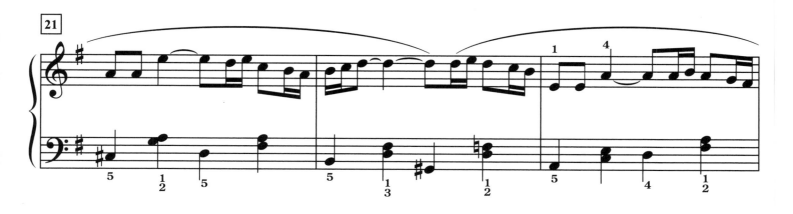

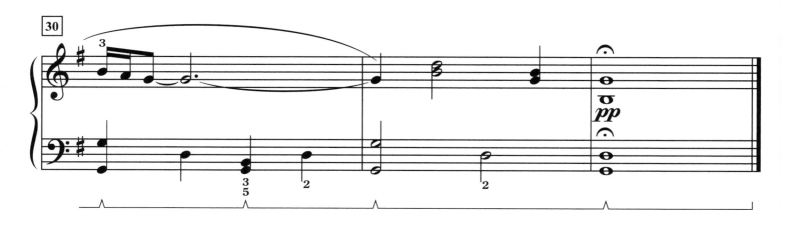

Hungarian Dance No. 5 in F-sharp Minor

Johannes Brahms (1833–1897)
WoO 1
Arranged by Carol Matz

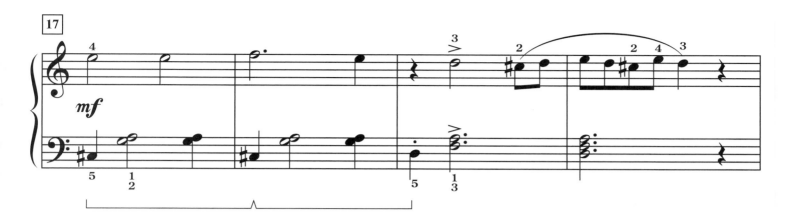

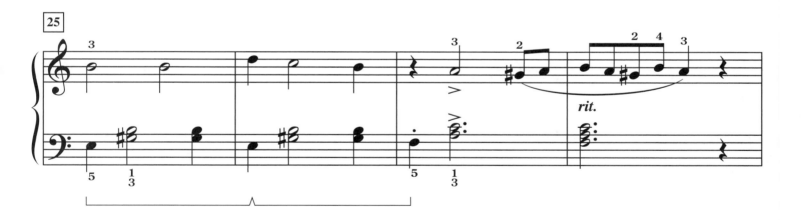

Waltz in A-flat Major

Johannes Brahms (1833–1897)
Op. 39, No. 15
Arranged by Carol Matz

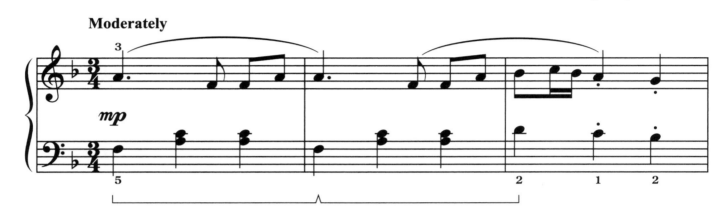

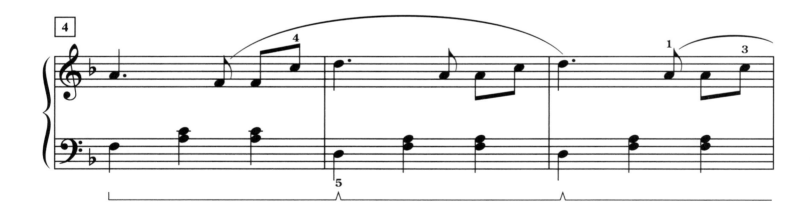

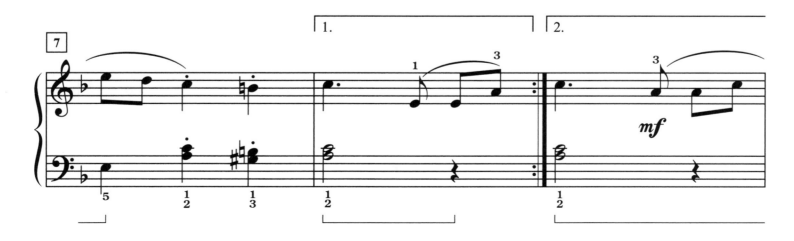

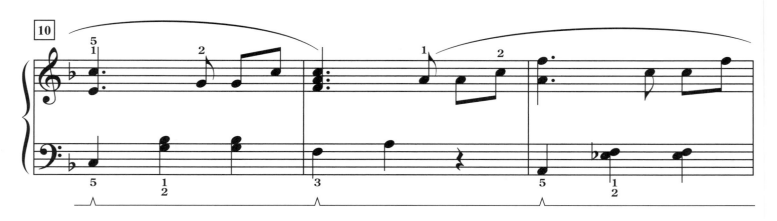

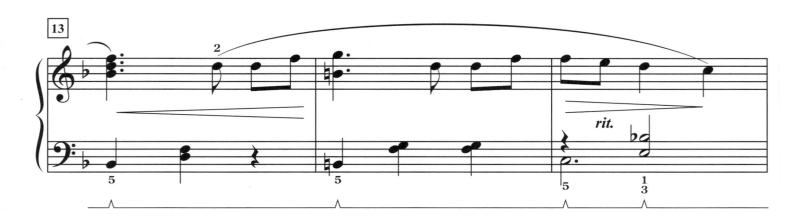

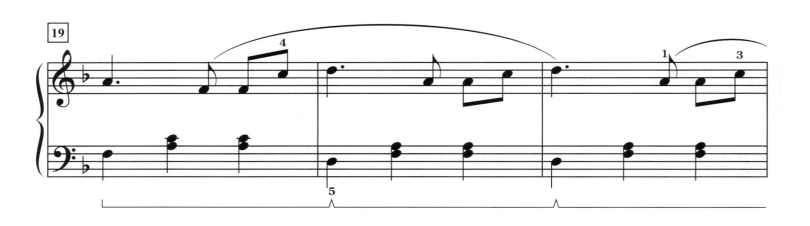

Ballade No. 1 in G Minor

Frédéric Chopin (1810–1849)
Op. 23
Arranged by Jerry Ray

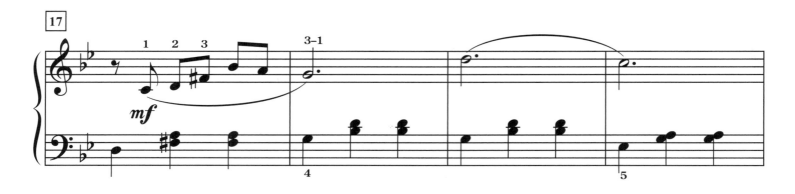

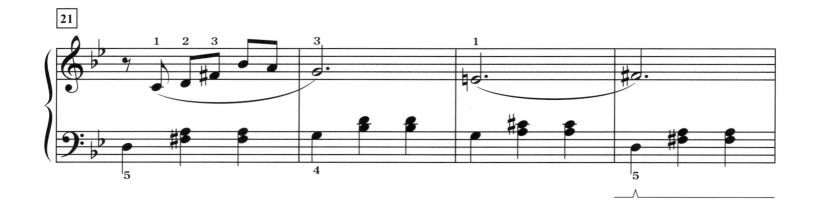

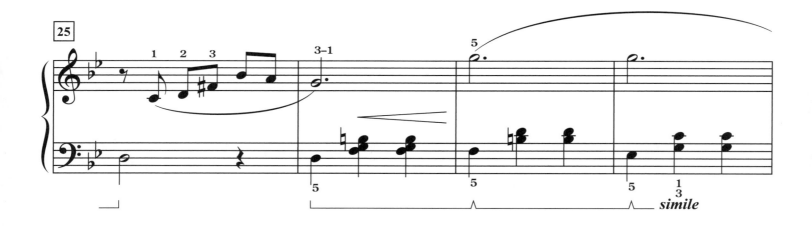

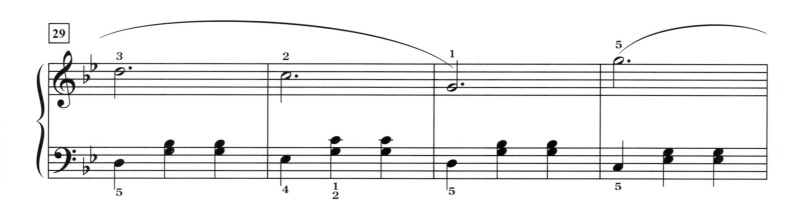

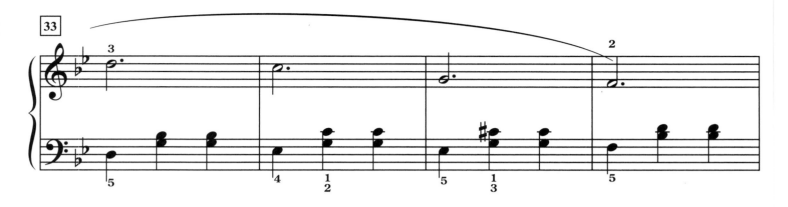

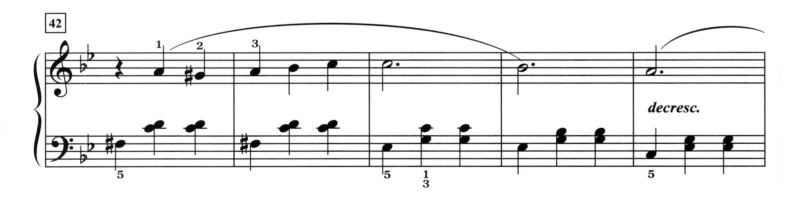

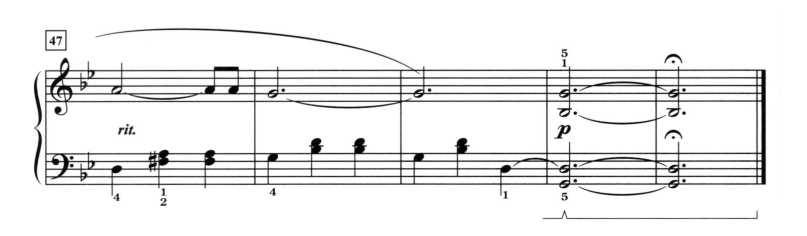

Etude in E Major

Frédéric Chopin (1810–1849)
Op. 10, No. 3
Arranged by Jerry Ray

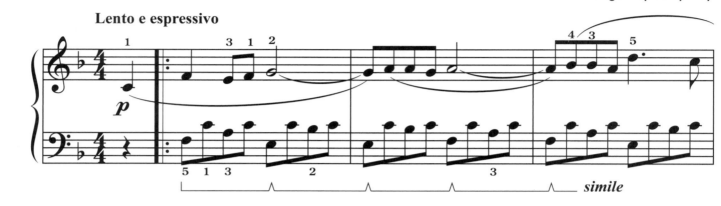

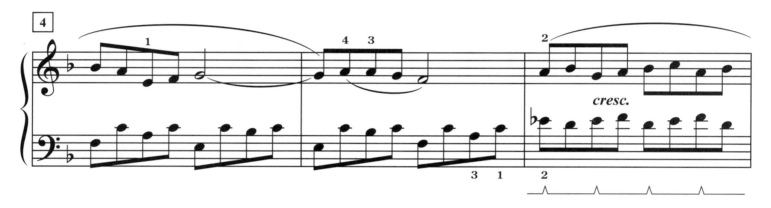

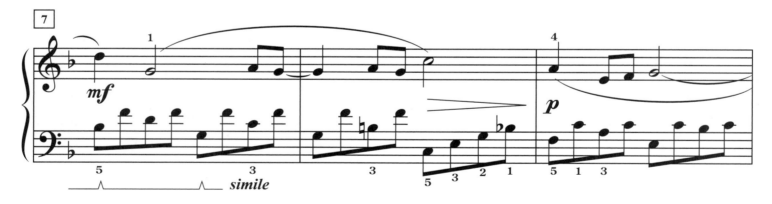

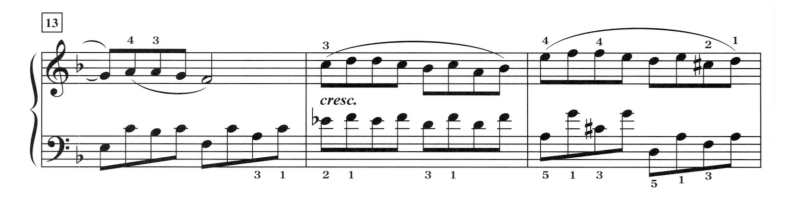

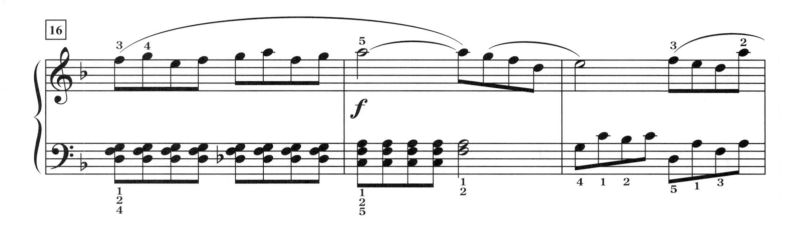

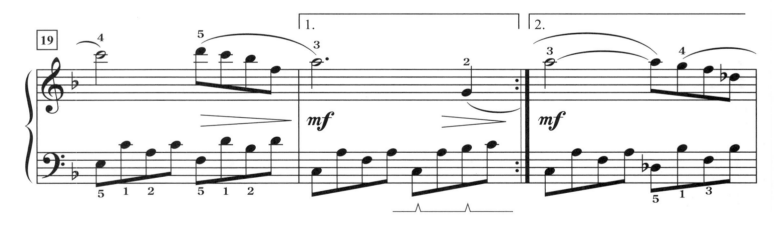

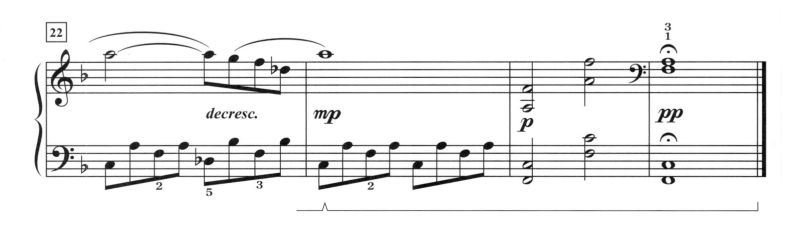

Fantaisie-Impromptu

Frédéric Chopin (1810–1849)
Op. 66
Arranged by Jerry Ray

Moderato cantabile

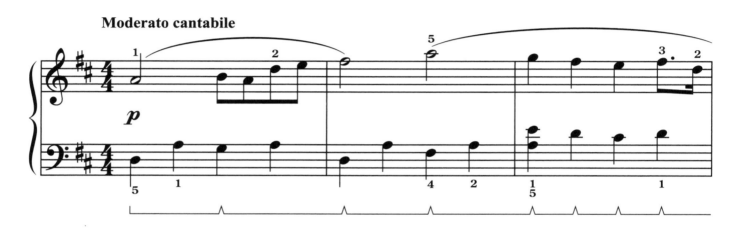

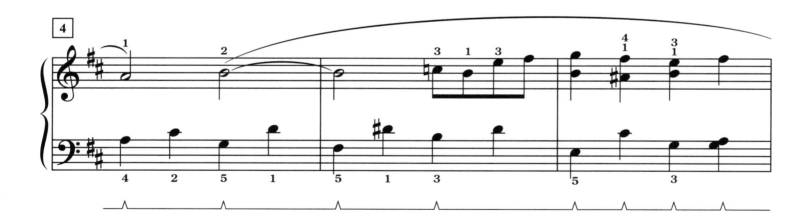

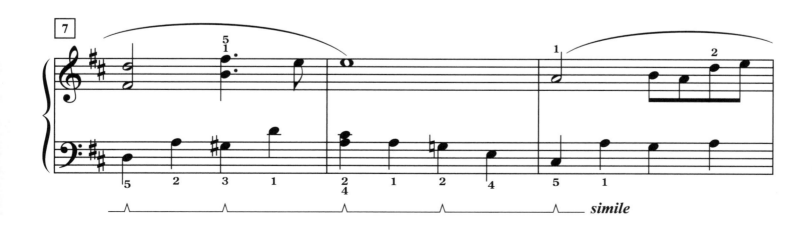

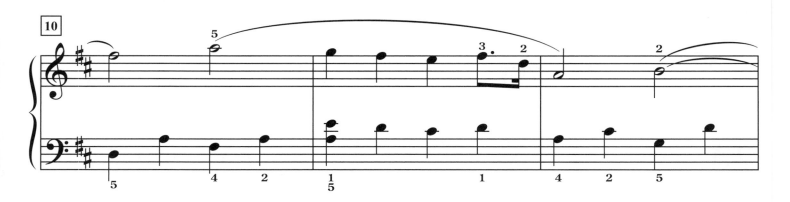

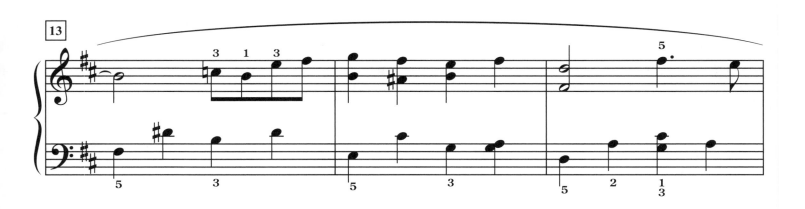

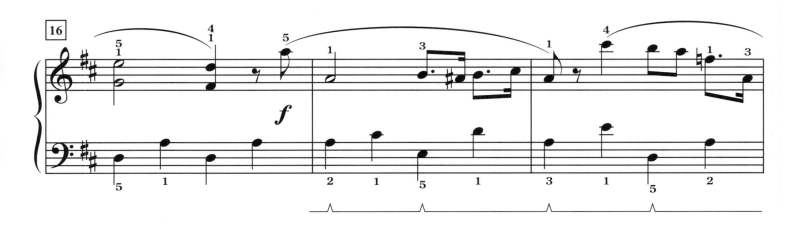

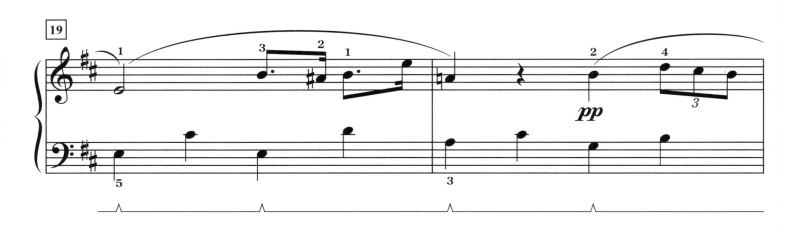

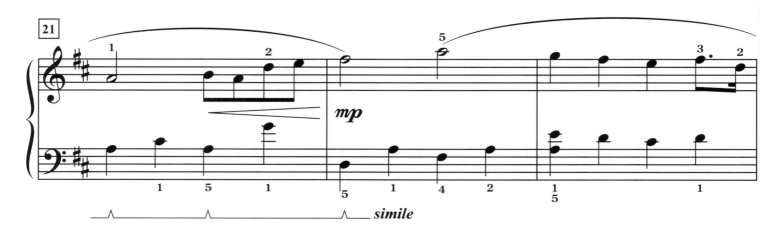

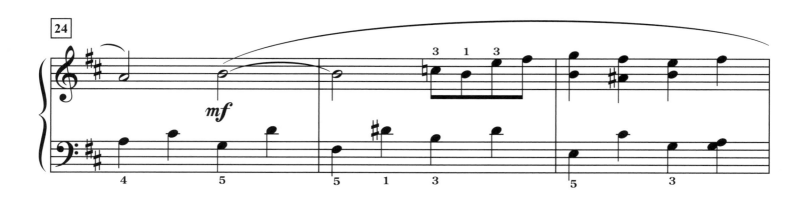

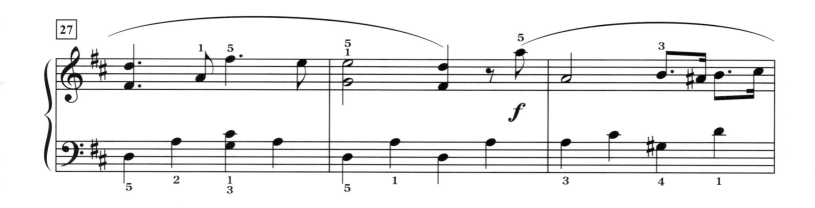

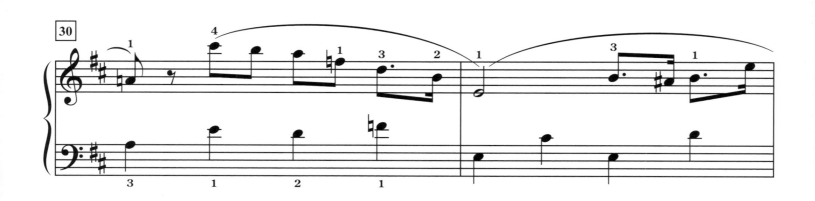

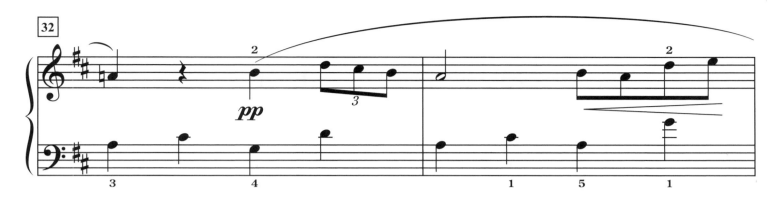

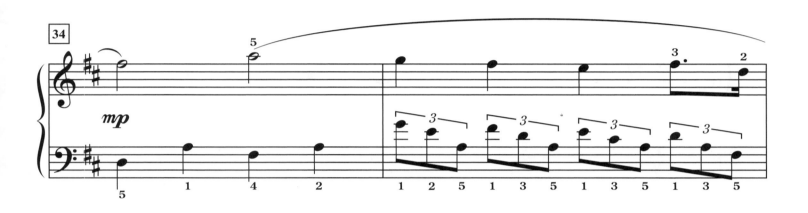

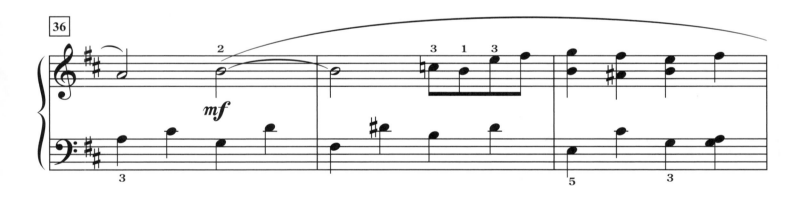

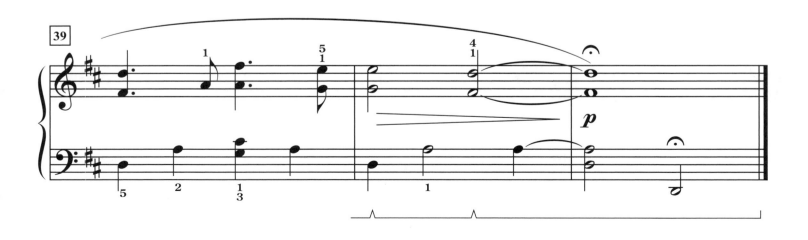

Nocturne in F Minor

Frédéric Chopin (1810–1849)
Op. 55, No. 1
Arranged by Jerry Ray

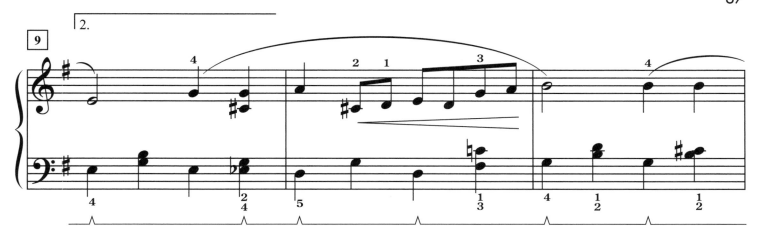

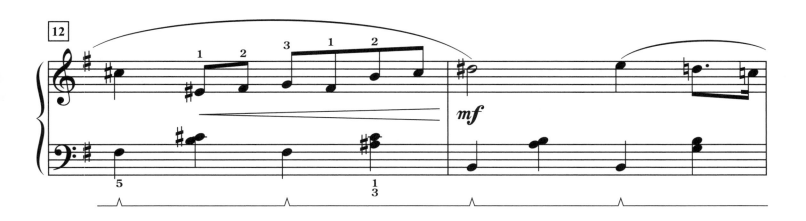

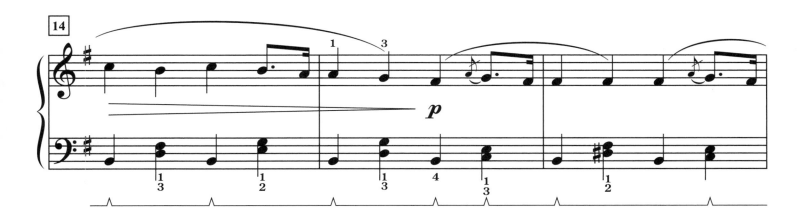

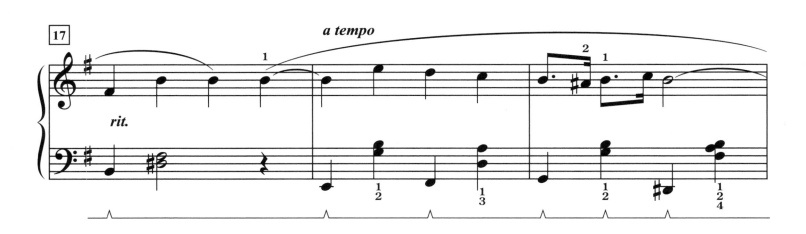

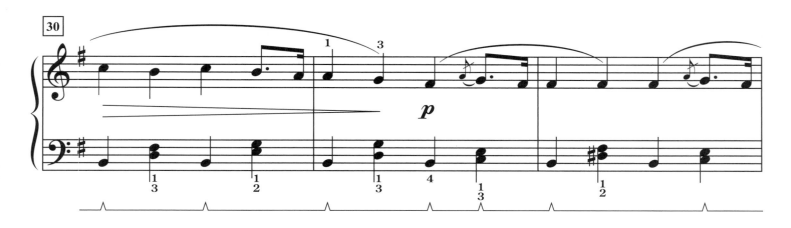

Etude in C Minor—Revolutionary

Frédéric Chopin (1810–1849)
Op. 10, No. 12
Arranged by Jerry Ray

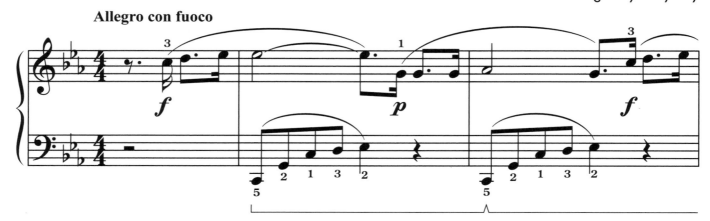

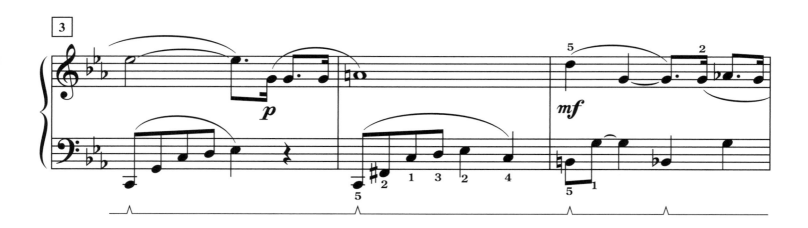

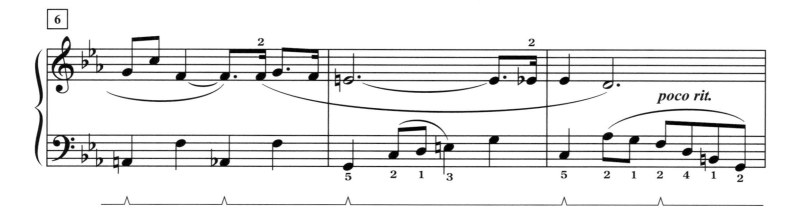

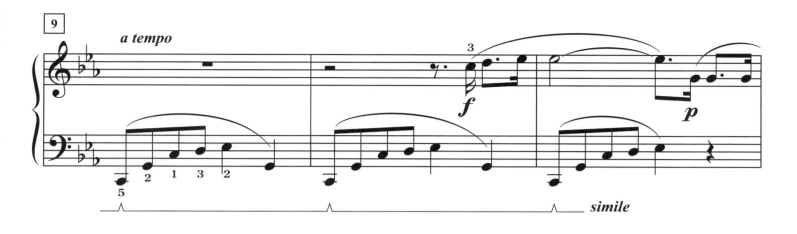

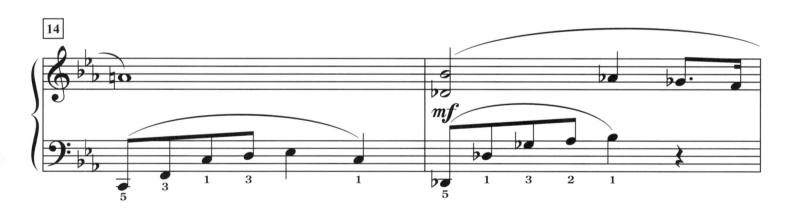

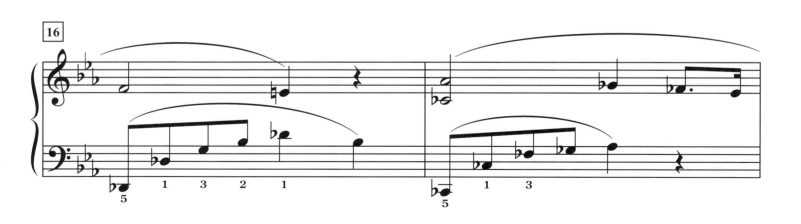

Piano Sonata No. 2 in B-flat Minor

(Third Movement)
"Funeral March"

Frédéric Chopin (1810–1849)
Op. 35
Arranged by Jerry Ray

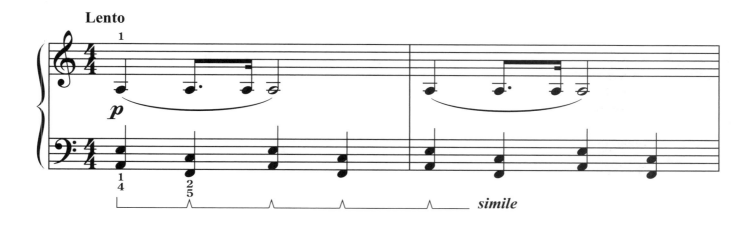

Prelude in D-flat Major—Raindrop

Frédéric Chopin (1810–1849)
Op. 28, No. 15
Arranged by Jerry Ray

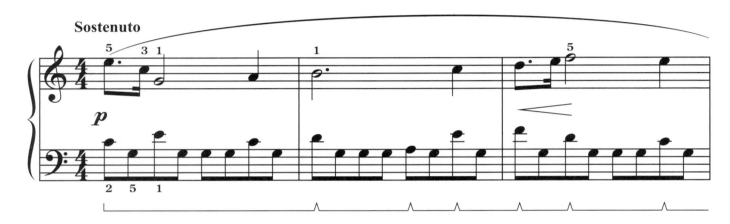

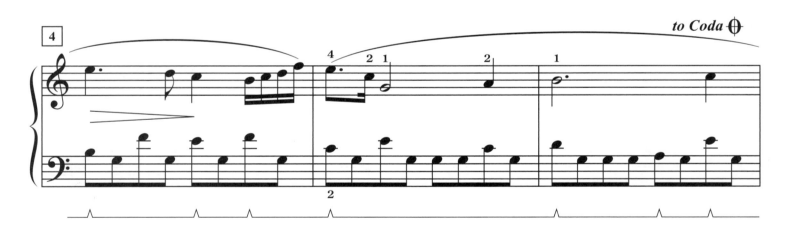

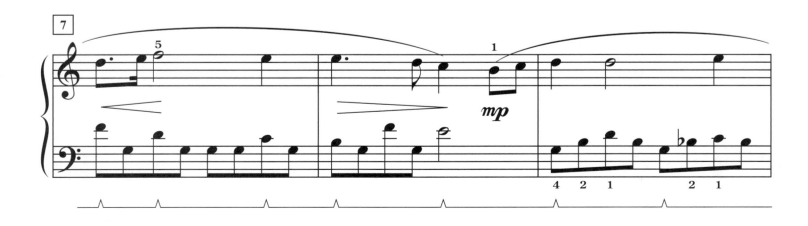

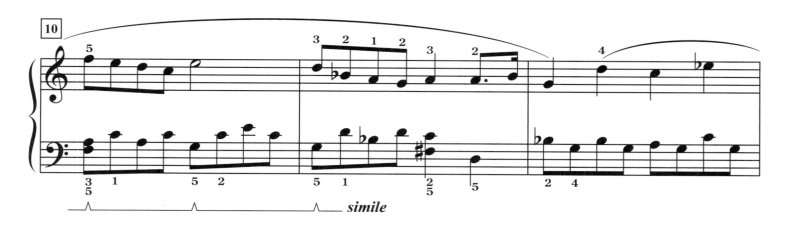

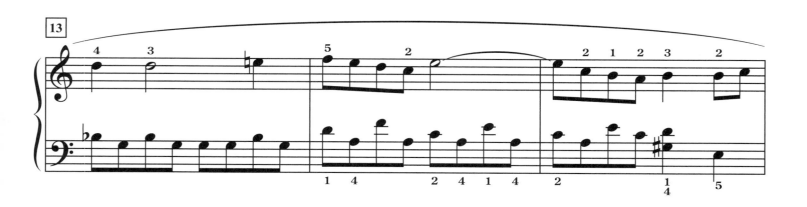

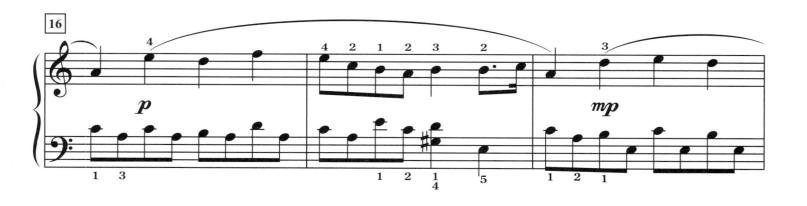

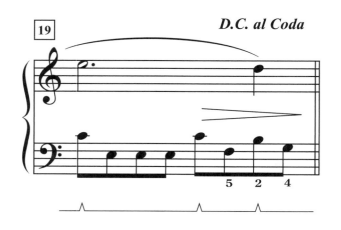

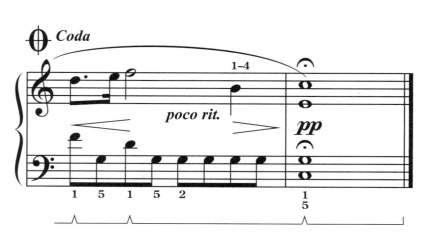

Prelude in E Minor

Frédéric Chopin (1810–1849)
Op. 28, No. 4
Arranged by Jerry Ray

Polonaise in A Major—Military

Frédéric Chopin (1810–1849)
Op. 40, No. 1
Arranged by Jerry Ray

Waltz in D-flat Major—Minute

Frédéric Chopin (1810–1849)
Op. 64, No. 1
Arranged by Jerry Ray

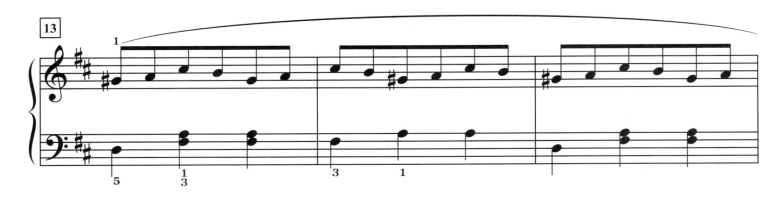

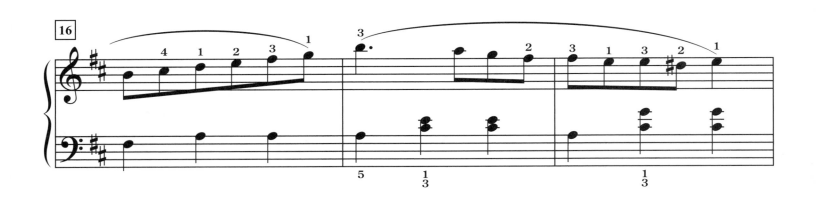

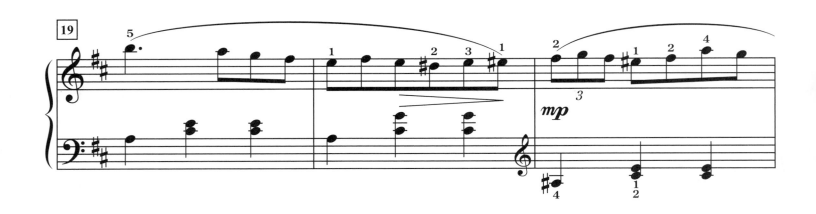

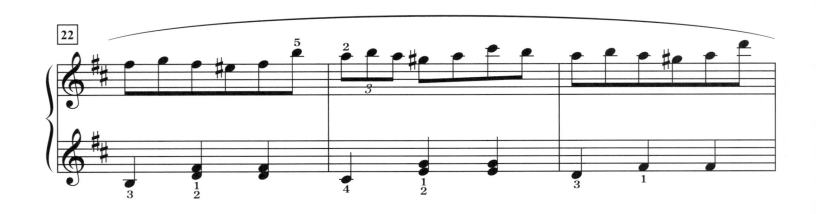

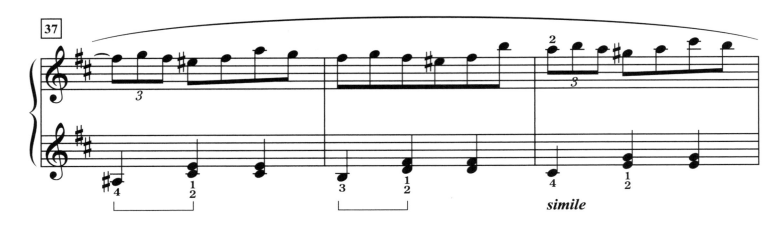

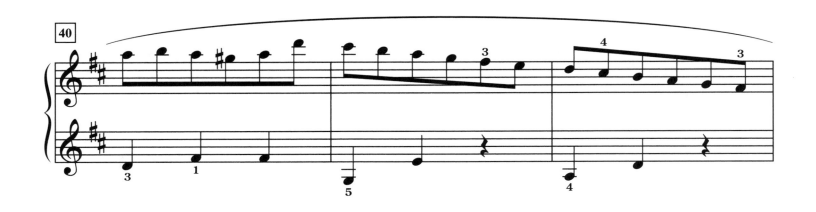

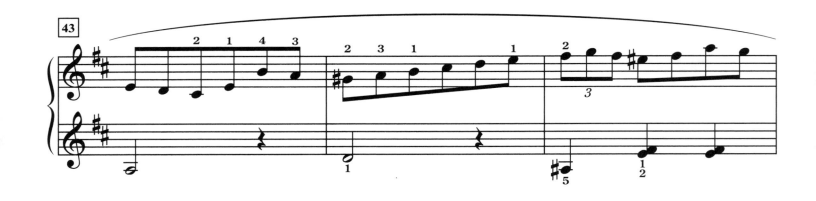

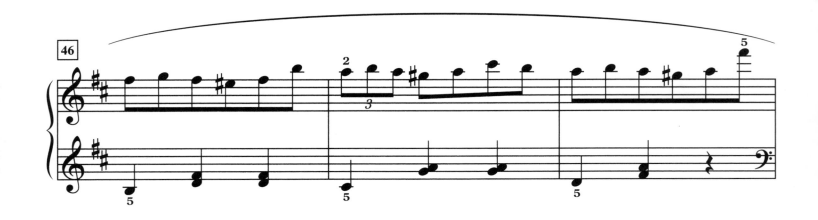

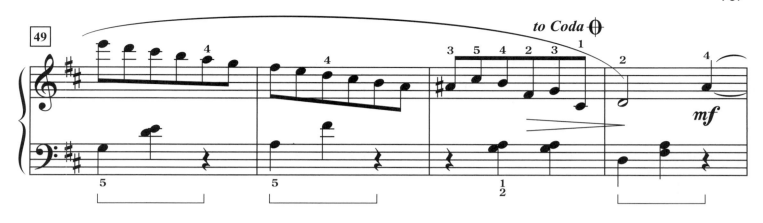

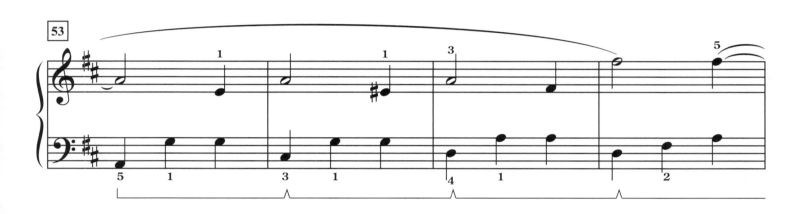

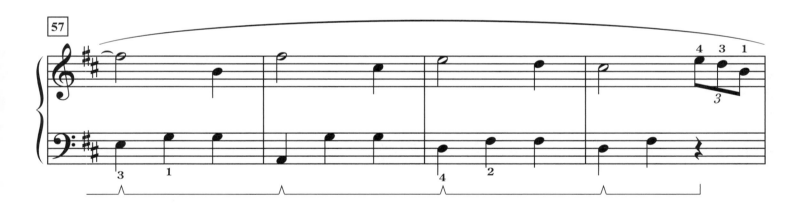

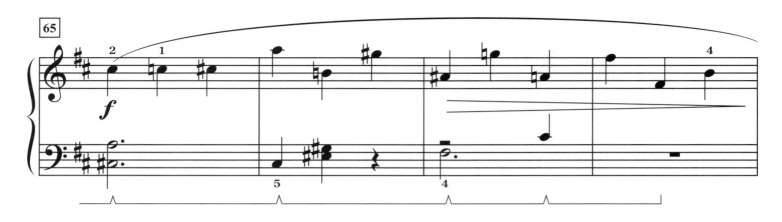

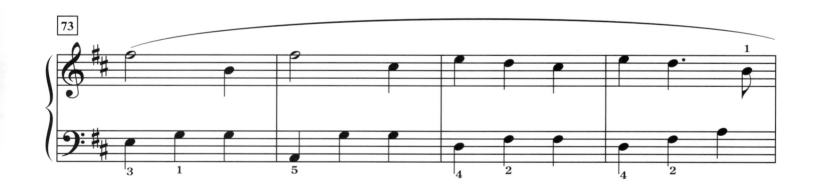

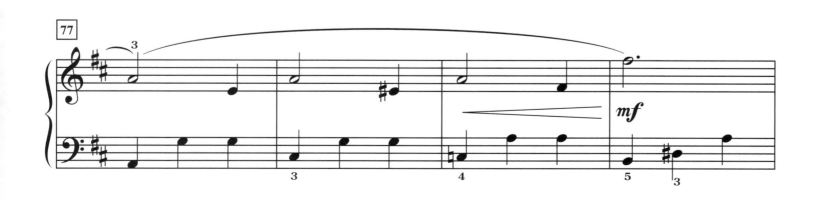

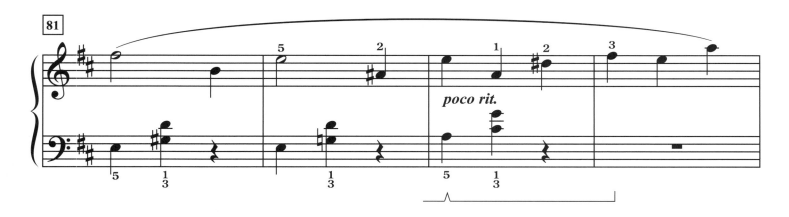

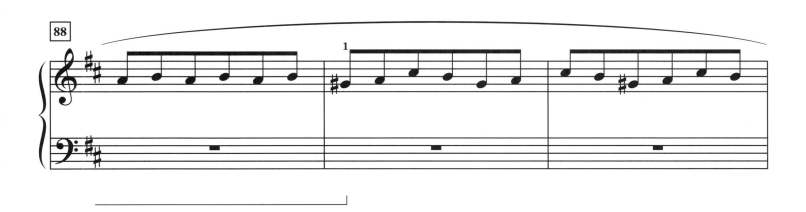

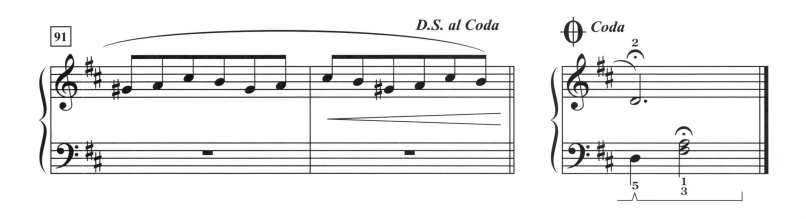

Prince of Denmark's March

Jeremiah Clarke
(1673–1707)
Arranged by Bruce Nelson

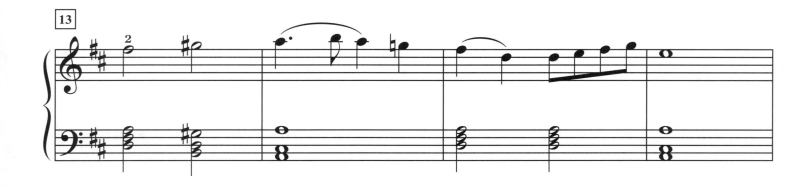

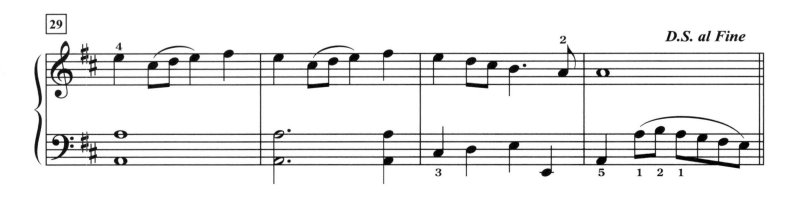

Clair de lune

(from *Suite Bergamasque*)

Claude Debussy
(1862–1918)
Arranged by E. L. Lancaster

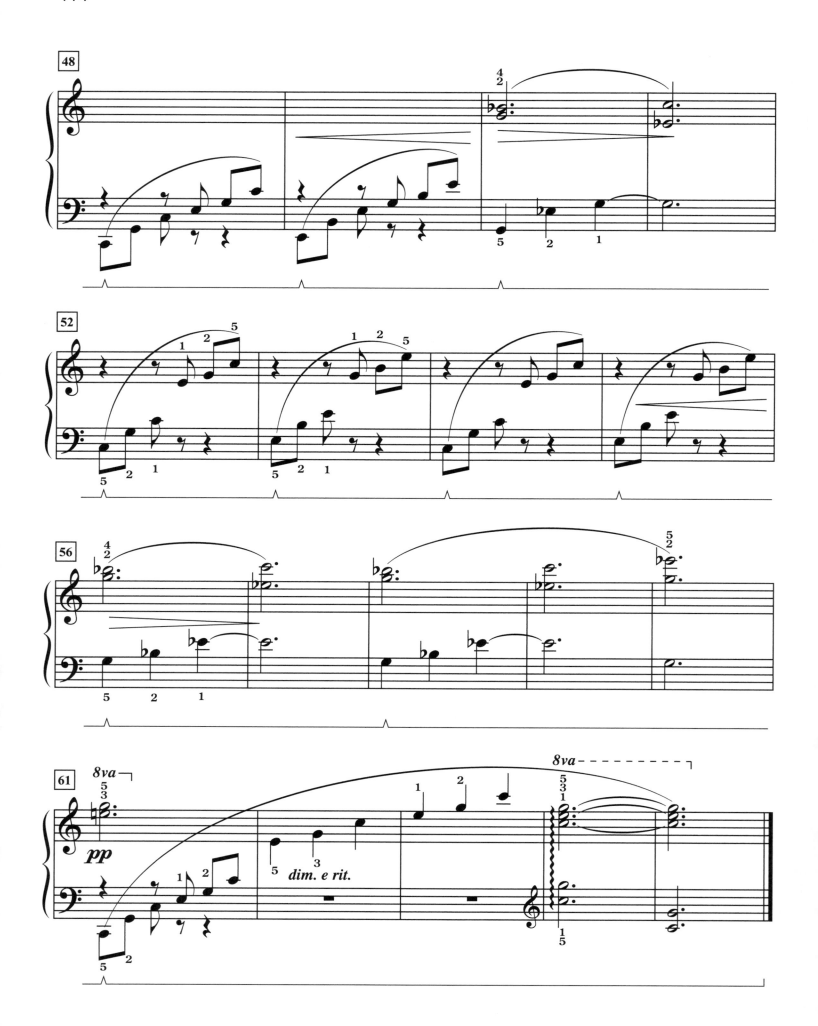

Andaluza No. 5

(from *12 Spanish Dances*)

Enrique Granados
(1867–1916)
Arranged by Carol Matz

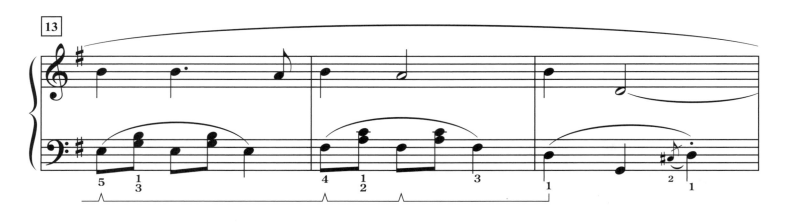

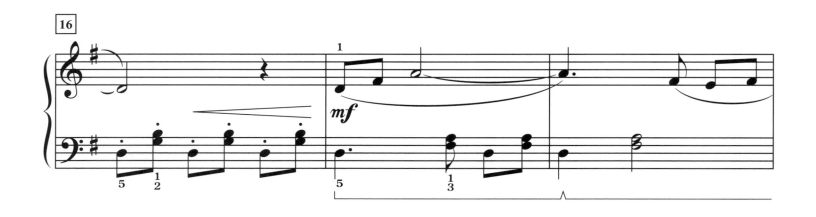

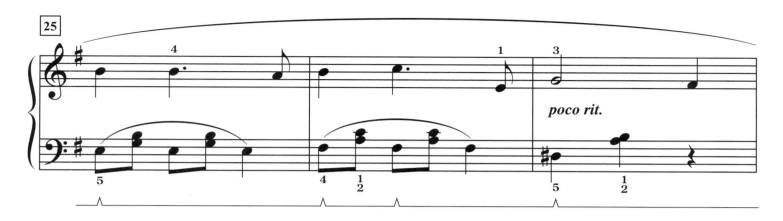

Flower Duet

(from *Lakmé*)

Léo Delibes
(1836–1891)
Arranged by Tom Gerou

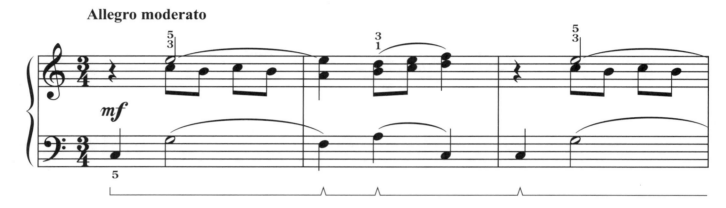

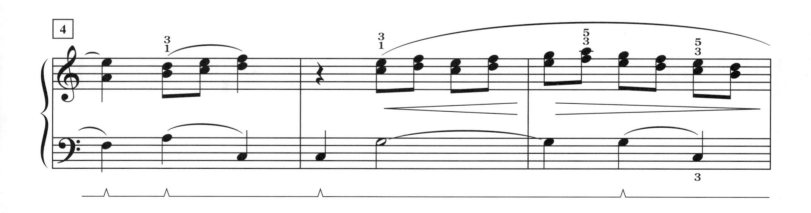

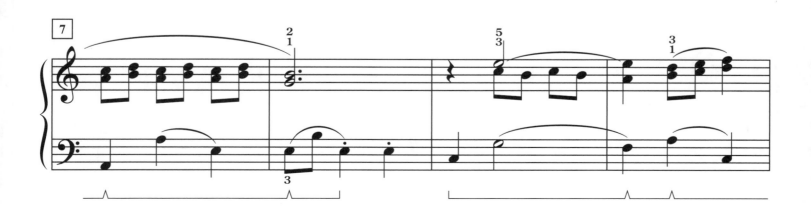

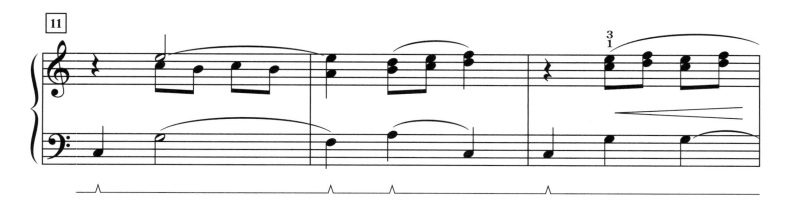

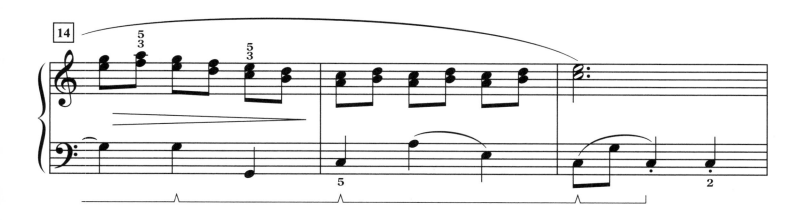

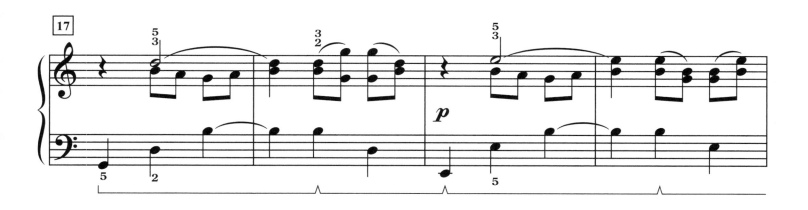

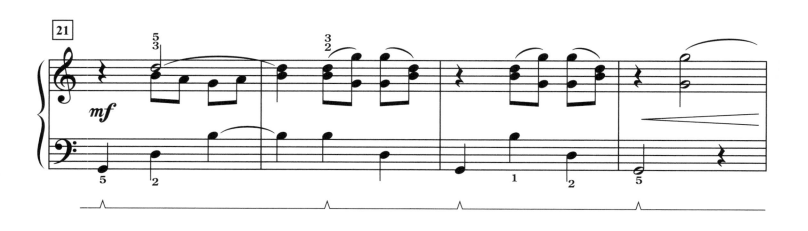

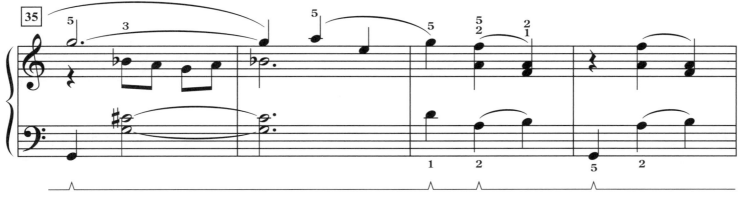

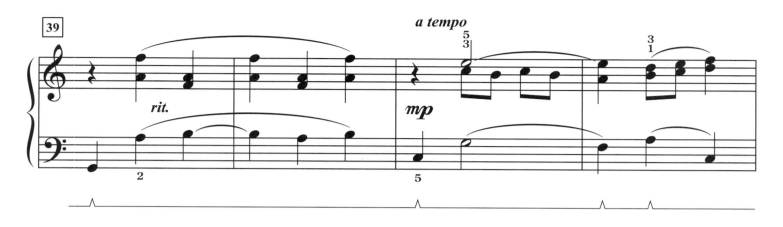

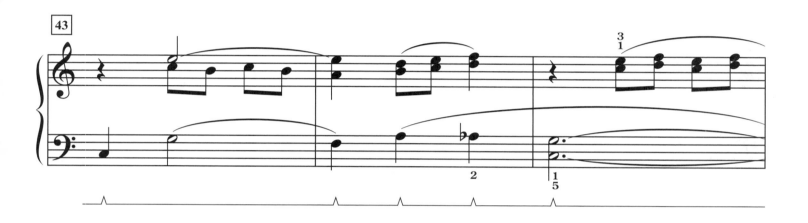

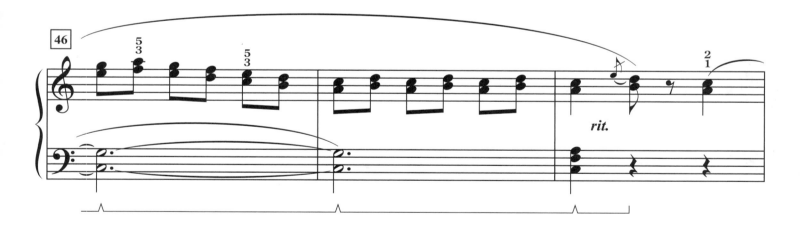

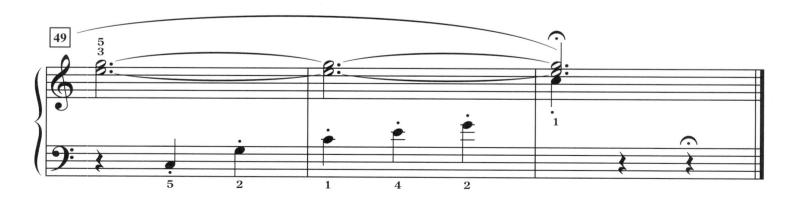

The Sorcerer's Apprentice

Paul Dukas
(1865–1935)
Arranged by Robert Schultz

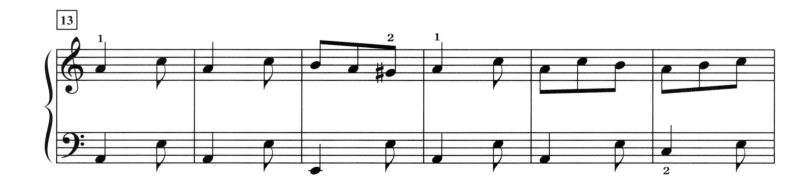

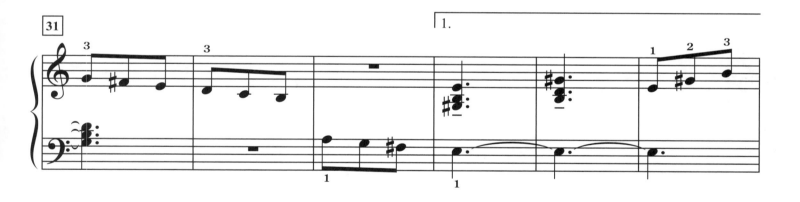

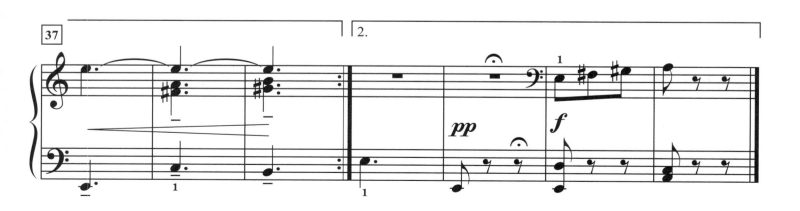

Symphony No. 9 in E Minor—New World

(Second Movement)

Antonín Dvořak (1841–1904)
Op. 95
Arranged by Robert Schultz

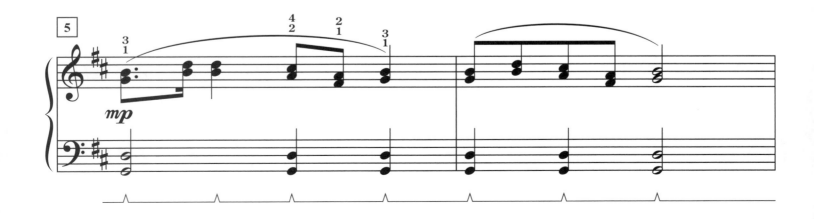

Pomp and Circumstance

(March No. 1)

Edward Elgar (1857–1934)
Op. 39
Arranged by Robert Schultz

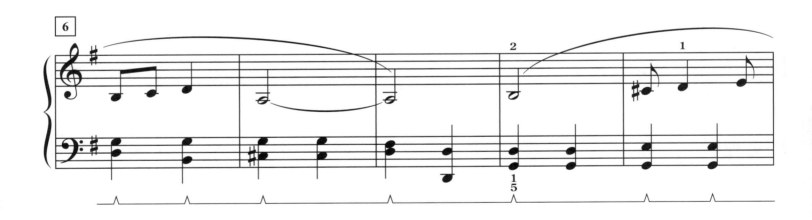

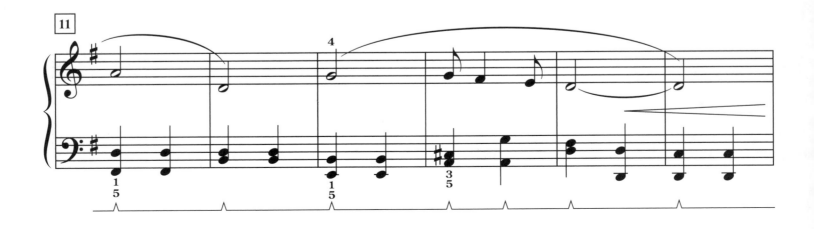

Pavane

Gabriel Fauré (1845–1924)
Op. 50
Arranged by Robert Schultz

Allegro moderato

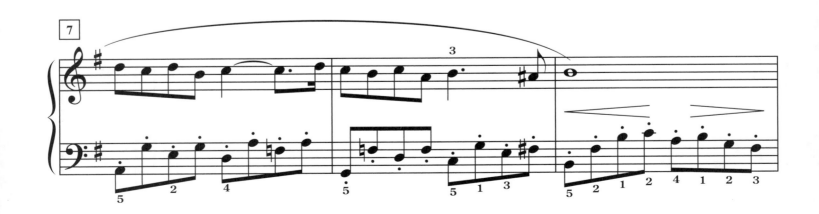

Ave Maria

Johann Sebastian Bach (1685–1750)
Charles Gounod (1818–1893)
Arranged by Jerry Ray

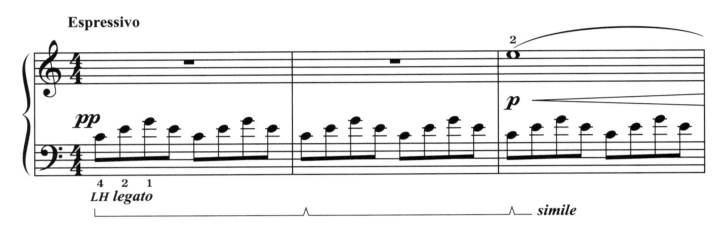

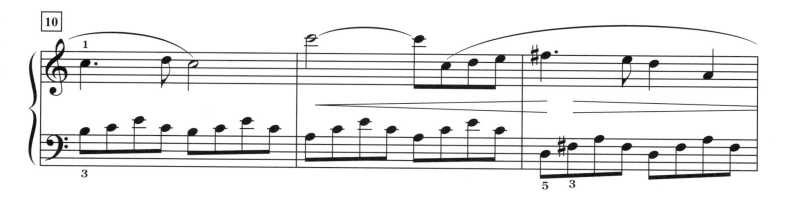

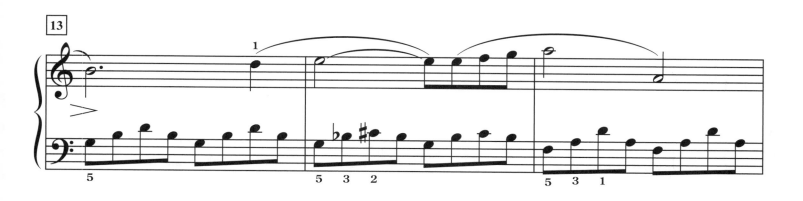

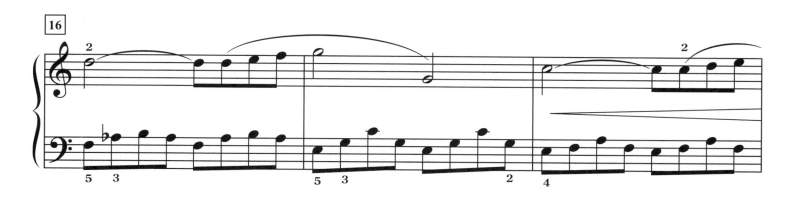

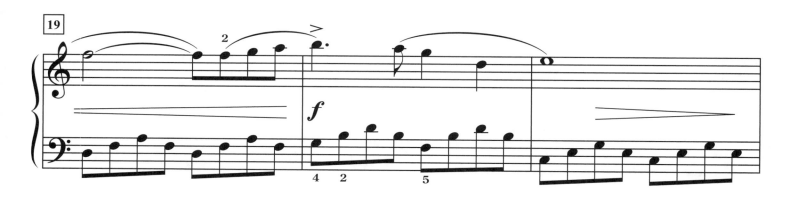

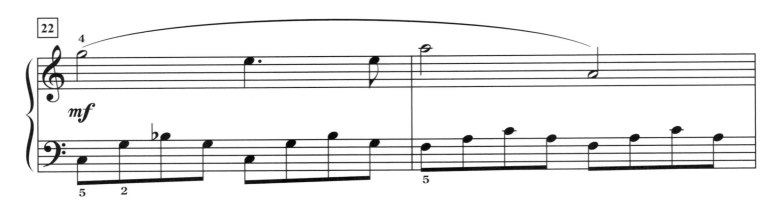

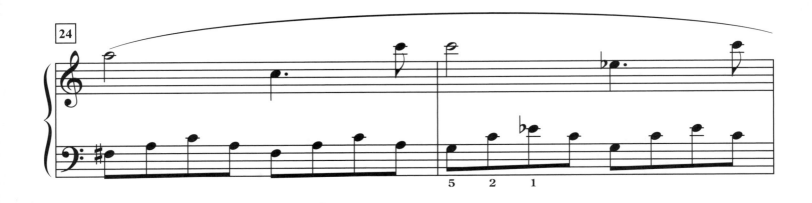

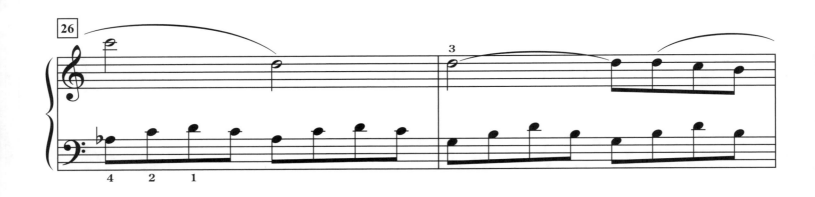

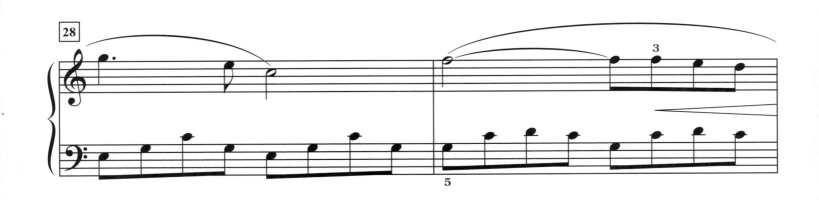

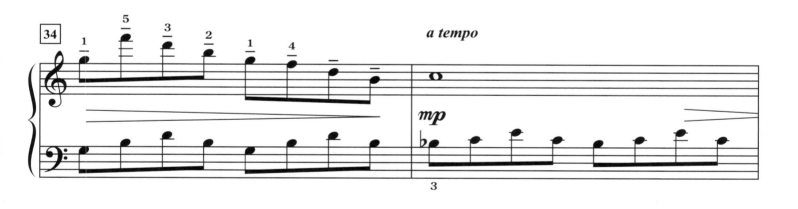

Funeral March of a Marionette

Charles Gounod
(1818–1893)
Arranged by Carol Matz

Moderately

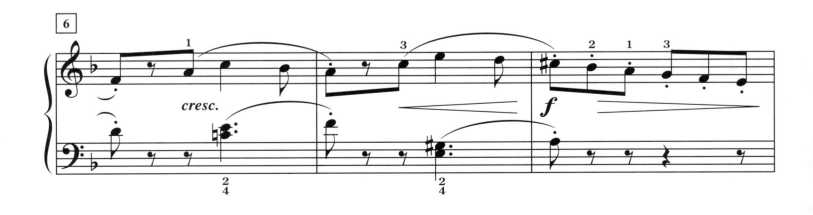

In the Hall of the Mountain King

(from *Peer Gynt Suite No. 1*)

Edvard Grieg (1843–1907)
Op. 46, No. 4
Arranged by Carol Matz

Moderately fast

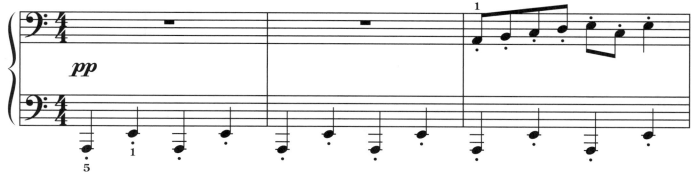

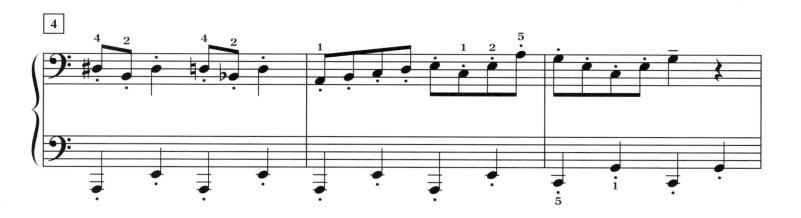

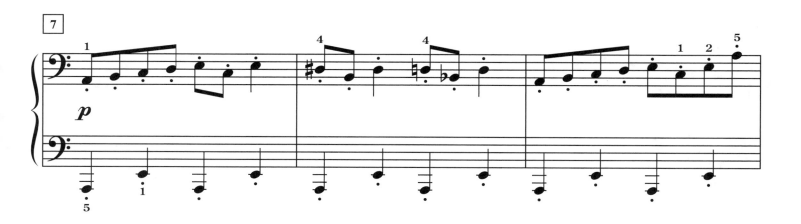

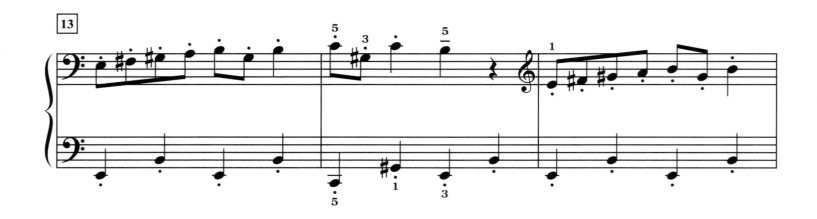

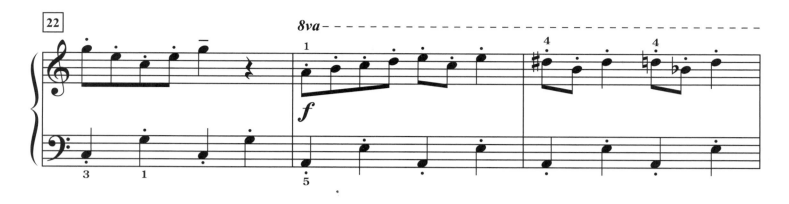

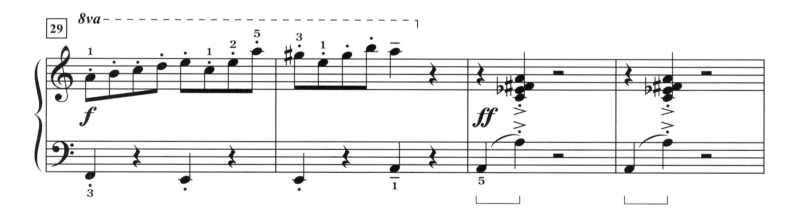

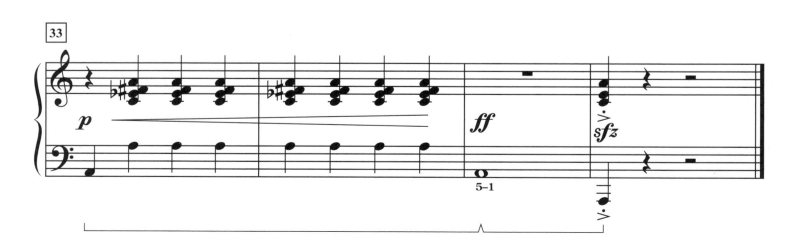

Morning Mood

(from *Peer Gynt Suite No. 1*)

Edvard Grieg (1843–1907)
Op. 46, No. 1
Arranged by Carol Matz

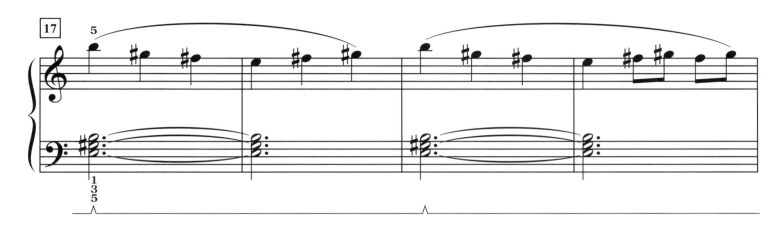

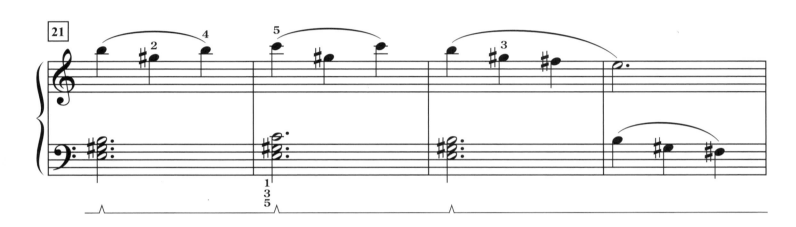

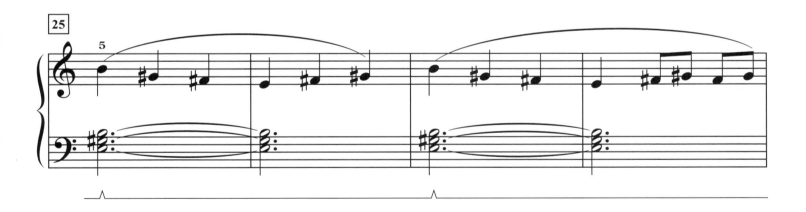

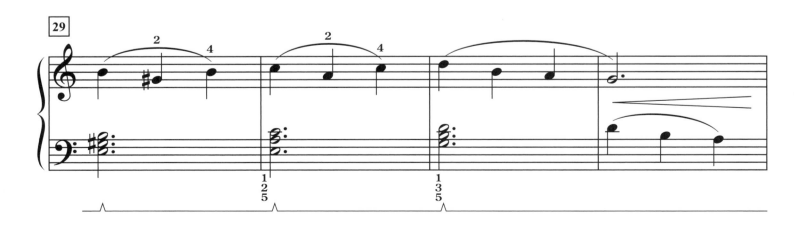

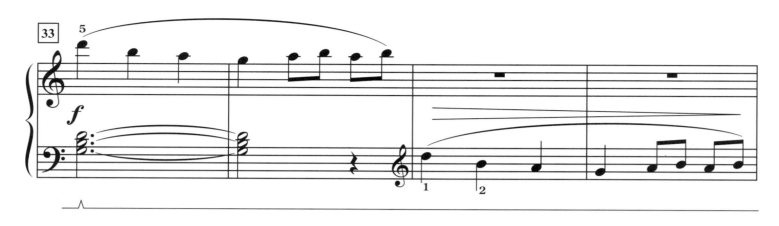

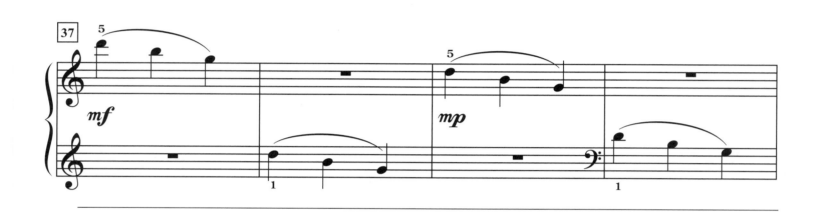

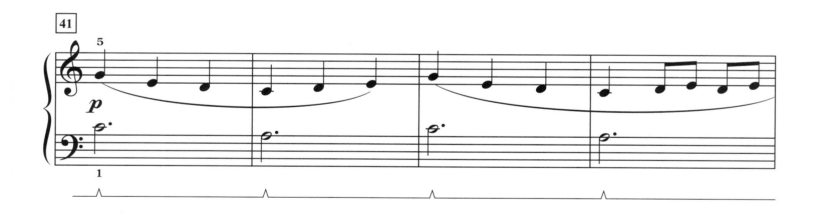

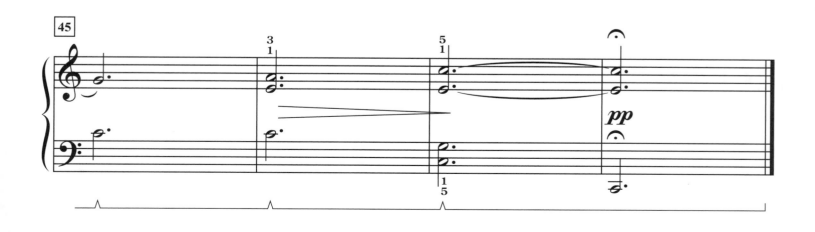

Hallelujah Chorus

(from *Messiah*)

George Frideric Handel (1685–1759)
HWV 56
Arranged by Bruce Nelson

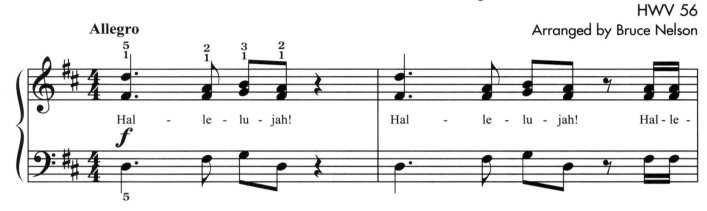

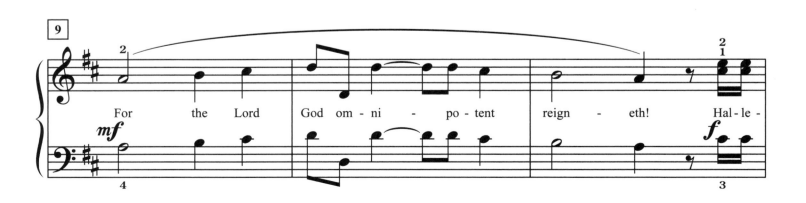

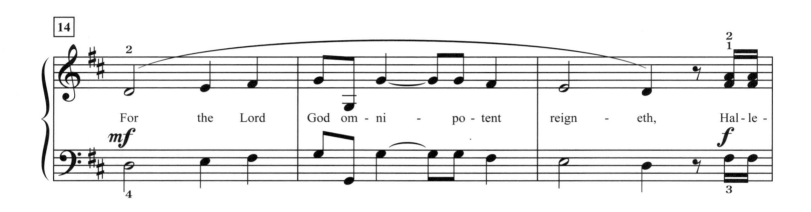

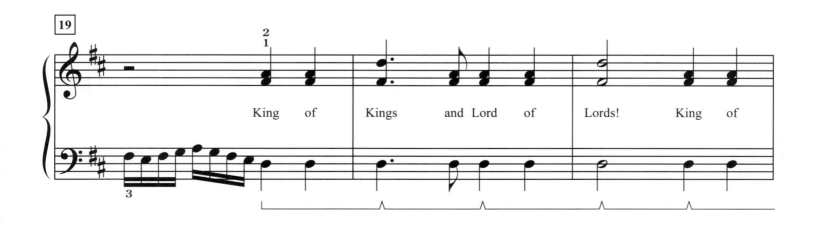

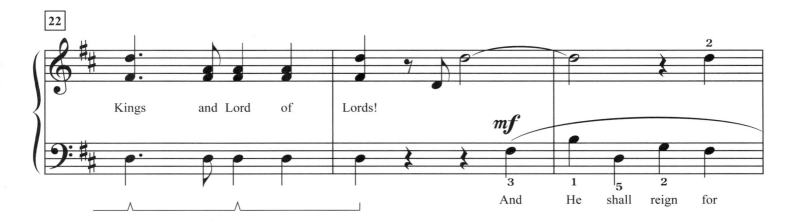

Kings   and Lord   of   Lords!

And   He   shall   reign   for

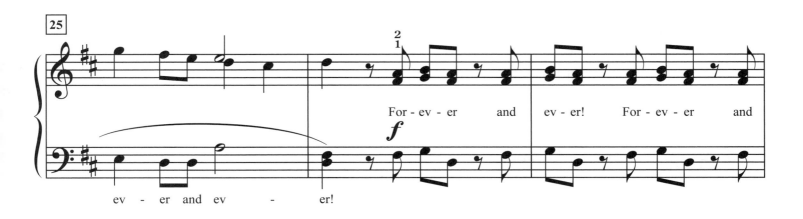

For - ev - er   and   ev - er!   For - ev - er   and

ev - er and ev - er!

ev - er!   Hal - le - lu - jah!   Hal - le - lu - jah!   Hal - le - lu - jah!   Hal - le -

cresc.

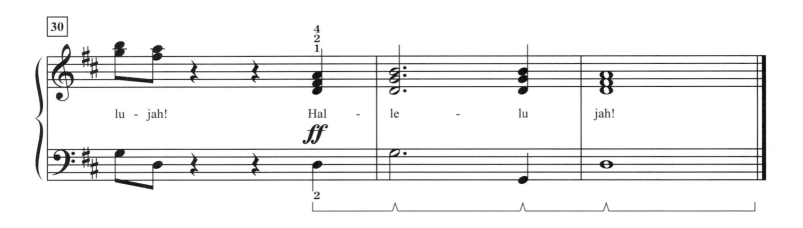

lu - jah!   Hal -   le -   lu   jah!

Hornpipe
(from *Water Music*)

George Frideric Handel (1685–1759)
HWV 349
Arranged by Bruce Nelson

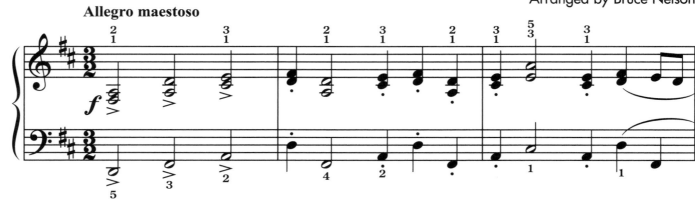

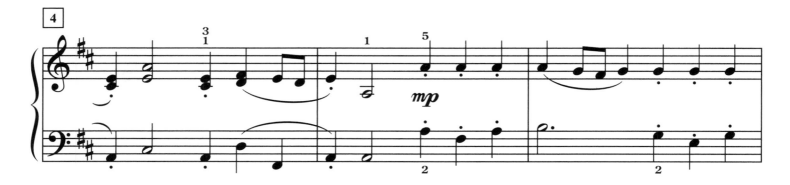

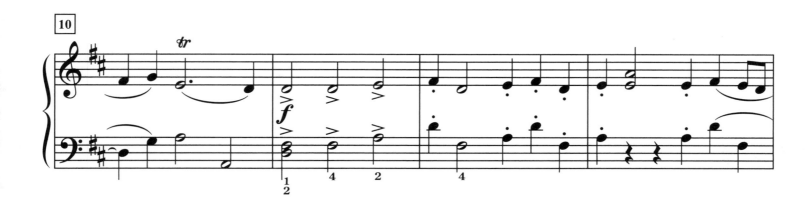

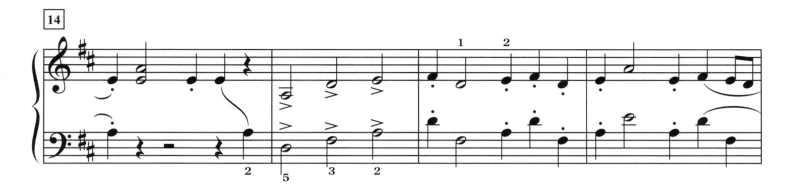

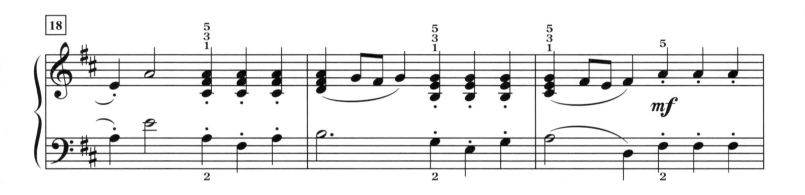

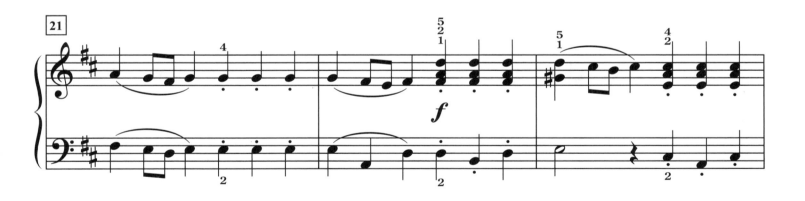

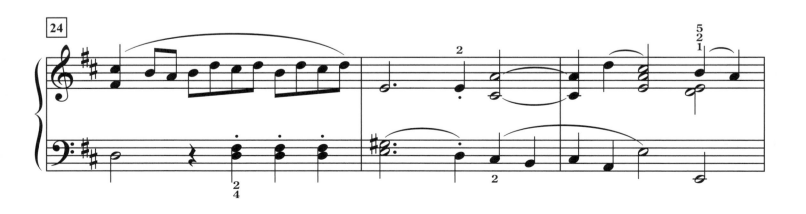

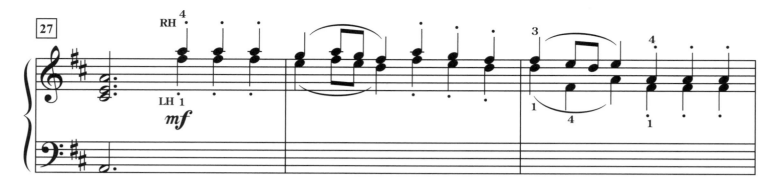

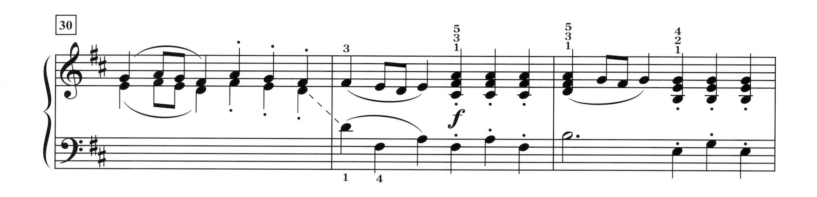

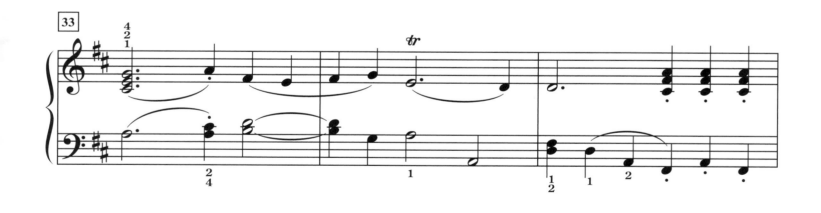

Solace
(A Mexican Serenade)

Scott Joplin
(1868–1917)
Arranged by Mary Sallee

Very slow march time

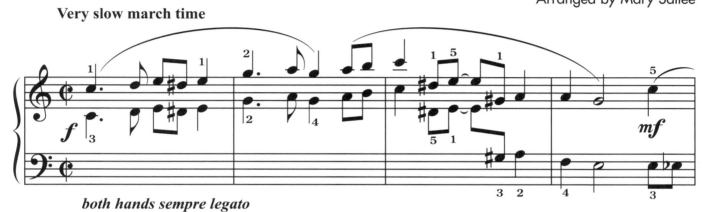

both hands sempre legato

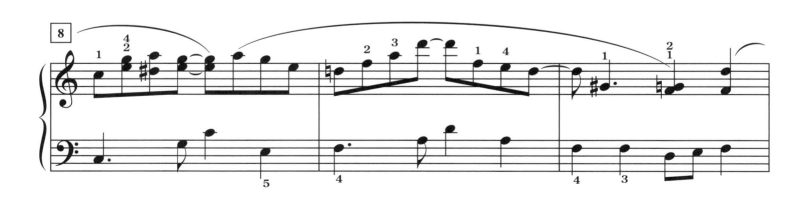

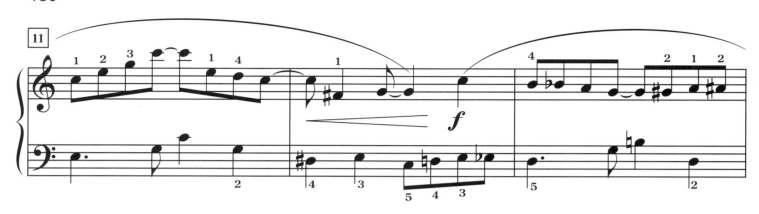

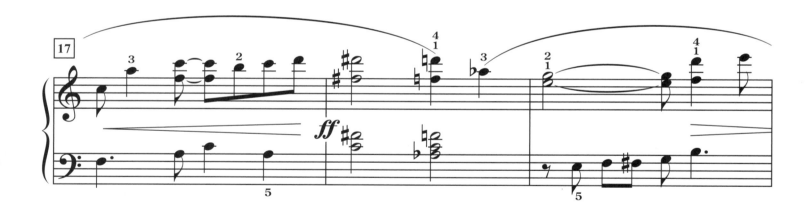

The Easy Winners

(A Ragtime Two-Step)

Scott Joplin
(1868–1917)
Arranged by Mary Sallee

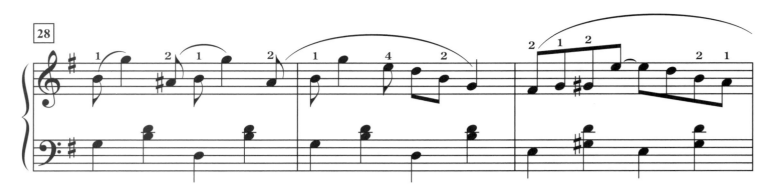

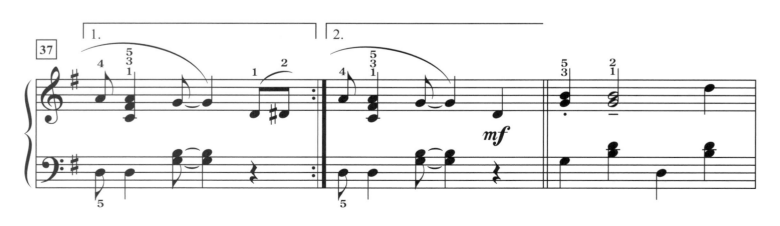

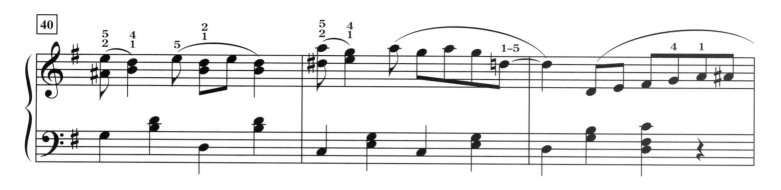

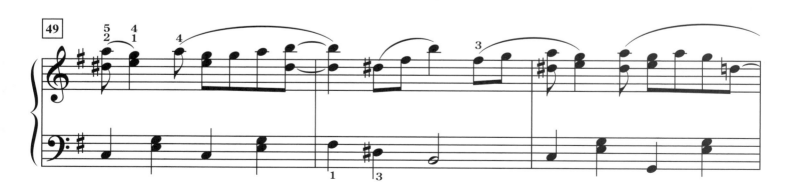

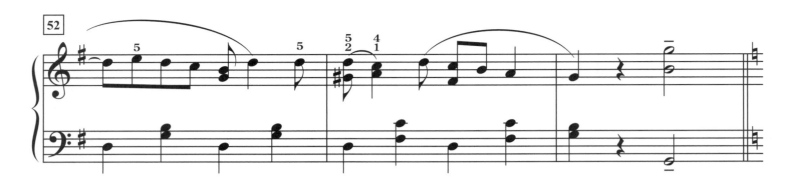

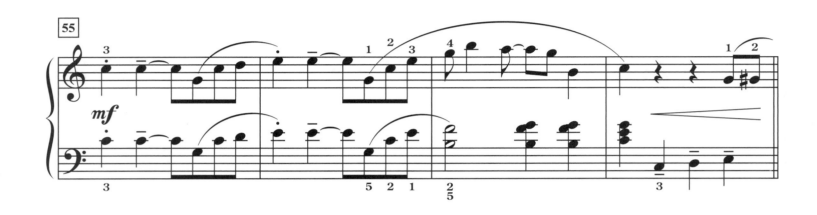

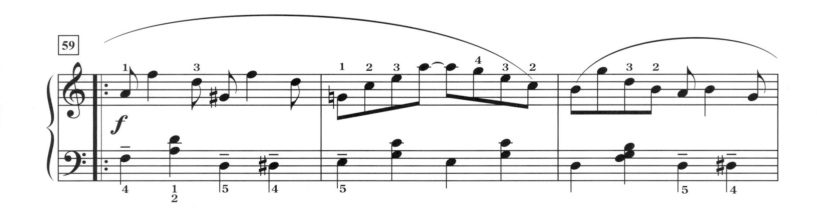

The Entertainer

Scott Joplin
(1868–1917)
Arranged by Mary Sallee

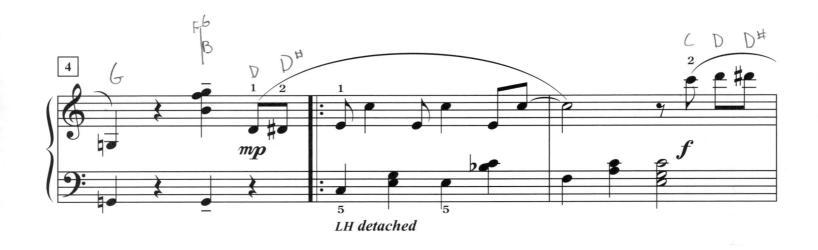

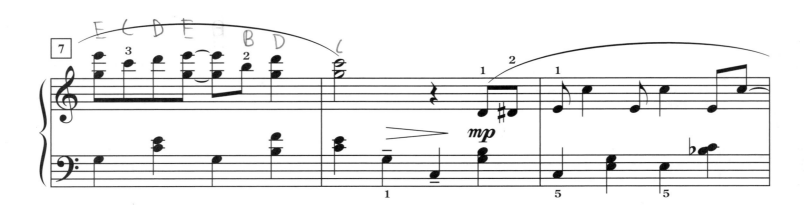

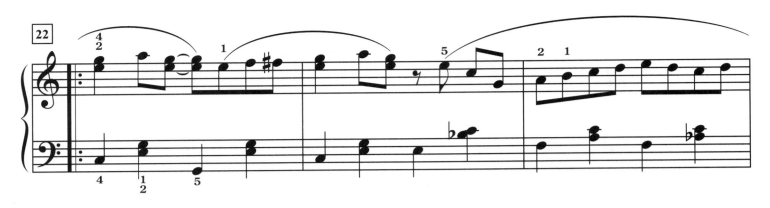

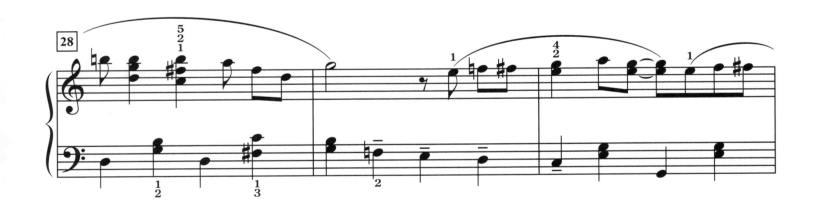

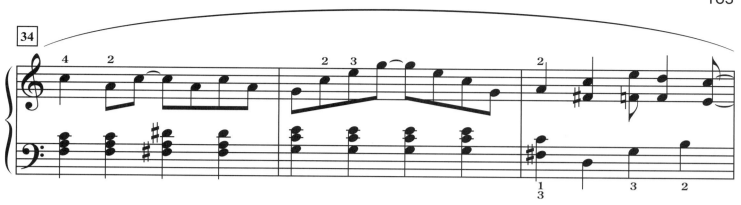

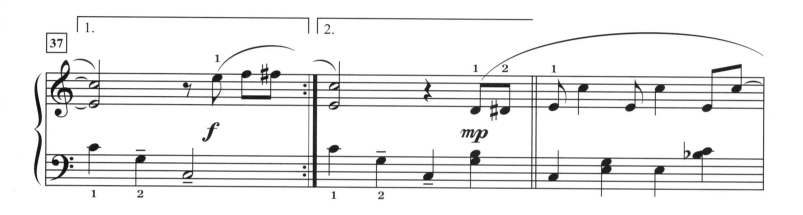

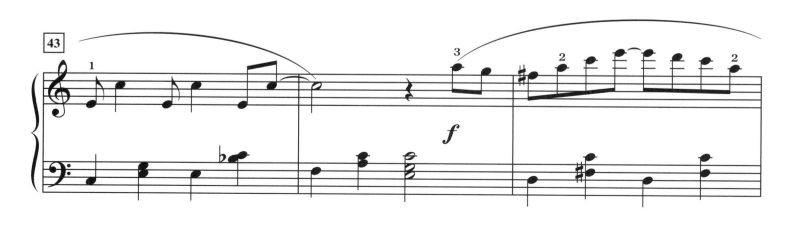

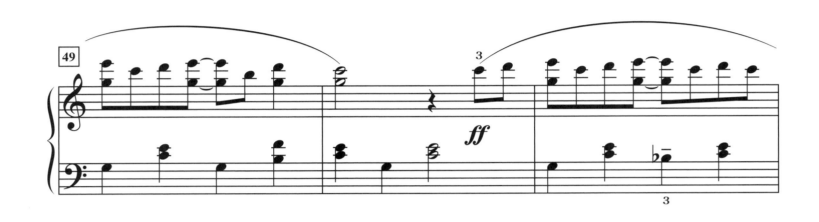

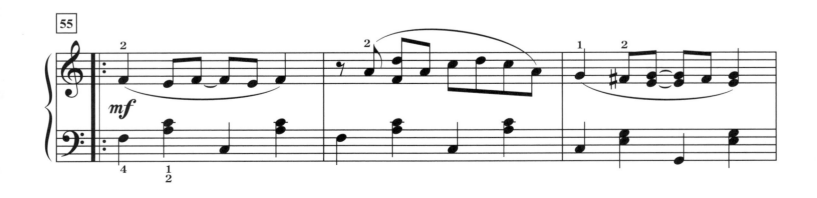

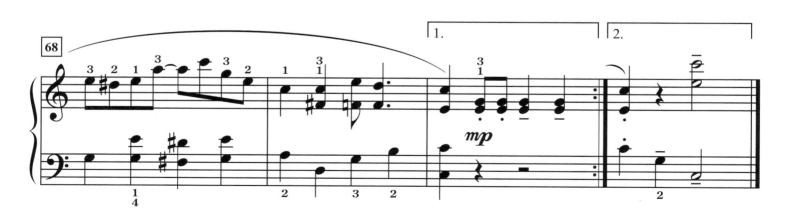

Maple Leaf Rag

Scott Joplin
(1868–1917)
Arranged by Mary Sallee

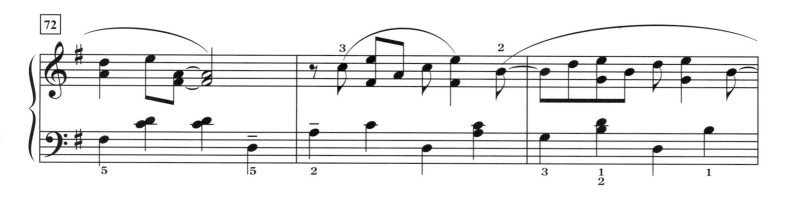

Symphony No. 94 in G Major—Surprise

(Second Movement)

Franz Joseph Haydn (1732–1809)
H. 94
Arranged by Robert Schultz

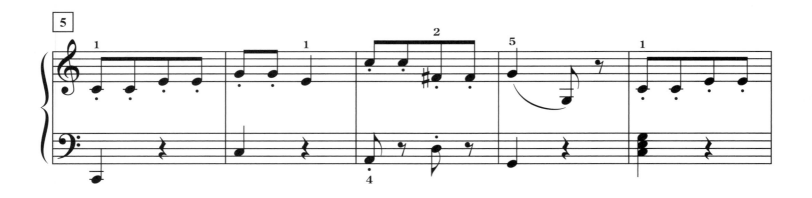

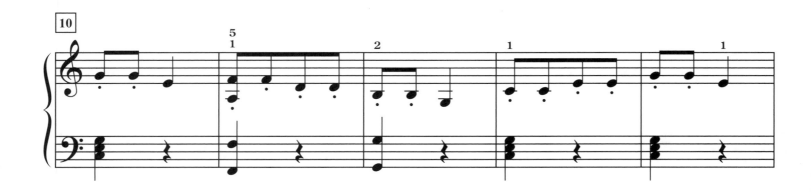

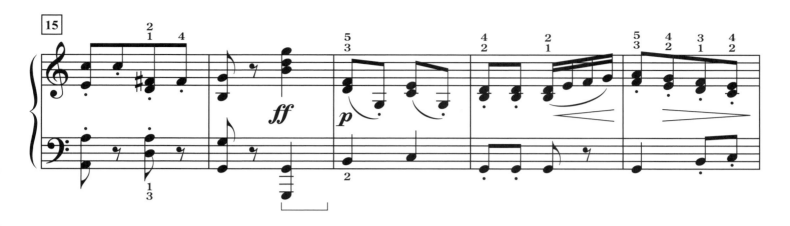

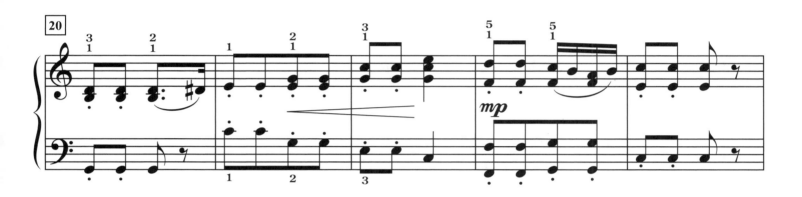

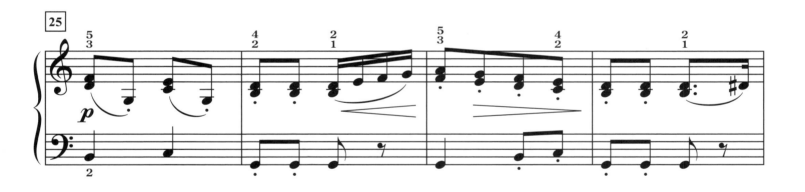

Waltz
(from *The Merry Widow*)

Franz Lehár
(1870–1948)
Arranged by Robert Schultz

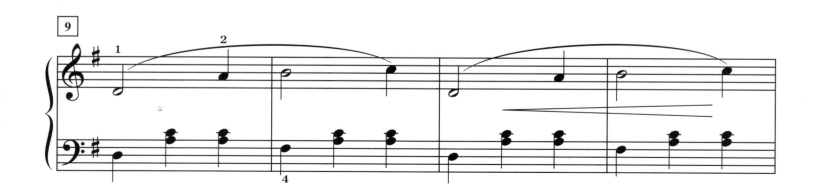

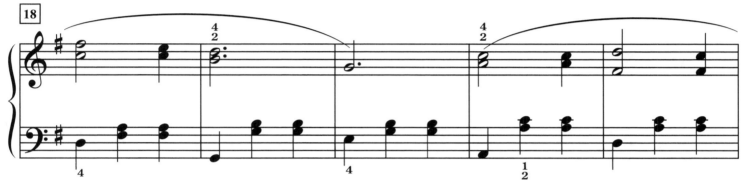

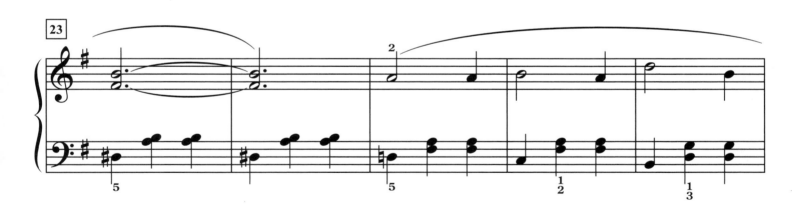

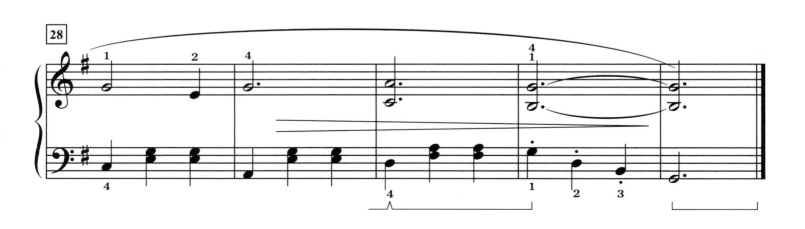

Intermezzo

(from *Cavalleria rusticana*)

Pietro Mascagni
(1863–1945)
Arranged by Tom Gerou

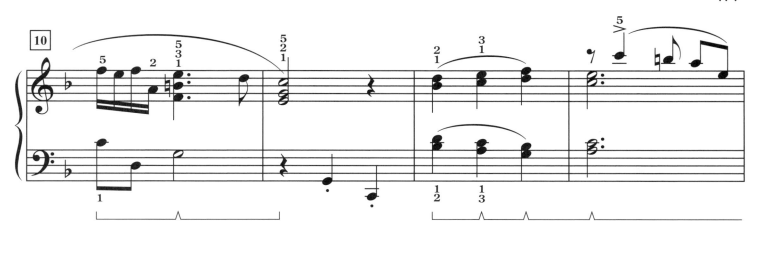

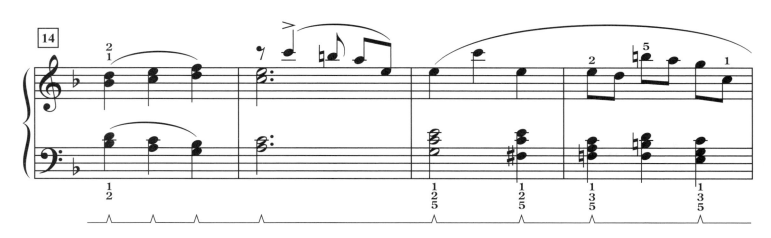

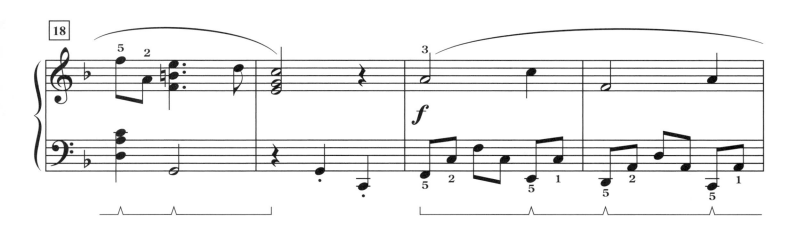

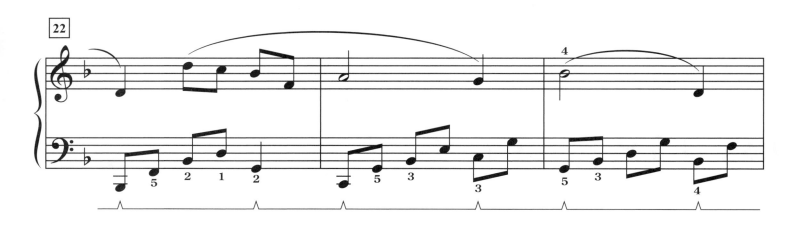

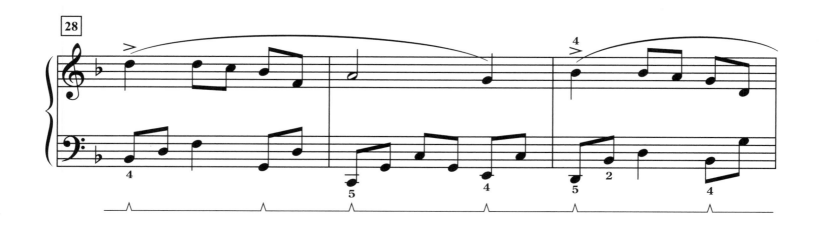

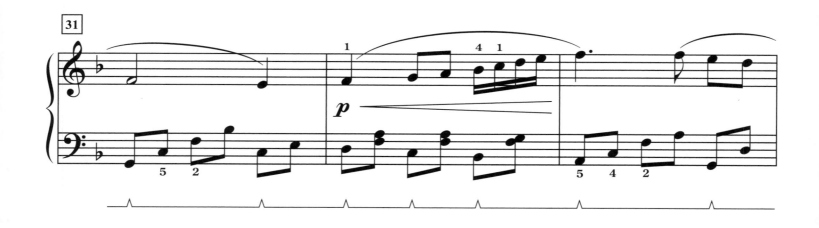

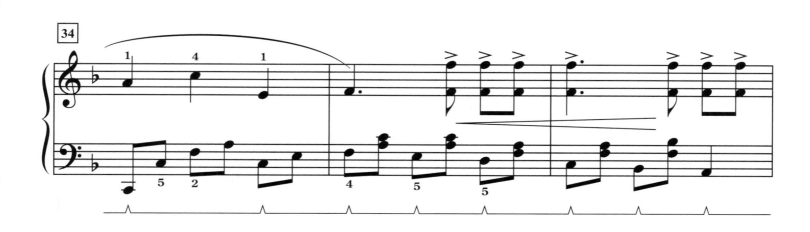

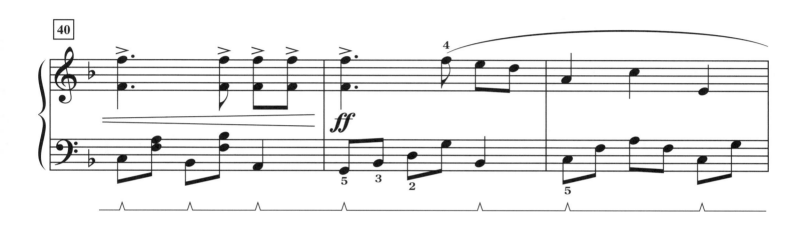

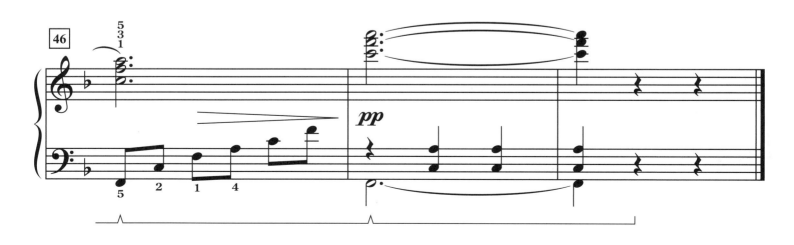

Meditation

(from *Thaïs*)

Jules Massenet
(1842–1912)
Arranged by Tom Gerou

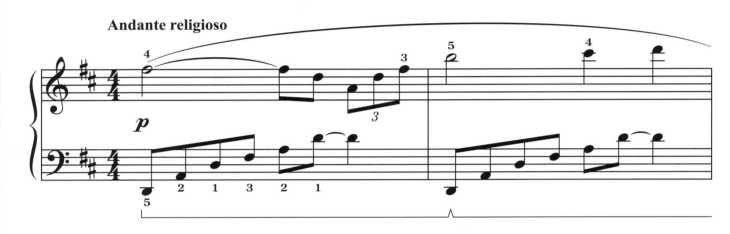

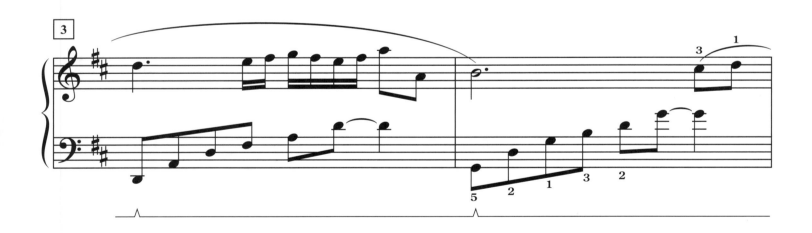

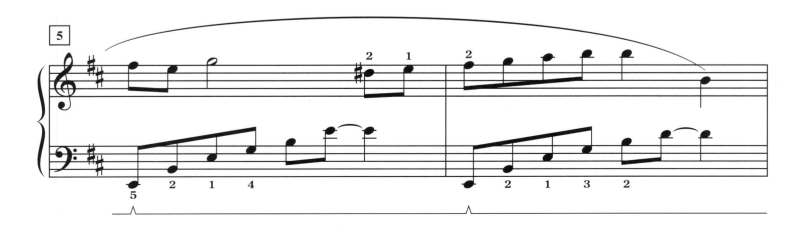

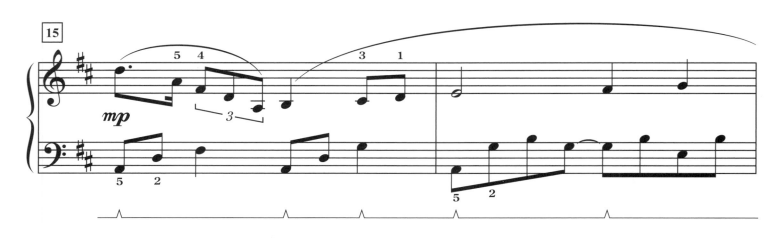

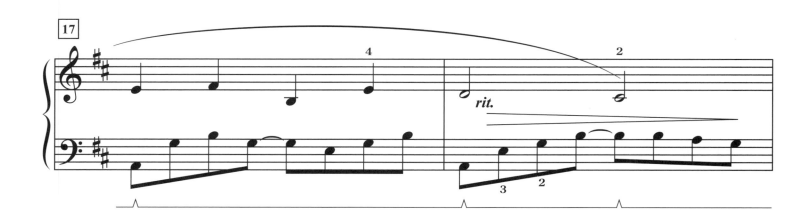

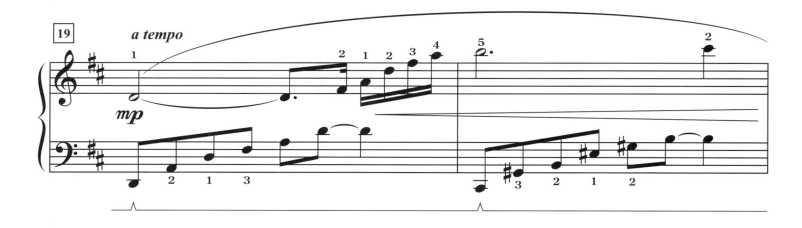

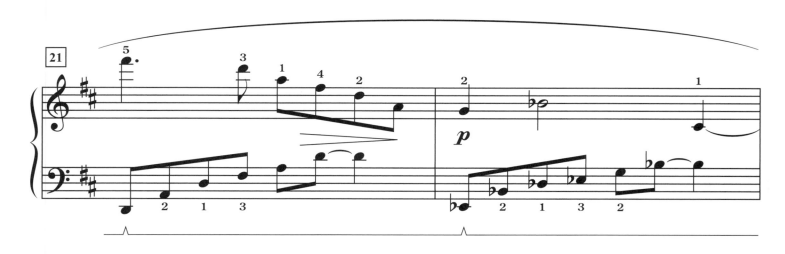

Wedding March

(from *A Midsummer Night's Dream*)

Felix Mendelssohn (1809–1847)
Op. 21
Arranged by Robert Schultz

Rondeau

(from *Suite de symphonies*)

Jean-Joseph Mouret
(1682–1738)
Arranged by Bruce Nelson

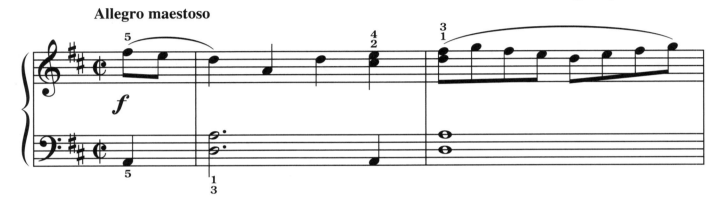

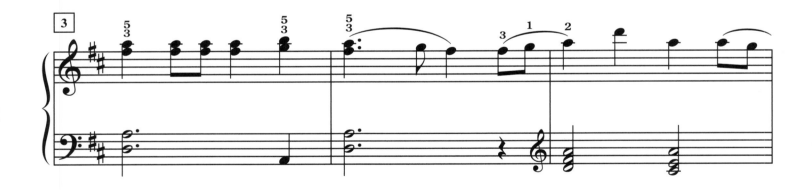

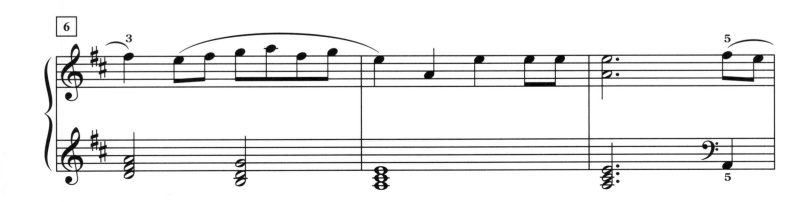

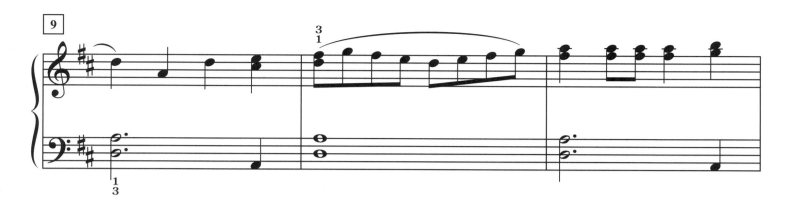

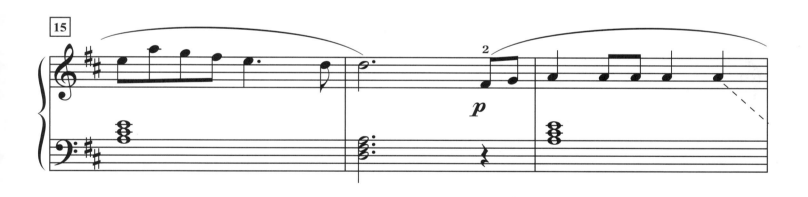

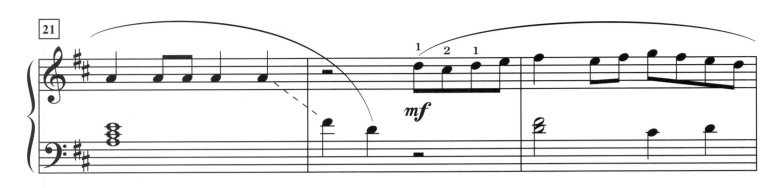

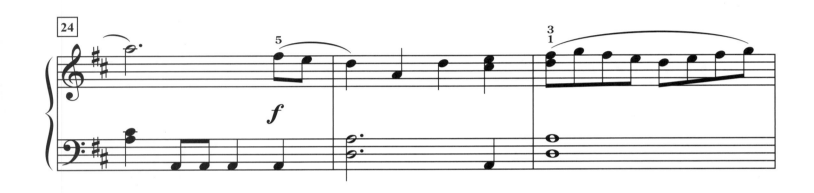

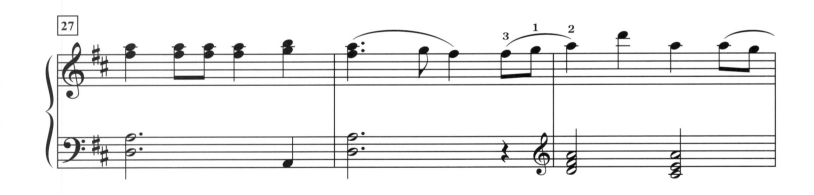

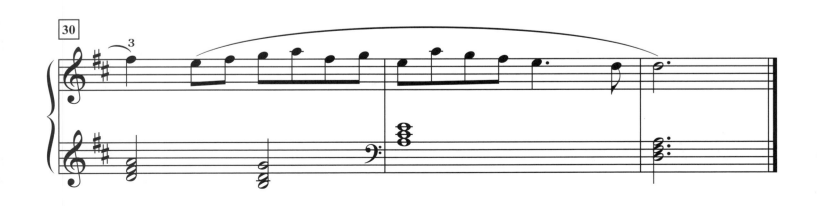

Eine kleine Nachtmusik

(First Movement)

Wolfgang Amadeus Mozart (1756–1791)
K. 525
Arranged by Mary K. Sallee

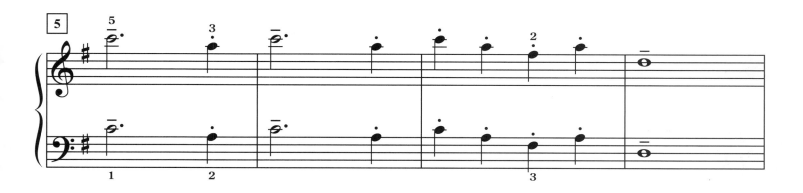

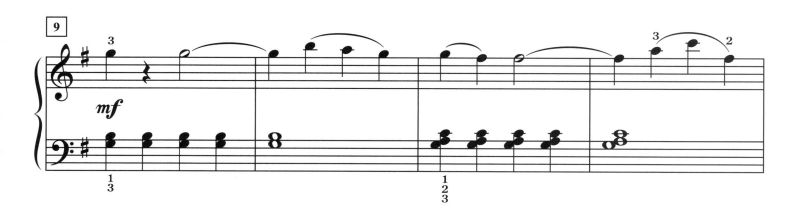

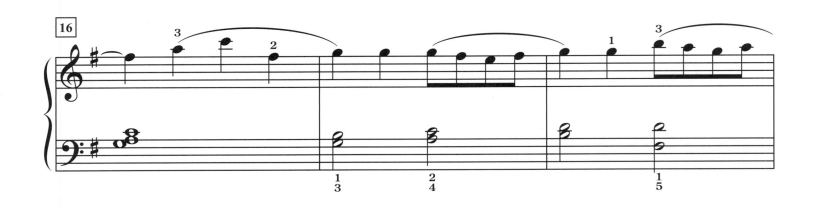

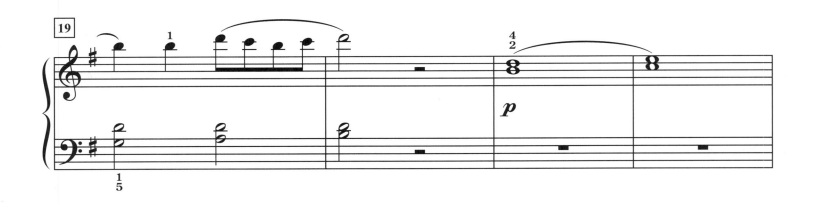

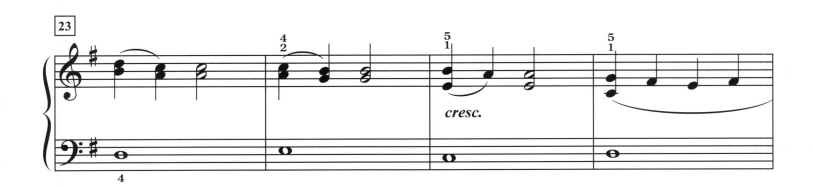

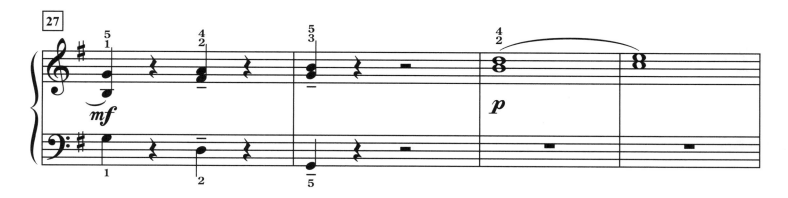

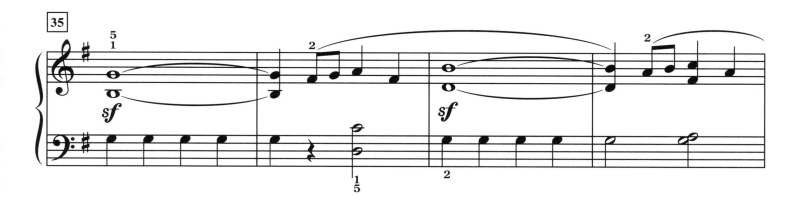

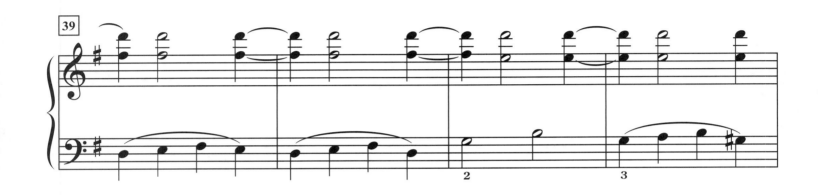

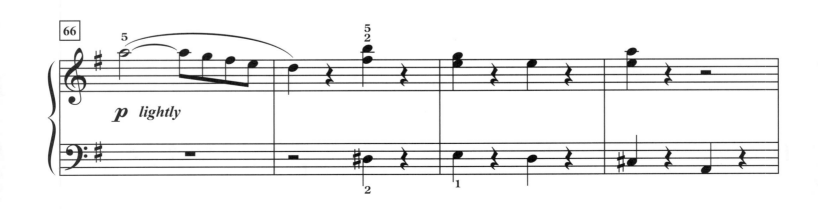

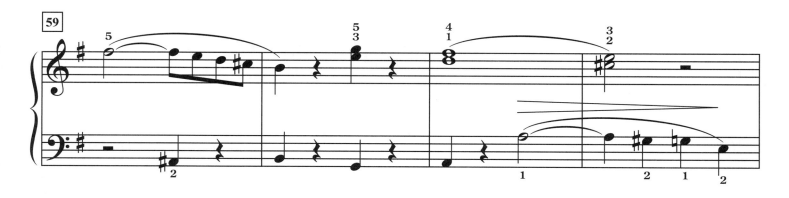

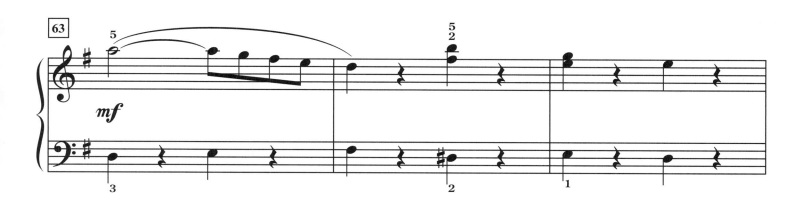

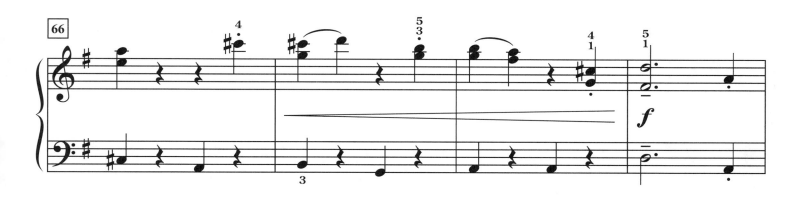

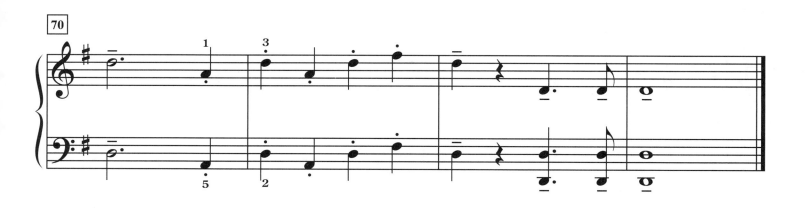

Variations on "Ah, vous dirai-je, Maman"

French Folk Song
Variations by Wolfgang Amadeus Mozart (1756–1791)
K. 265
Arranged by Jerry Ray

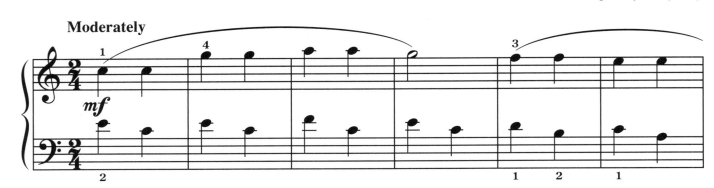

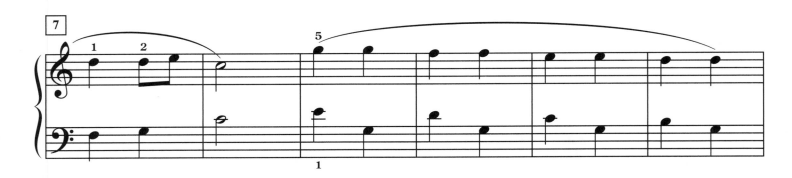

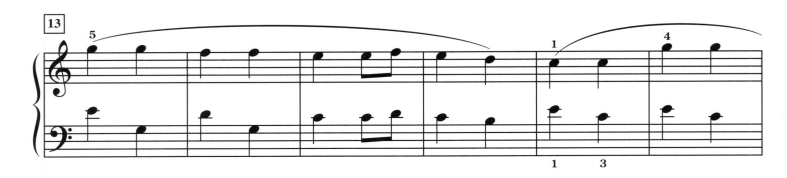

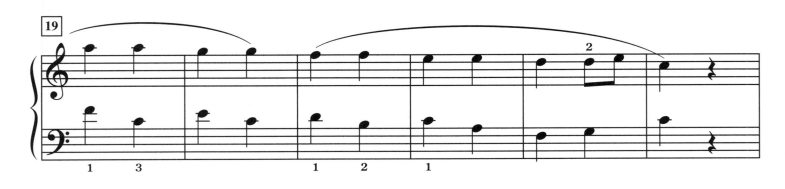

The Birdcatcher's Song

(from *The Magic Flute*)

Wolfgang Amadeus Mozart (1756–1791)
K. 620
Arranged by Jerry Ray

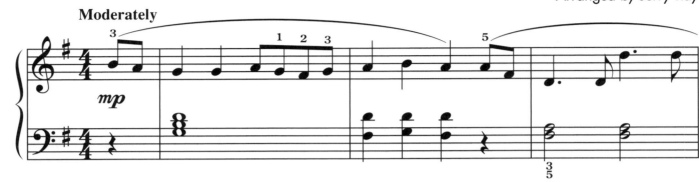

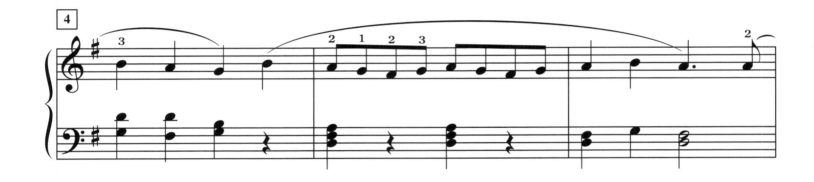

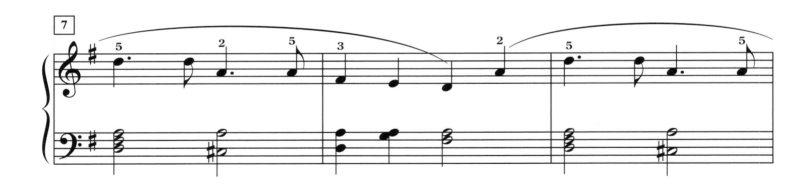

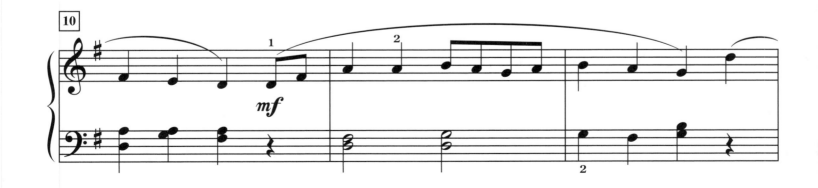

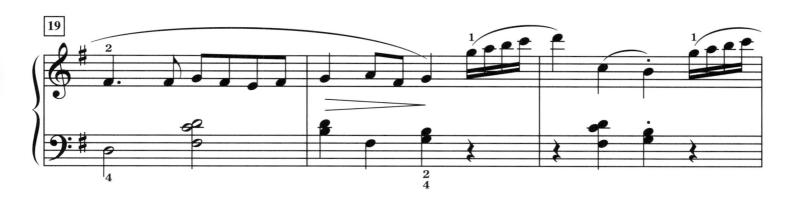

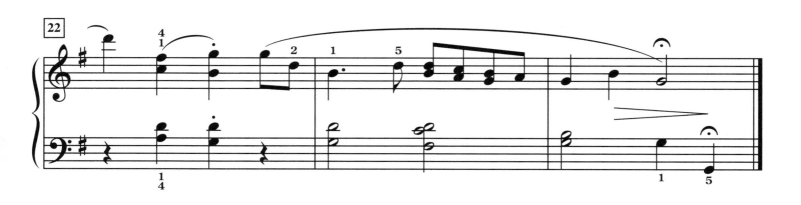

Piano Concerto No. 21 in C Major—Elvira Madigan

(Second Movement)

Wolfgang Amadeus Mozart (1756–1791)
K. 467
Arranged by Jerry Ray

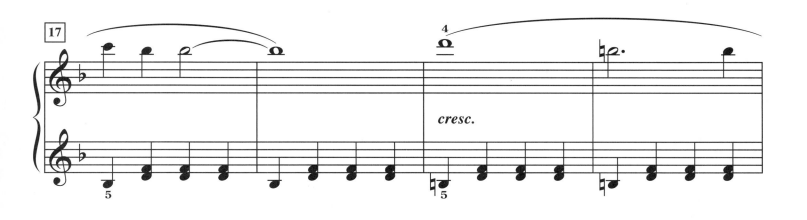

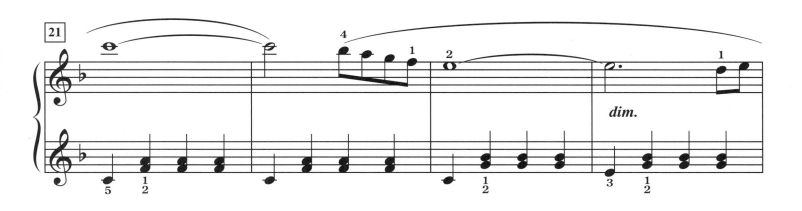

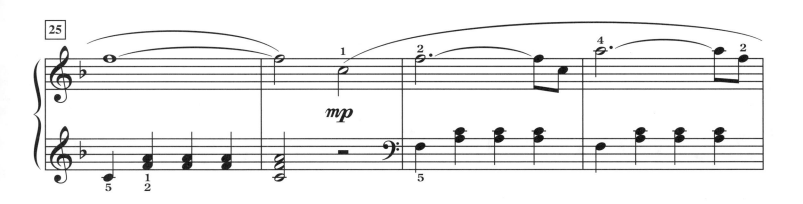

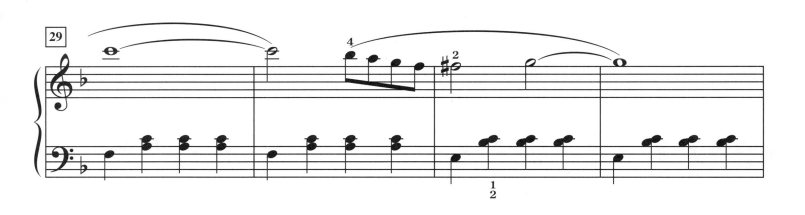

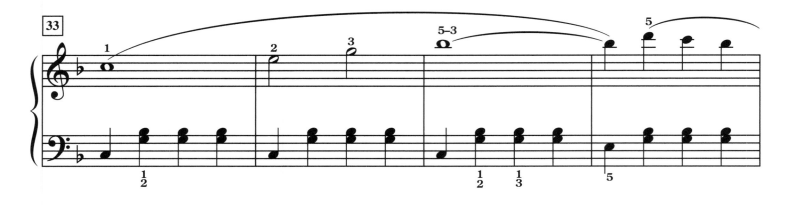

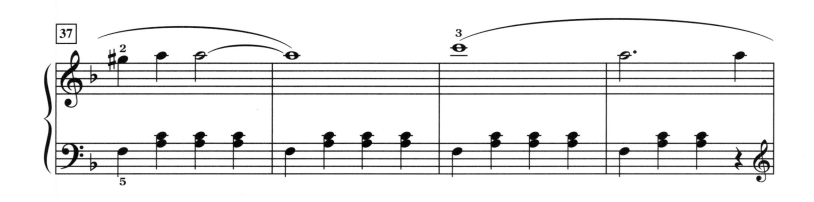

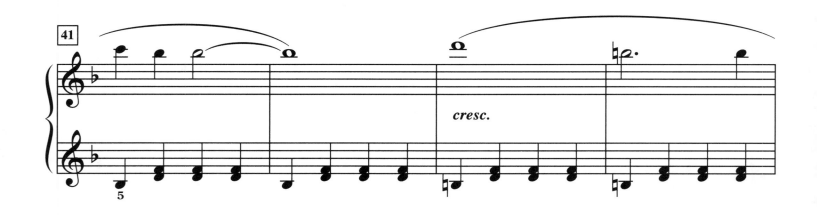

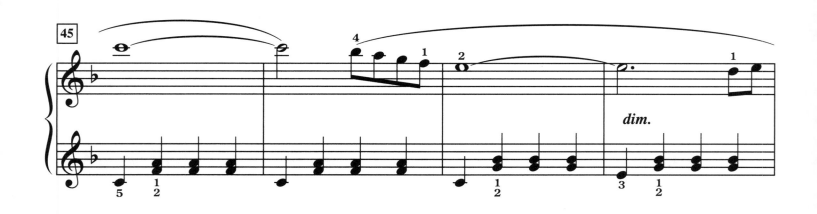

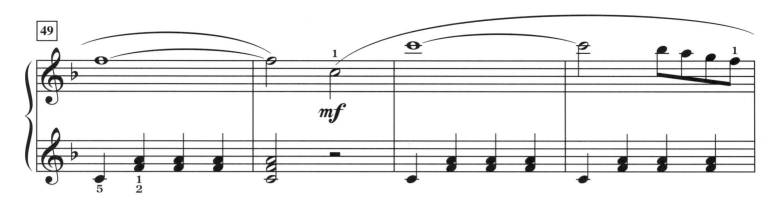

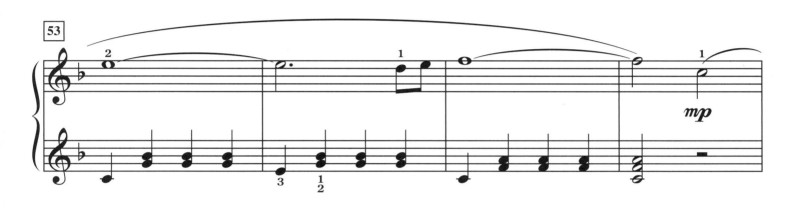

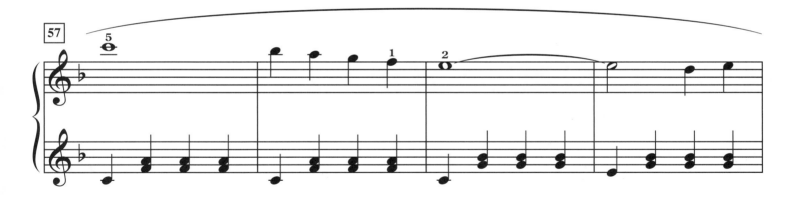

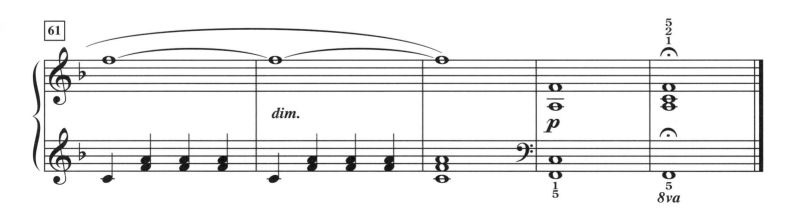

Là ci darem la mano

(from *Don Giovanni*)

Wolfgang Amadeus Mozart (1756–1791)
K. 527
Arranged by Tom Gerou

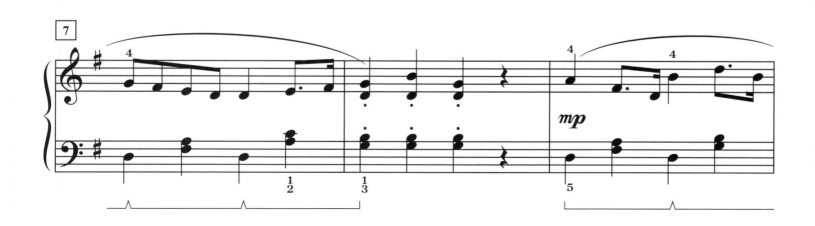

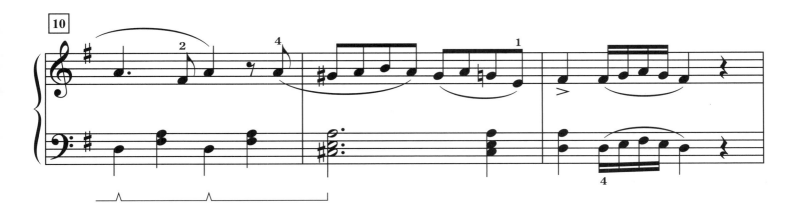

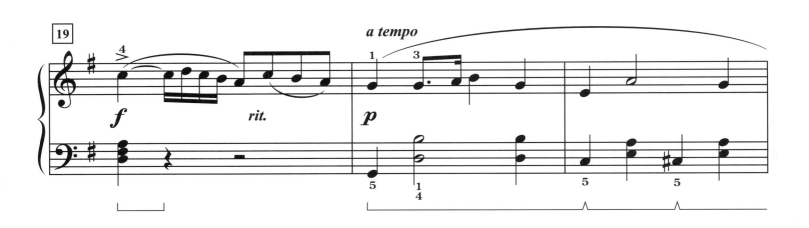

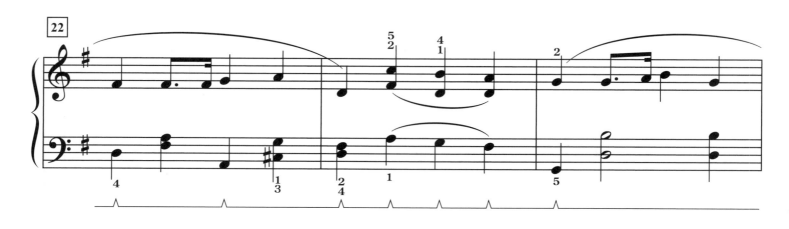

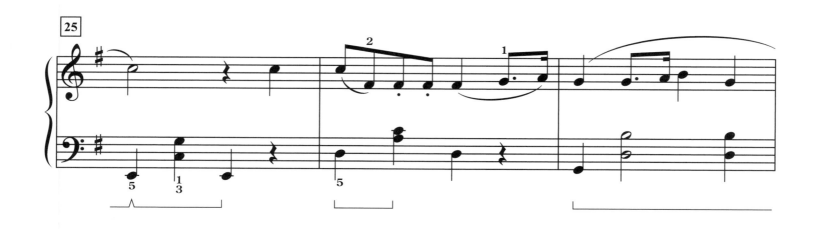

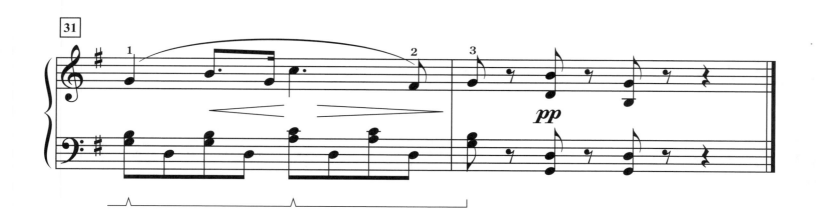

Laudate Dominum
(from *Vesperae solennes de confessore*)

Wolfgang Amadeus Mozart (1756–1791)
K. 339
Arranged by Mary K. Sallee

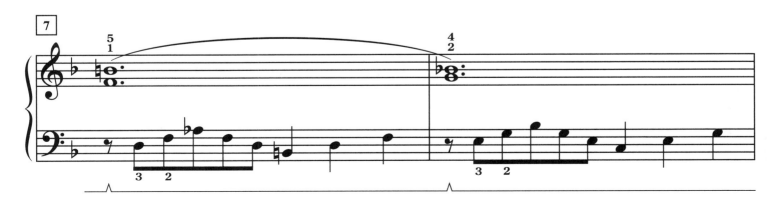

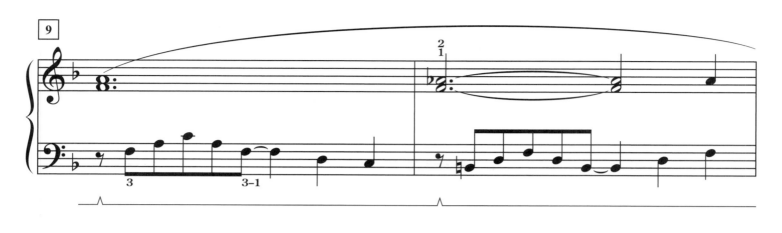

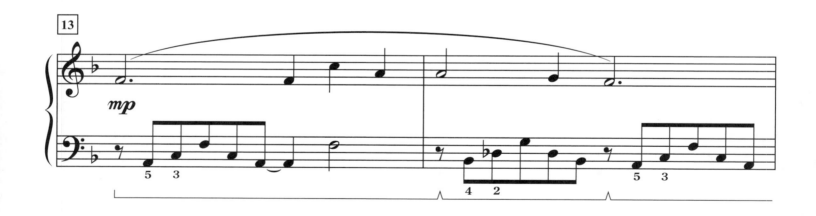

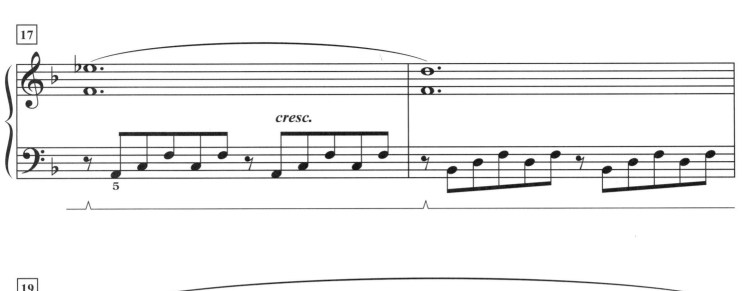

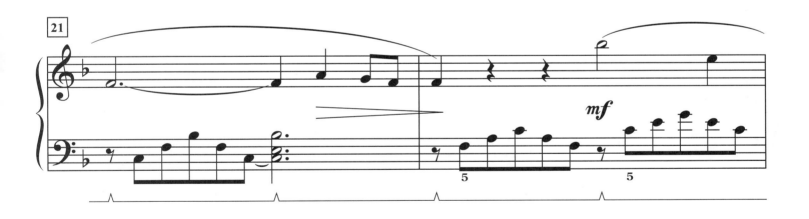

Overture from *The Marriage of Figaro*

Wolfgang Amadeus Mozart (1756–1791)
K. 492
Arranged by Jerry Ray

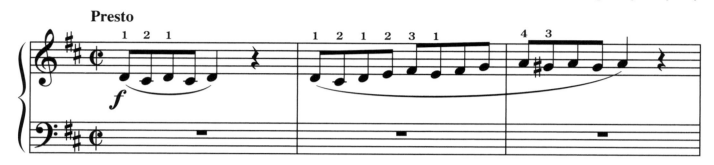

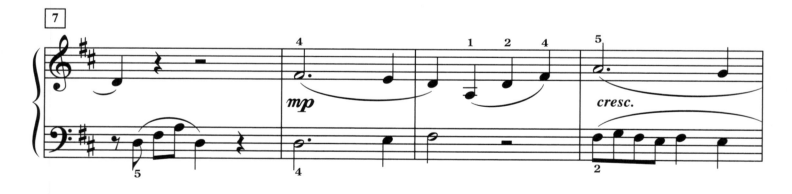

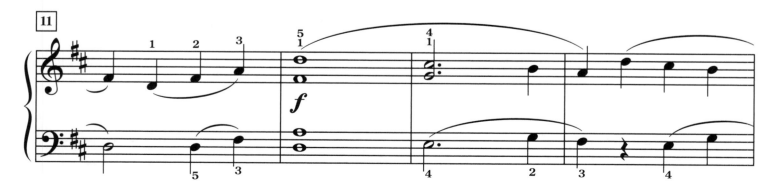

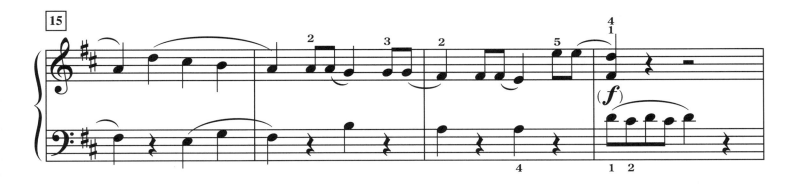

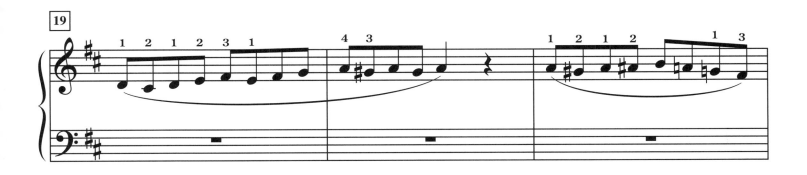

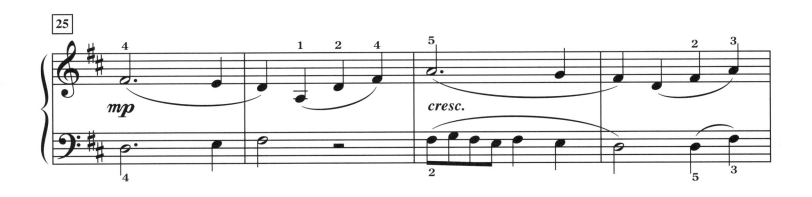

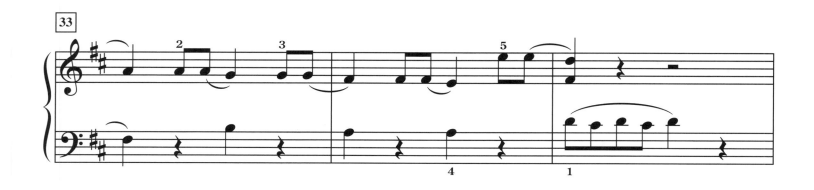

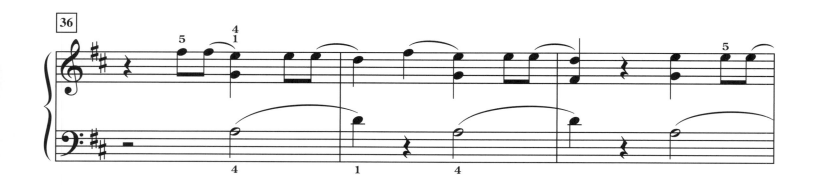

Queen of the Night Aria

(from *The Magic Flute*)

Wolfgang Amadeus Mozart (1756–1791)

K. 620

Arranged by Tom Gerou

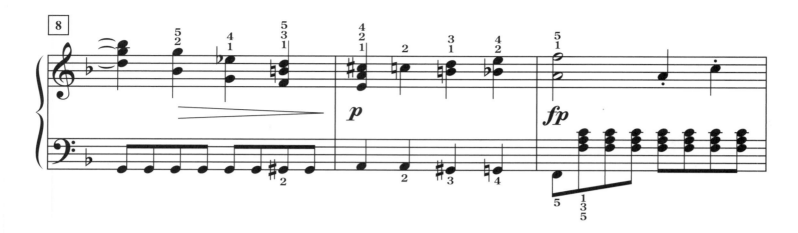

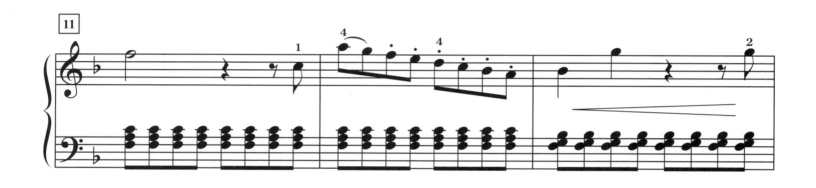

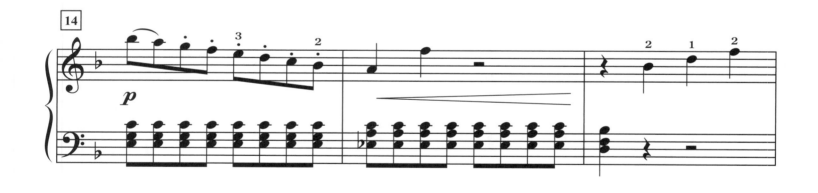

215

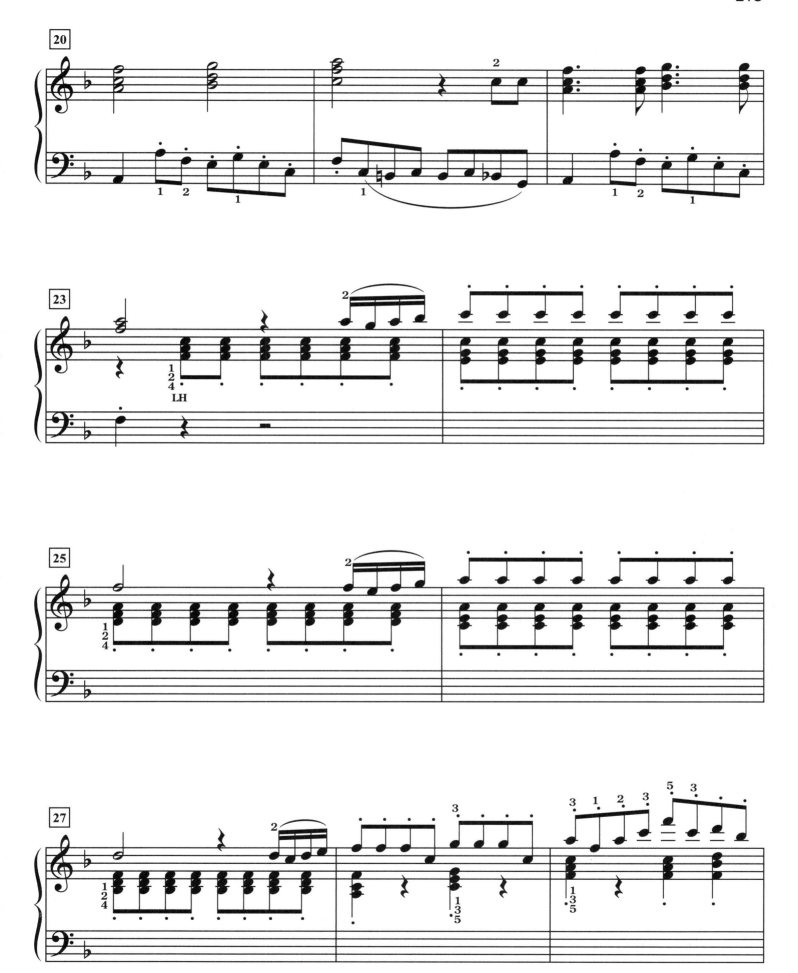

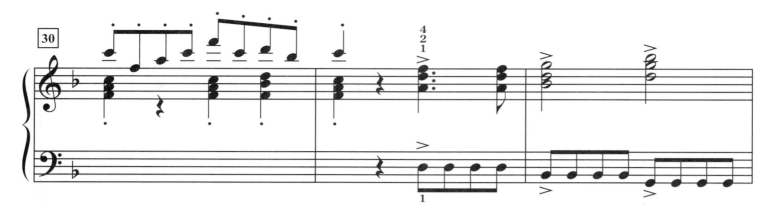

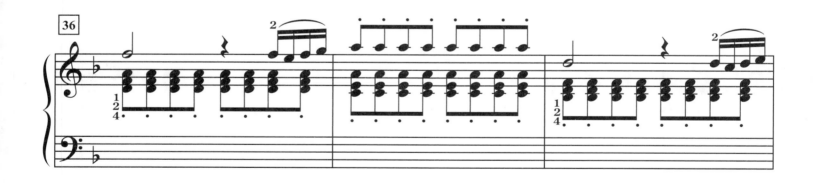

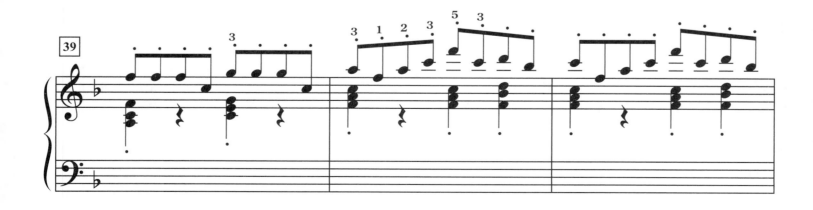

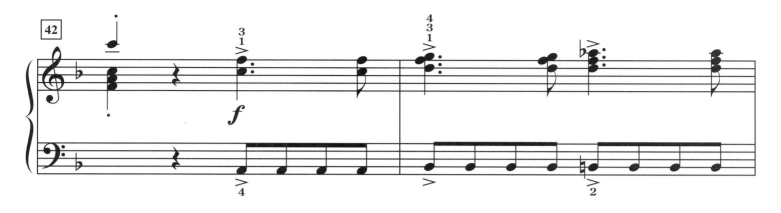

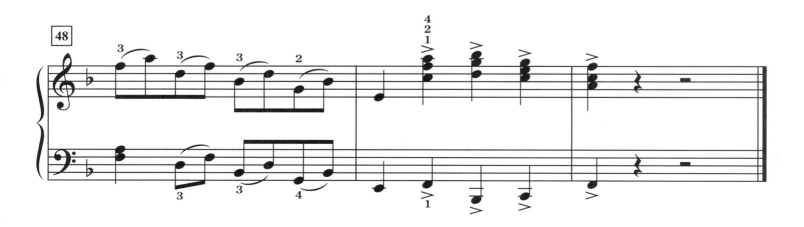

Piano Sonata No. 11 in A Major

(Third Movement)

"Rondo alla Turca"

Wolfgang Amadeus Mozart (1756–1791)

K. 331

Arranged by Mary K. Sallee

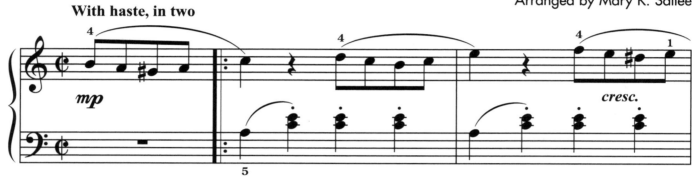

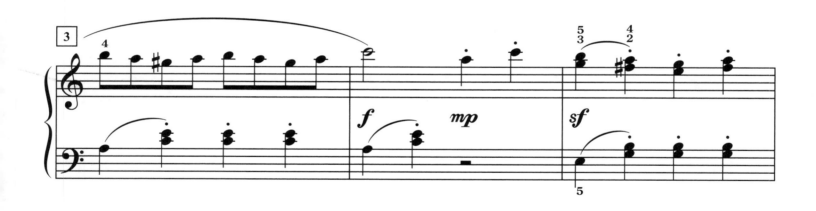

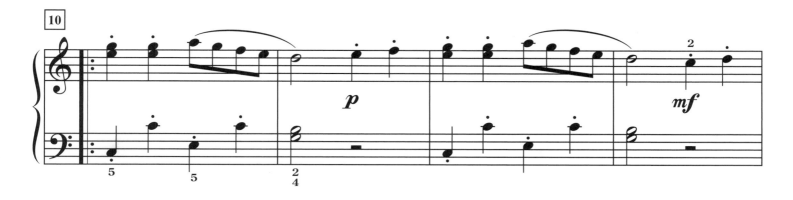

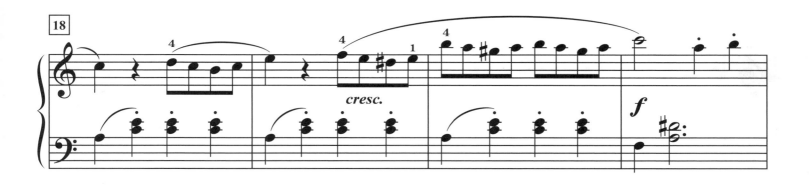

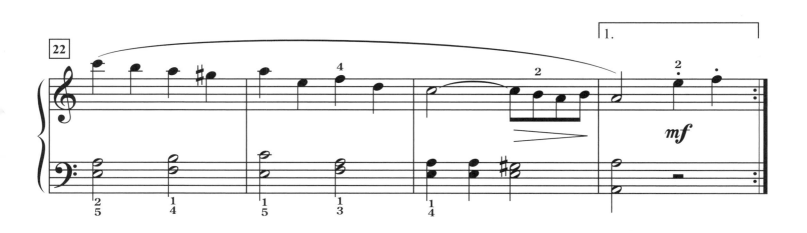

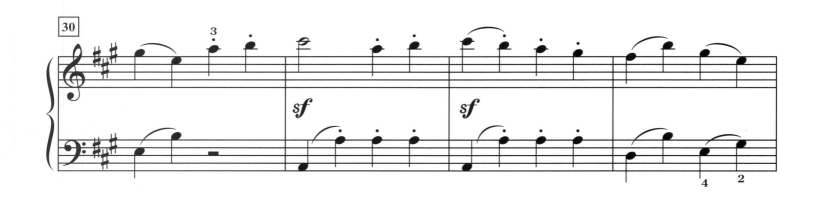

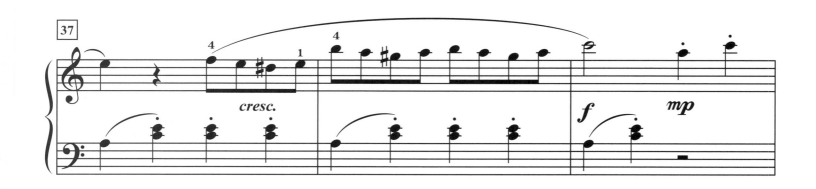

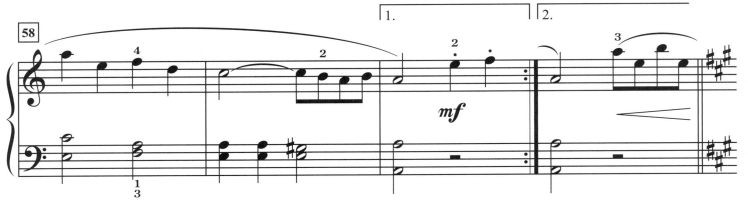

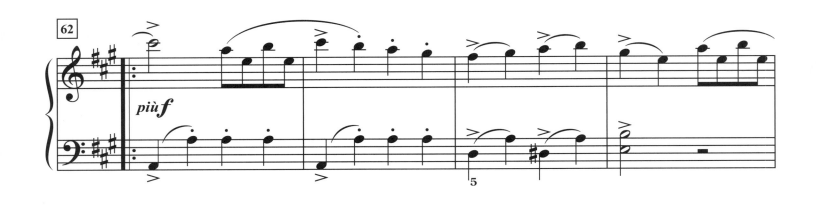

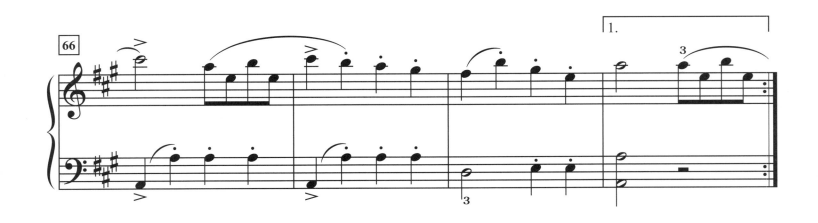

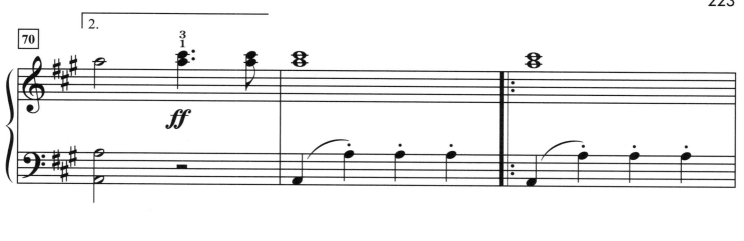

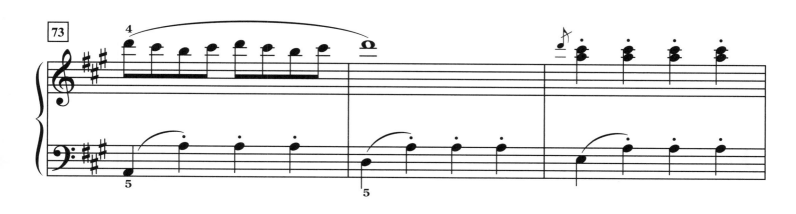

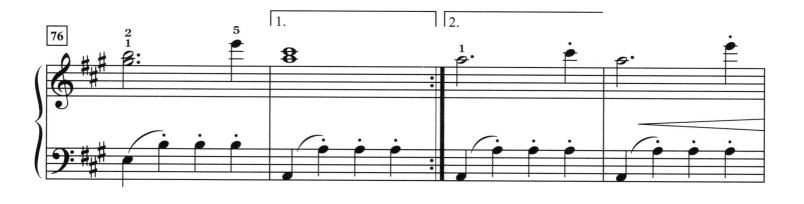

Piano Sonata No. 16 in C Major

(First Movement)

Wolfgang Amadeus Mozart (1756–1791)
K. 545
Arranged by Jerry Ray

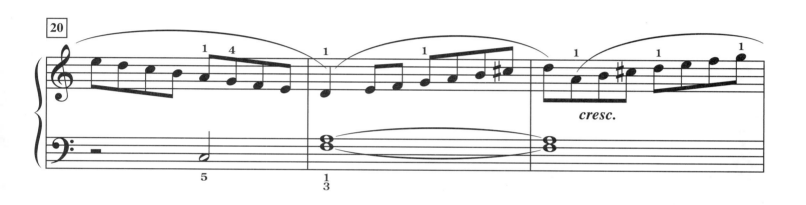

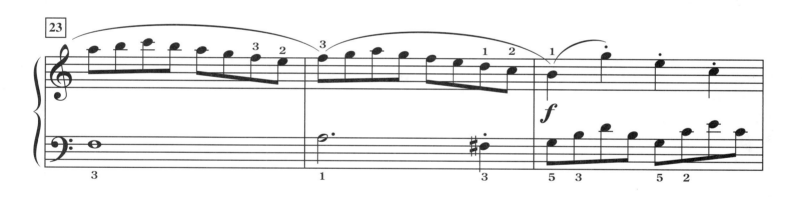

226

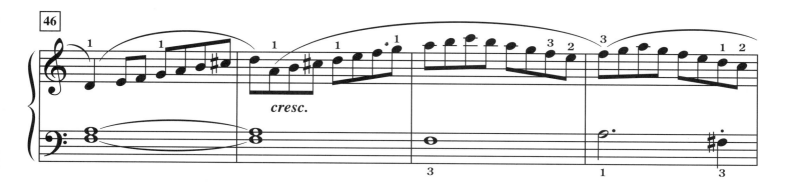

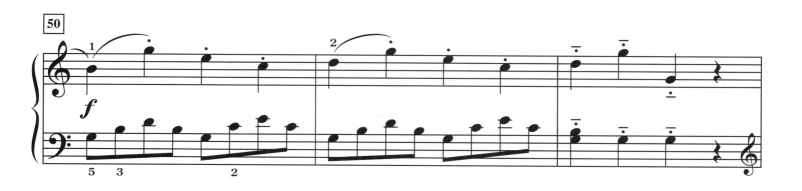

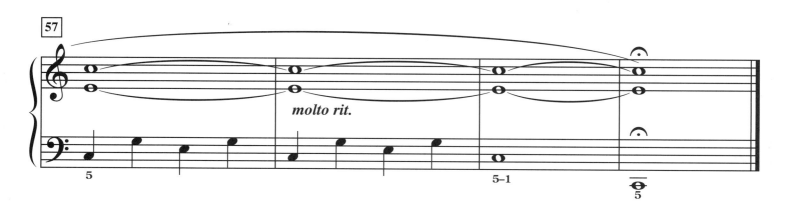

Symphony No. 40 in G Minor
(First Movement)

Wolfgang Amadeus Mozart (1756–1791)
K. 550
Arranged by Robert Schultz

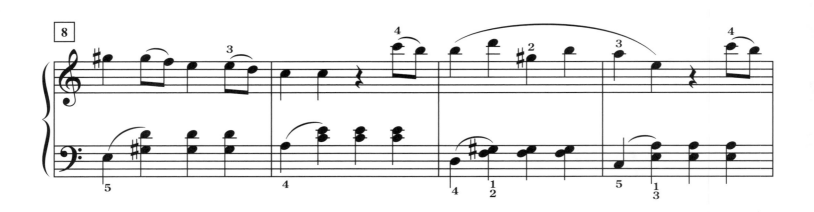

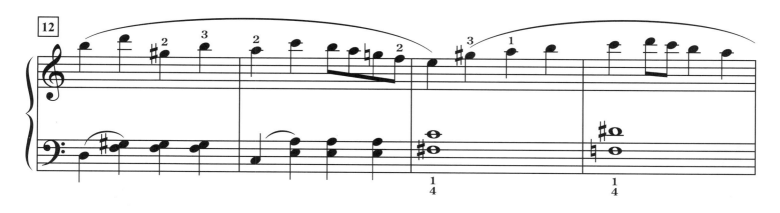

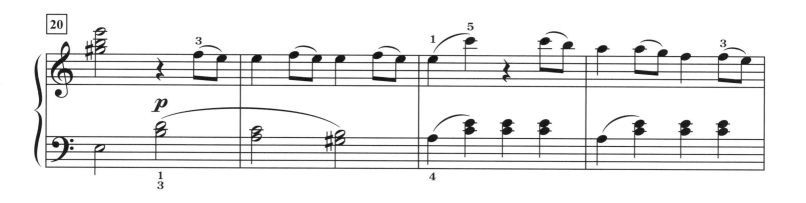

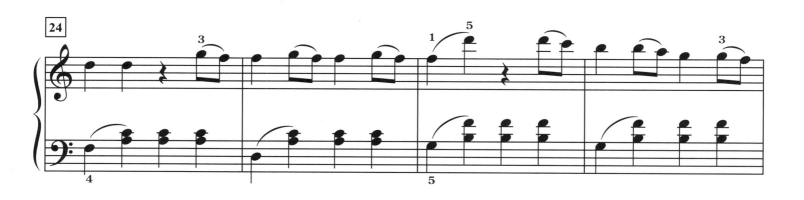

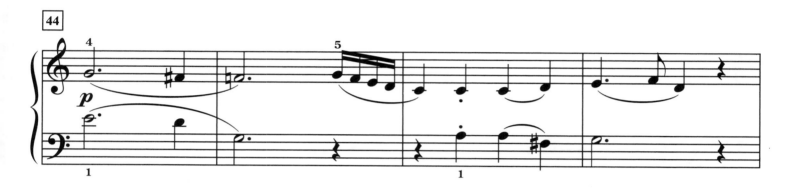

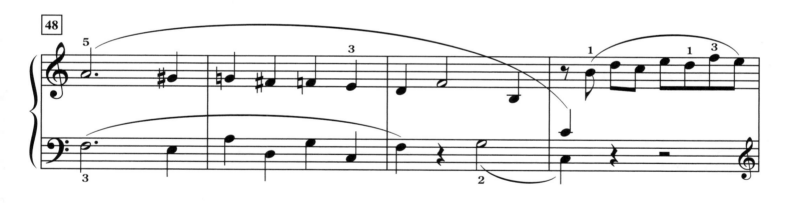

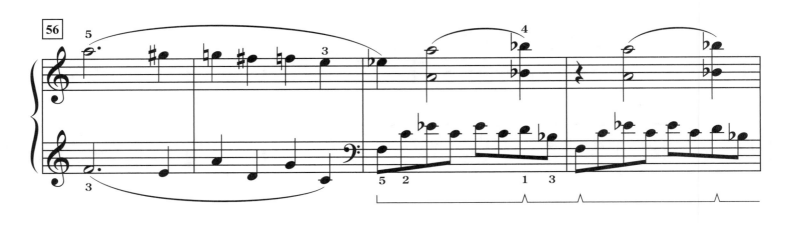

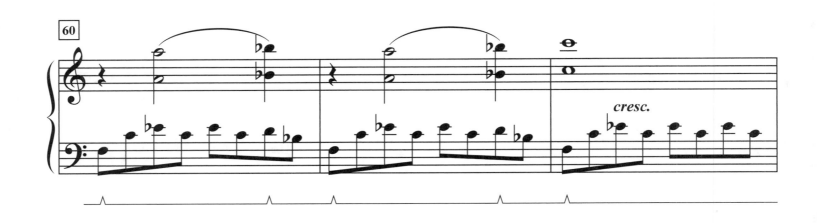

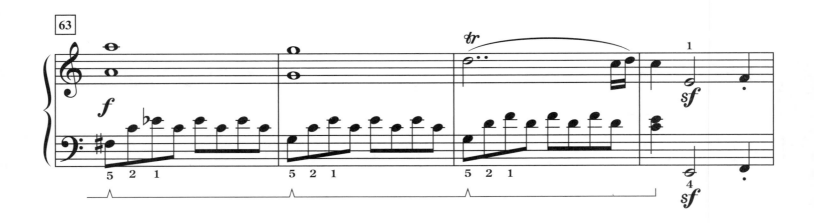

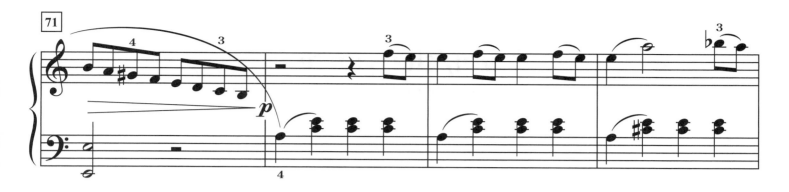

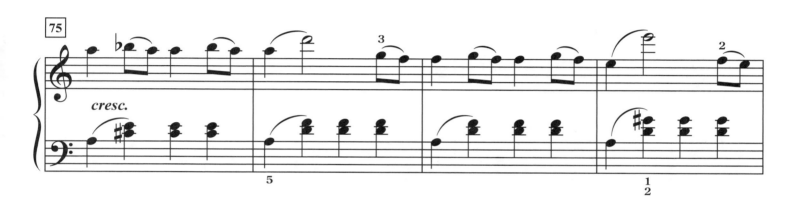

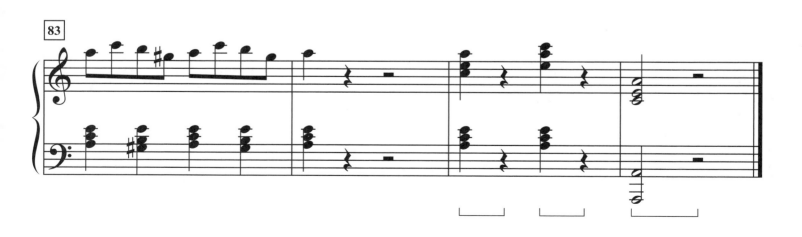

Voi, che sapete

(from *The Marriage of Figaro*)

Wolfgang Amadeus Mozart (1756–1791)
K. 492
Arranged by Tom Gerou

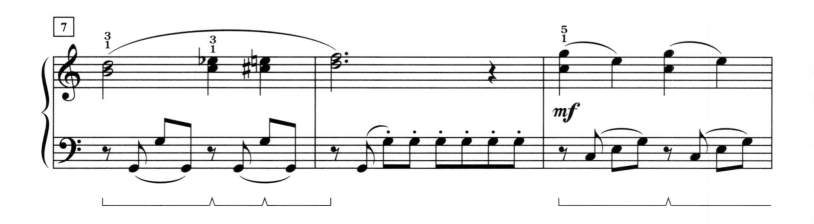

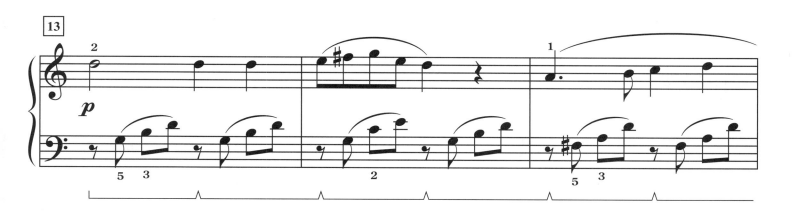

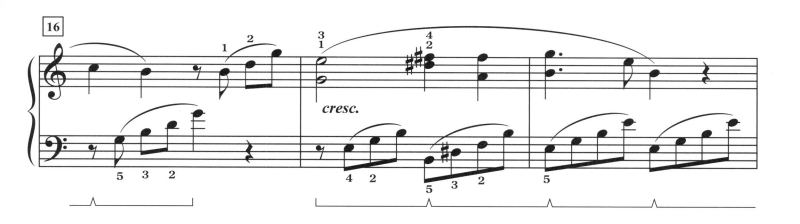

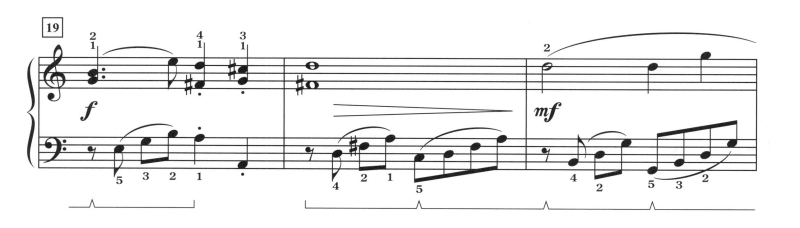

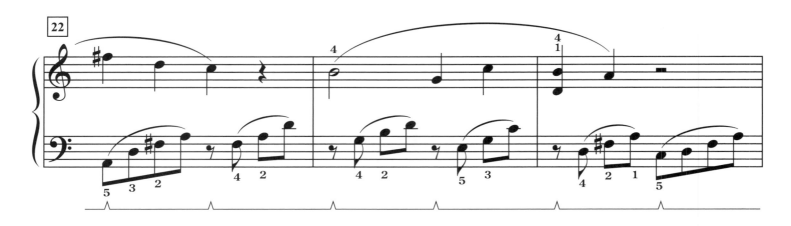

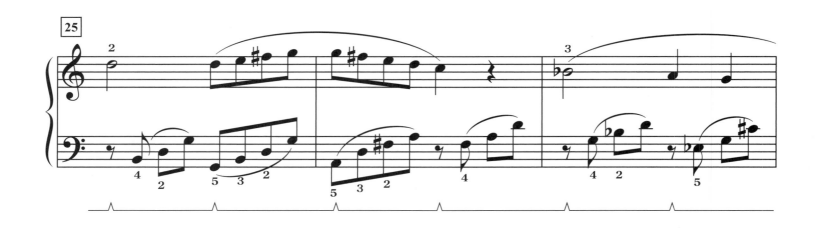

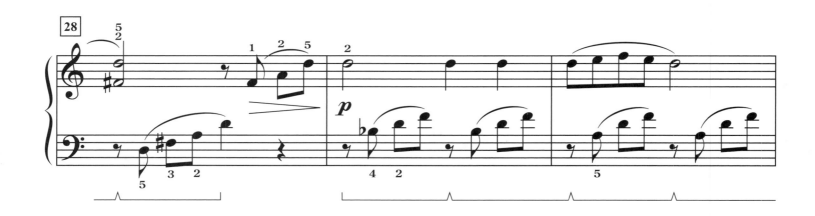

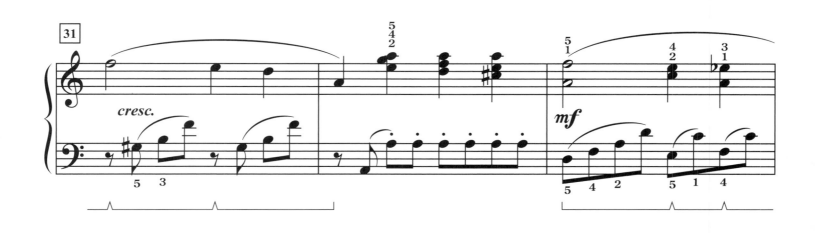

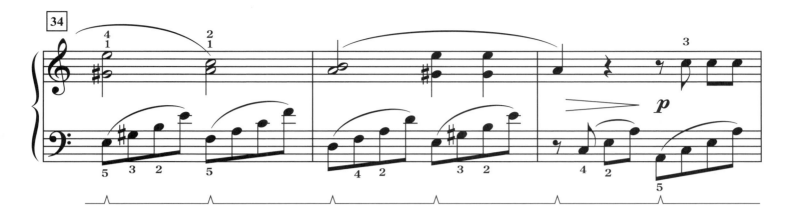

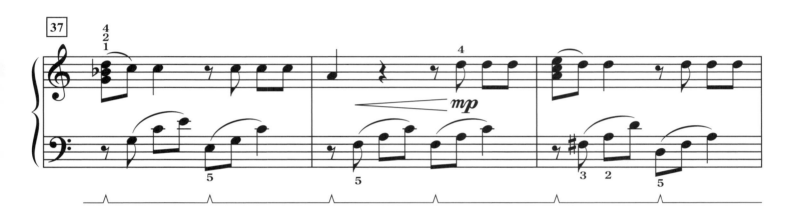

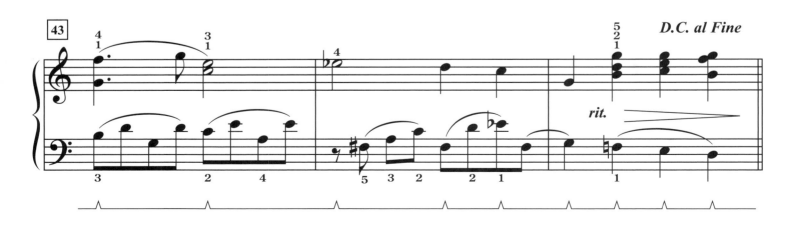

Piano Sonata No. 11 in A Major

(First Movement)

Wolfgang Amadeus Mozart (1756–1791)

K. 331

Arranged by Jerry Ray

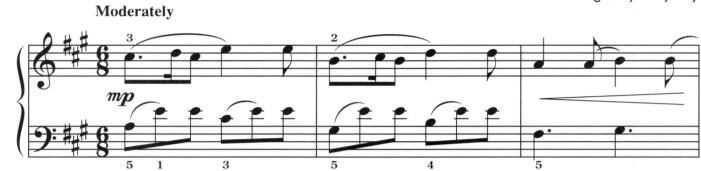

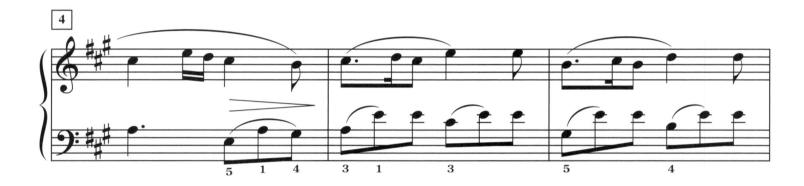

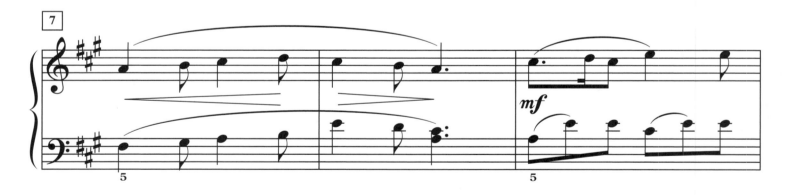

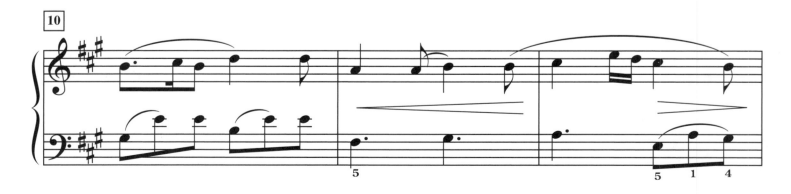

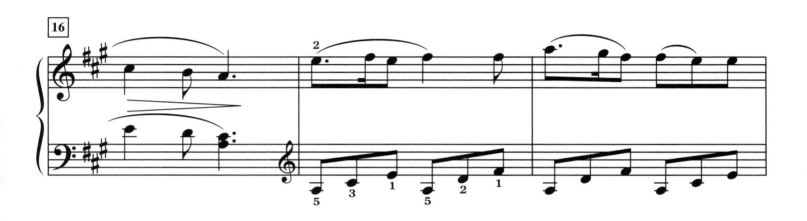

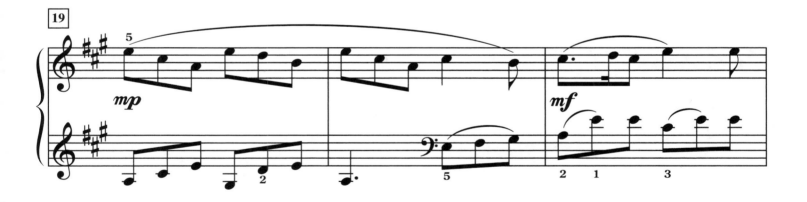

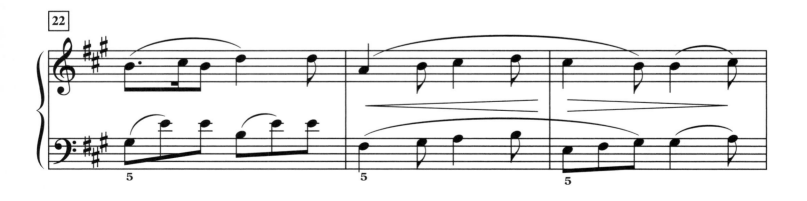

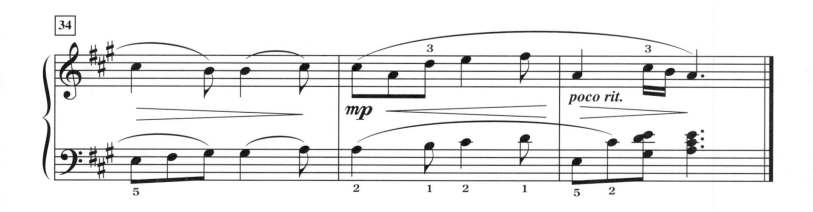

Barcarolle

(from *Tales of Hoffmann*)

Jacques Offenbach
(1819–1880)
Arranged by Tom Gerou

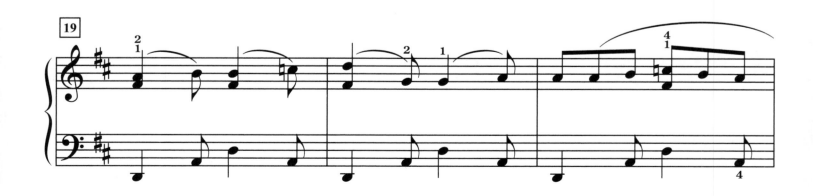

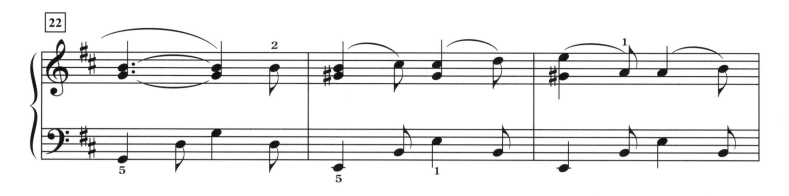

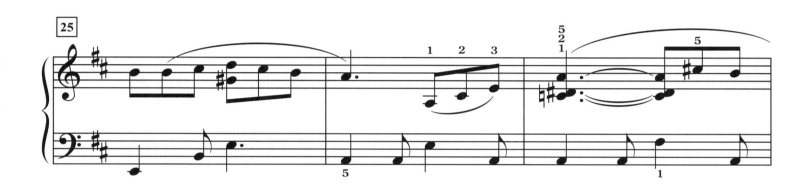

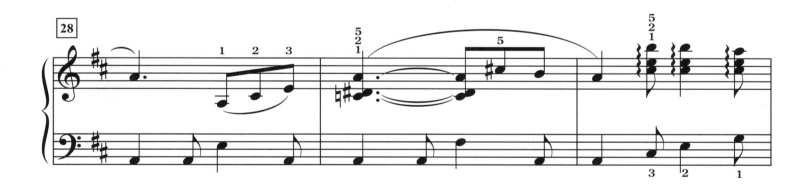

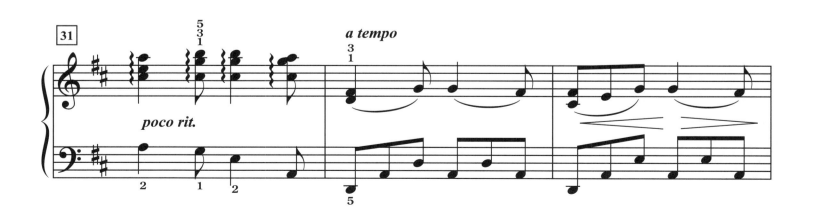

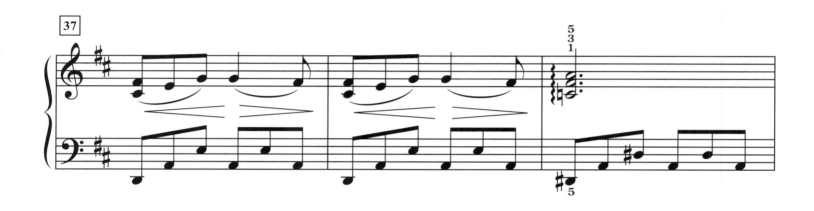

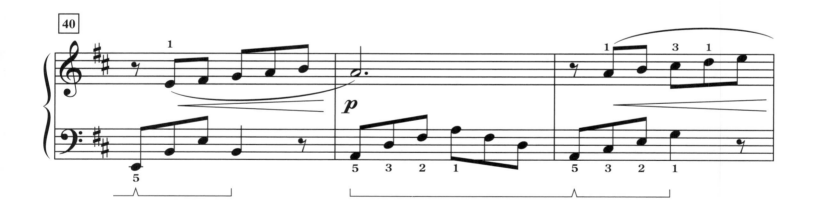

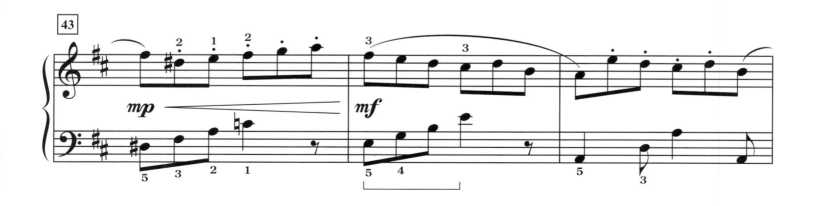

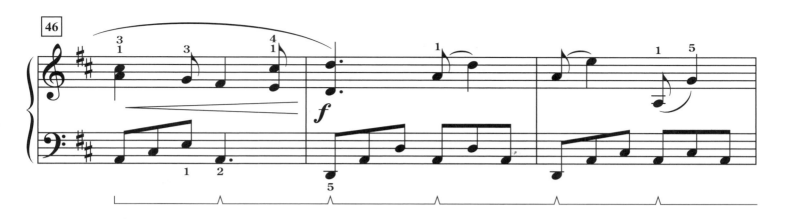

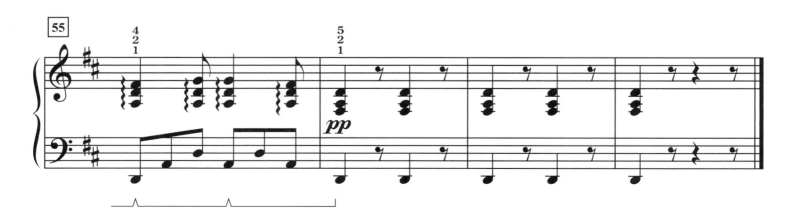

Can-Can

(from *Orpheus in the Underworld*)

Jacques Offenbach
(1819–1880)
Arranged by Carol Matz

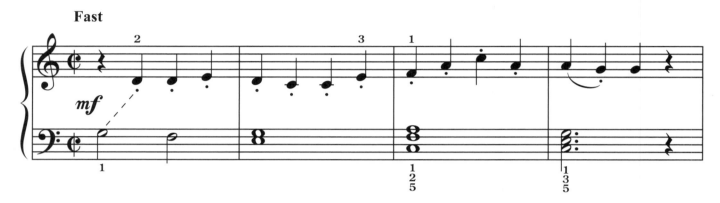

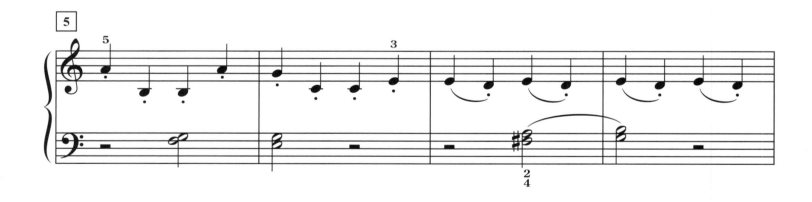

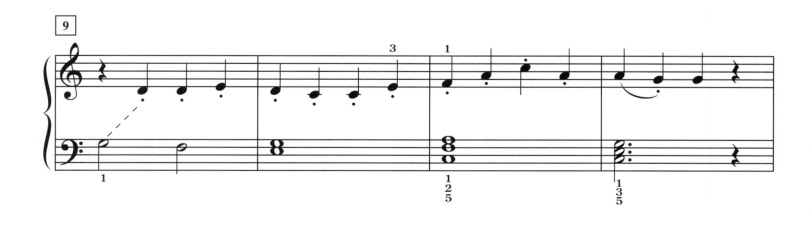

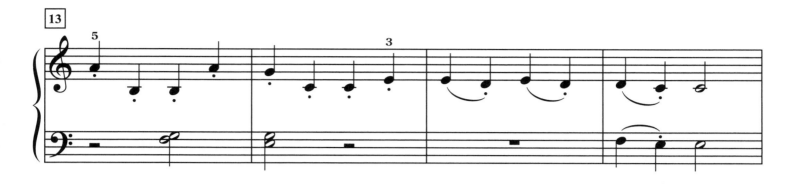

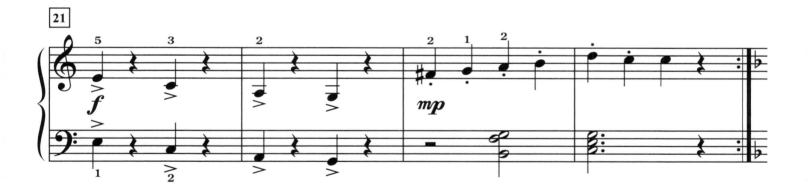

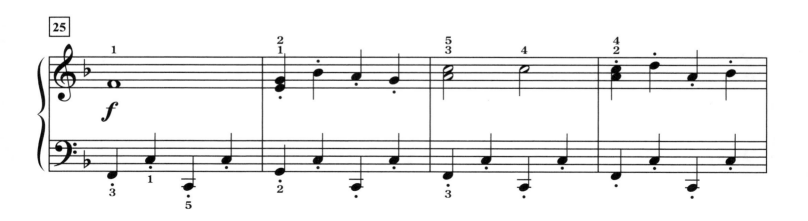

Doretta's Song

(from *La rondine*)

Giacomo Puccini
(1858–1924)
Arranged by Tom Gerou

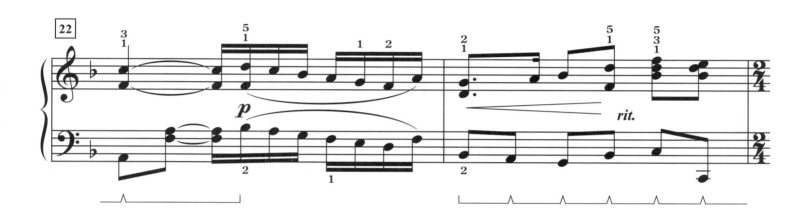

Broadly, sustained

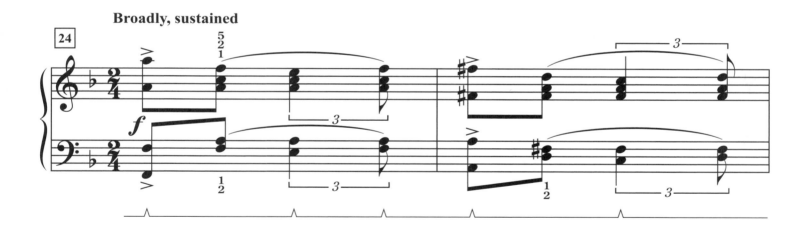

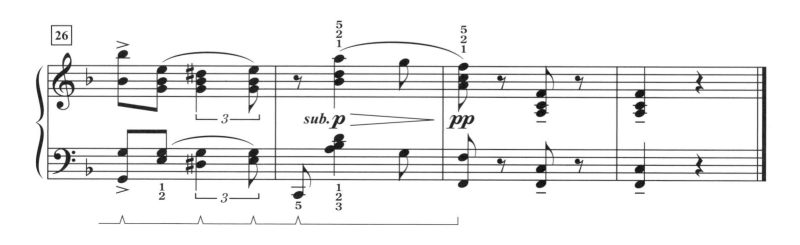

Canon in D

Johann Pachelbel
(1653–1706)
Arranged by Bruce Nelson

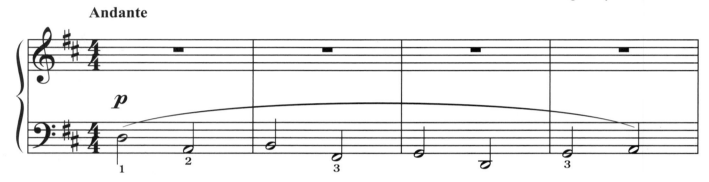

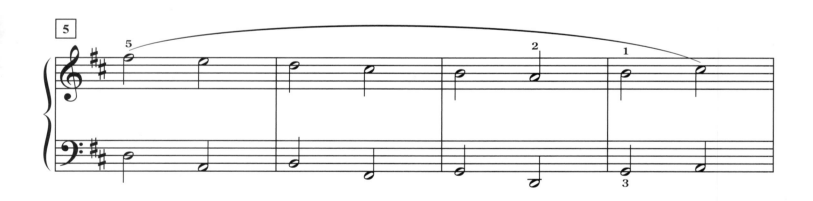

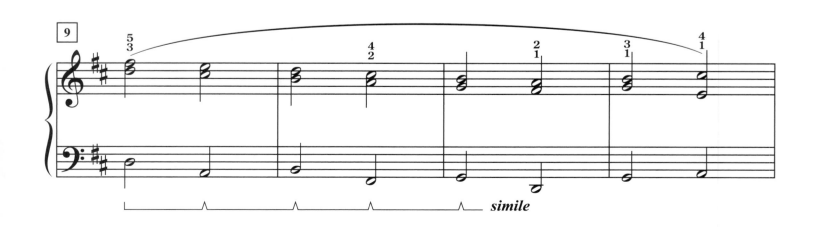

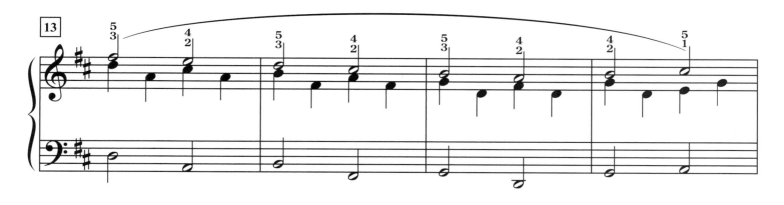

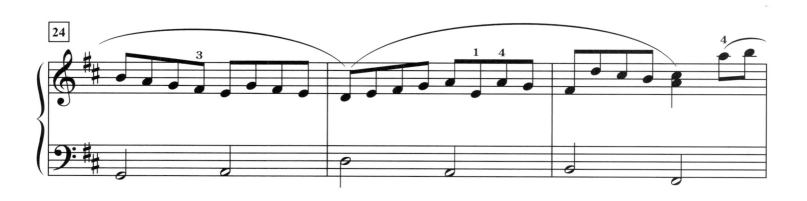

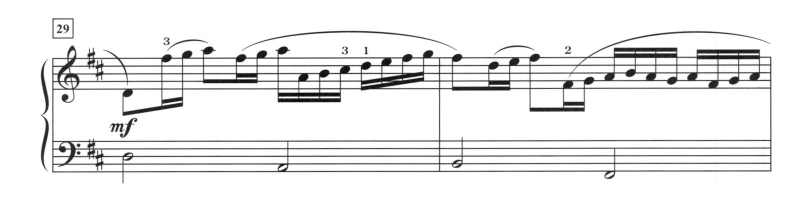

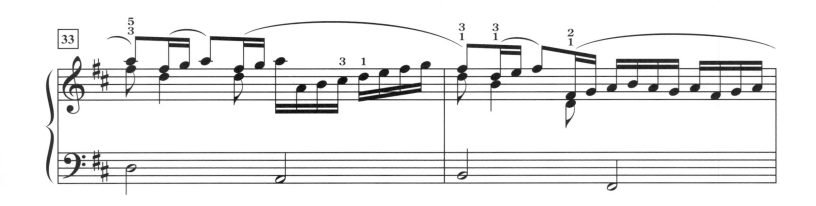

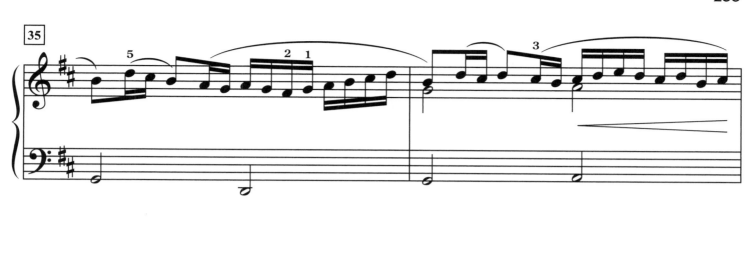

Musetta's Waltz

(from *La bohème*)

Giacomo Puccini
(1858–1924)
Arranged by Tom Gerou

Tempo di valse lento

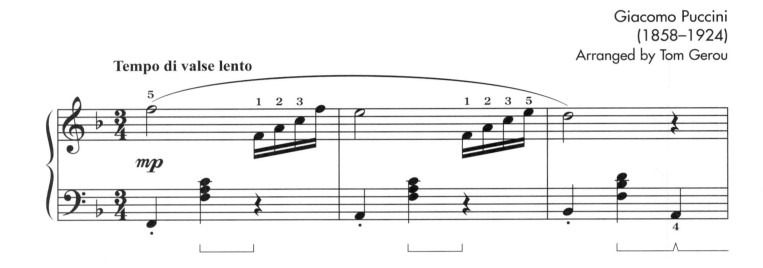

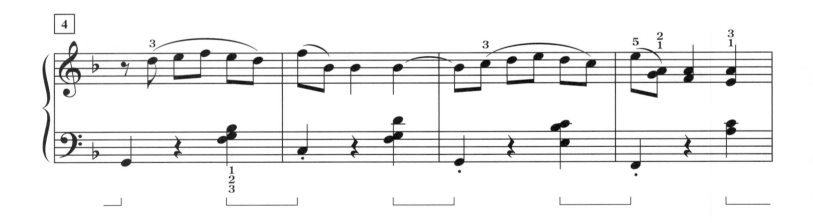

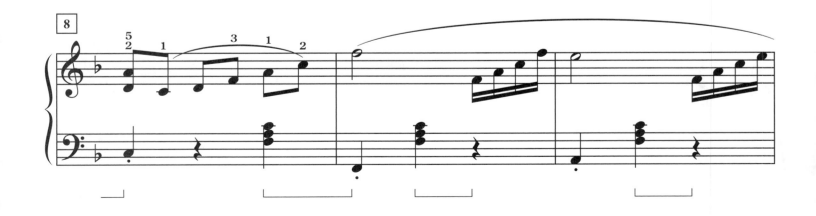

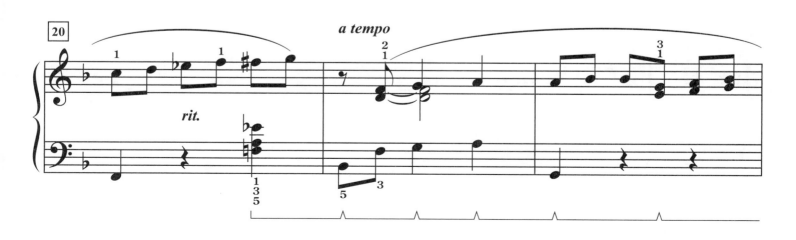

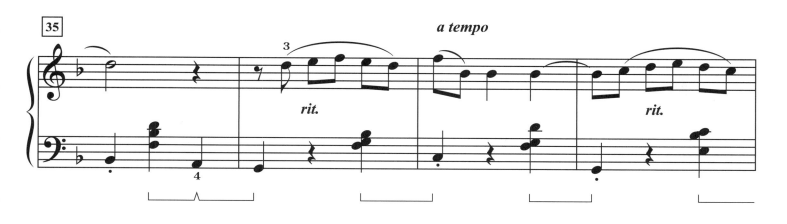

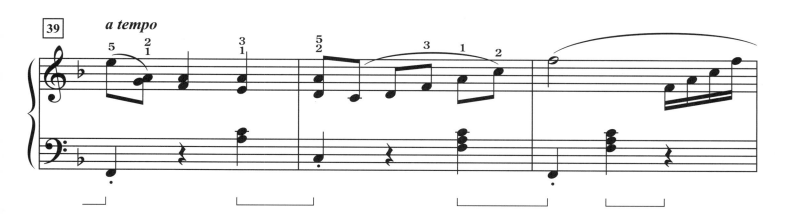

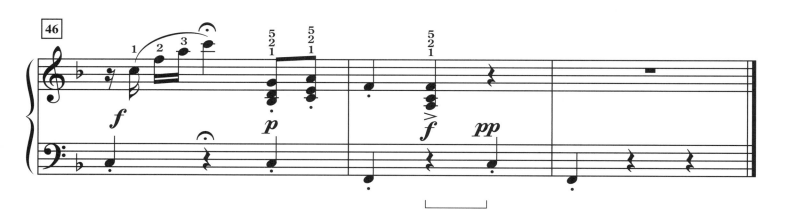

O mio babbino caro

(from *Gianni Schicchi*)

Giacomo Puccini
(1858–1924)
Arranged by Tom Gerou

Andante, con rubato

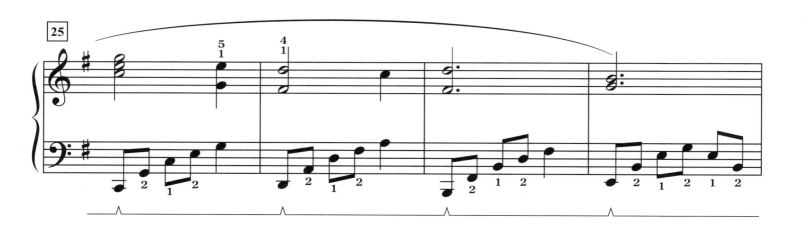

Un bel dì

(from *Madama Butterfly*)

Giacomo Puccini
(1858–1924)
Arranged by Tom Gerou

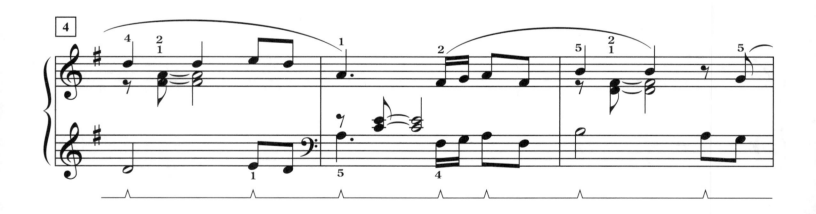

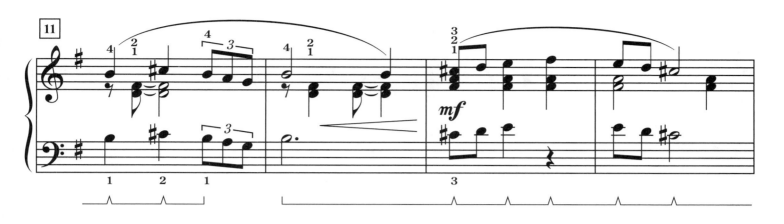

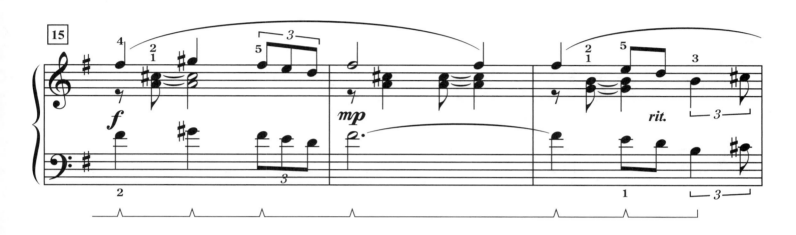

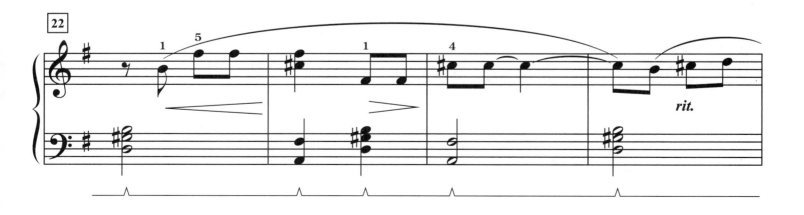

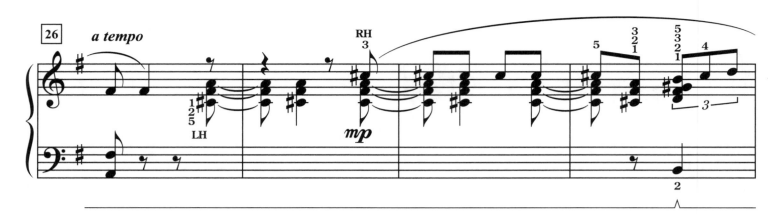

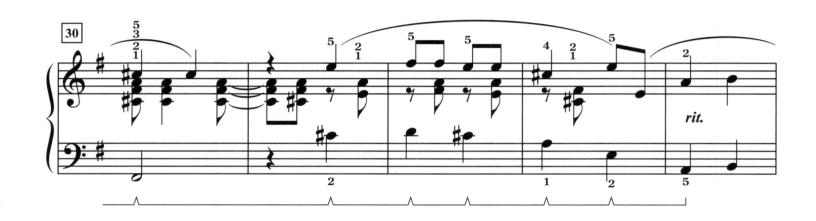

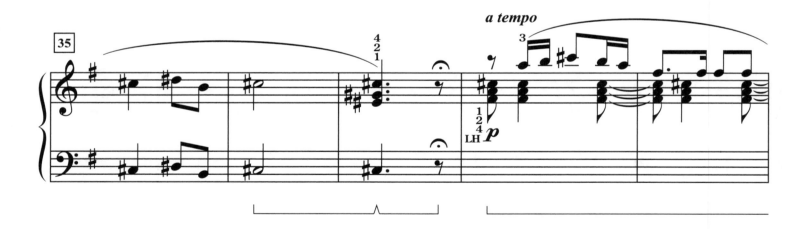

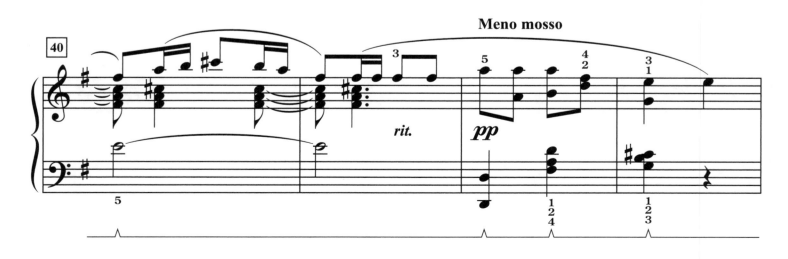

Ständchen

(Serenade)

Franz Schubert (1797–1828)
D. 957
Arranged by Carol Matz

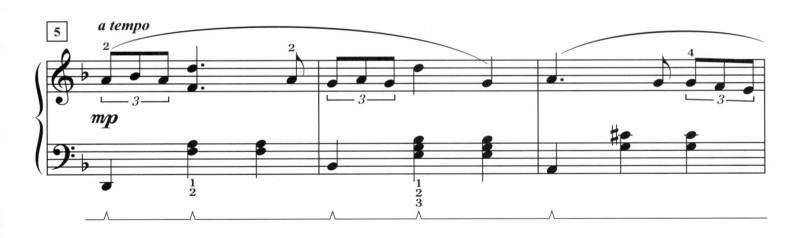

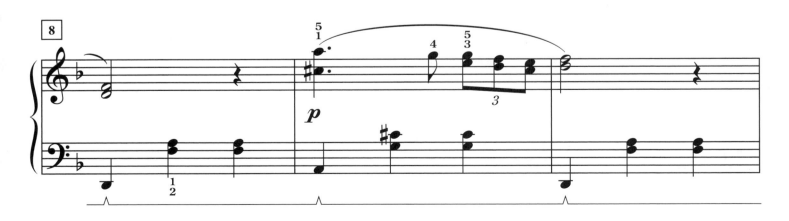

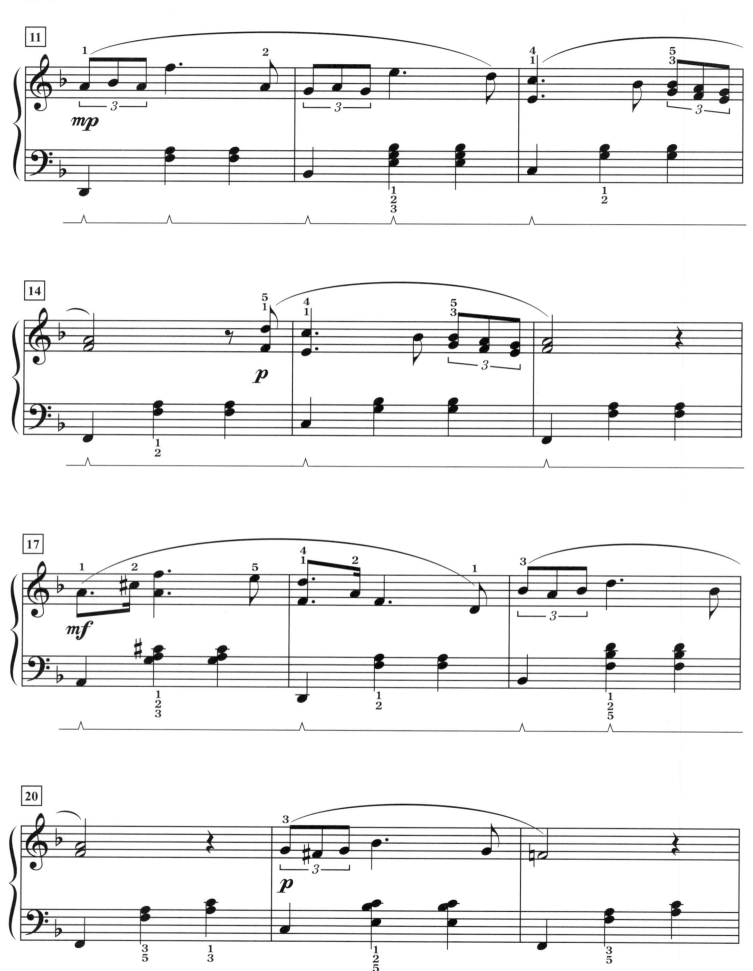

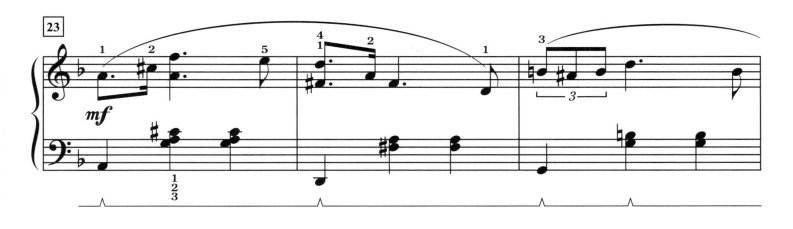

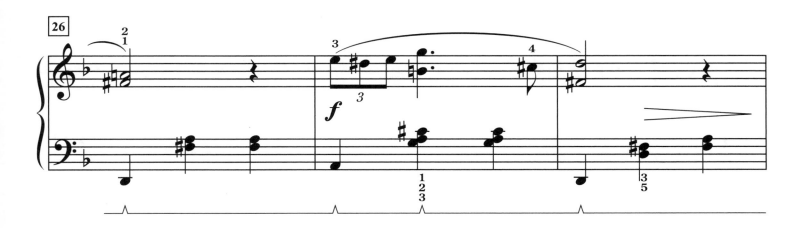

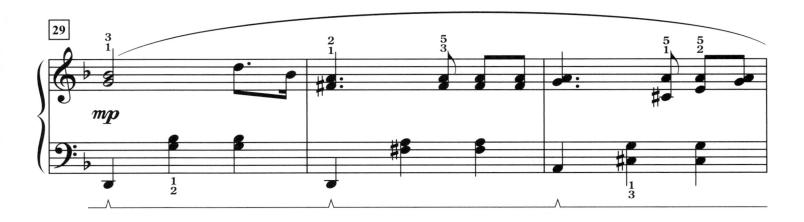

Symphony No. 8 in B Minor—Unfinished

(First Movement)

Franz Schubert (1797–1828)
D. 759
Arranged by Robert Schultz

Allegro moderato

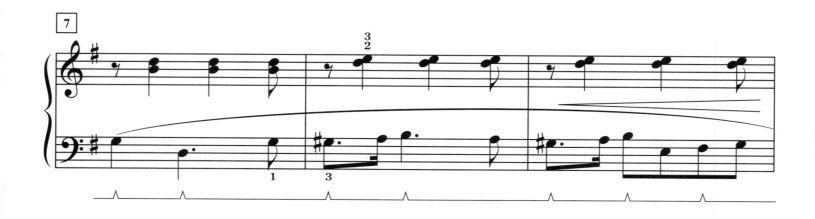

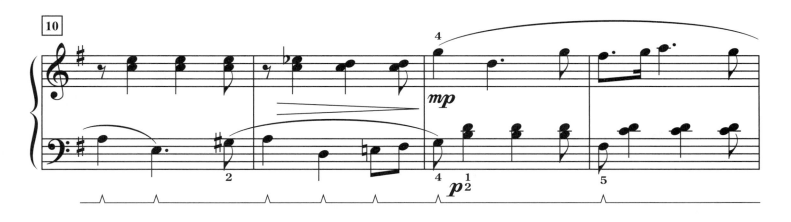

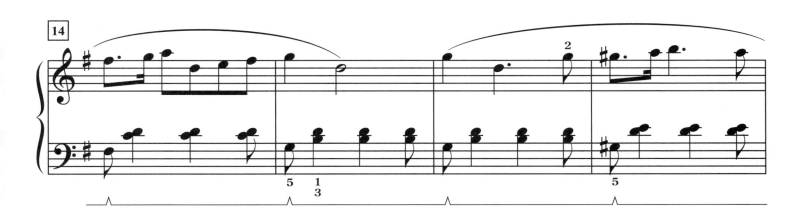

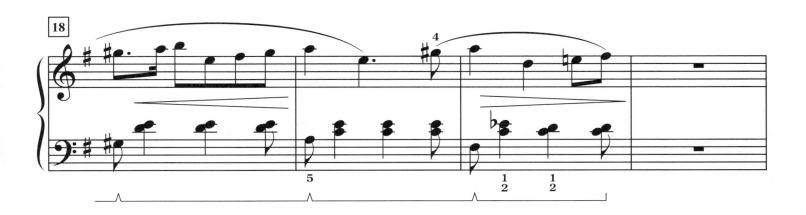

The Swan

(from *Carnival of the Animals*)

Camille Saint-Saëns
(1835–1921)
Arranged by Carol Matz

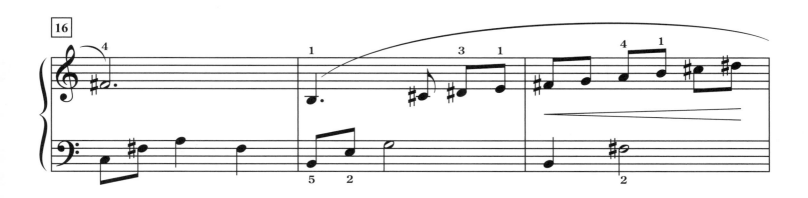

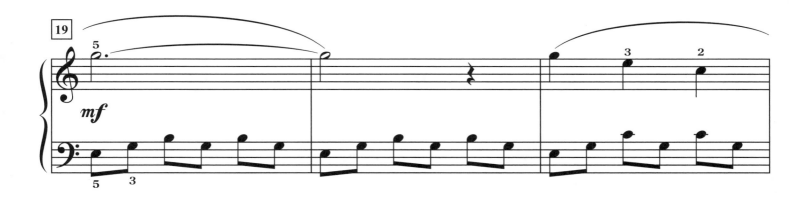

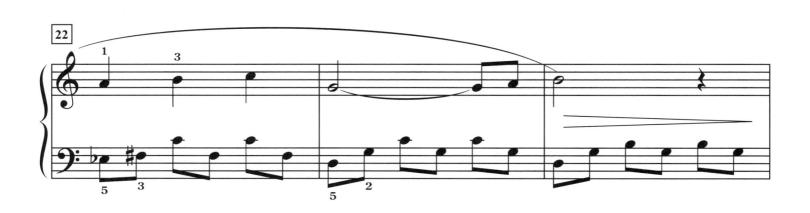

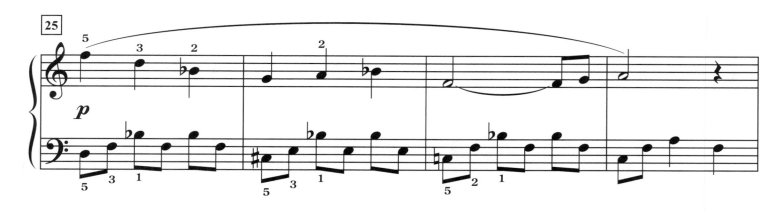

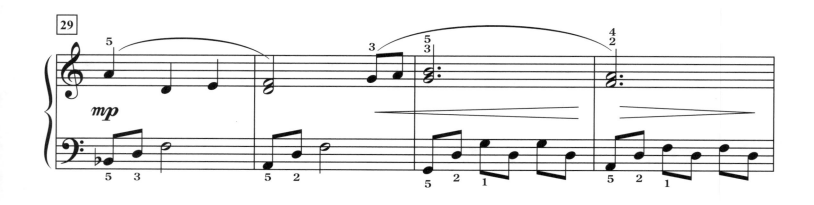

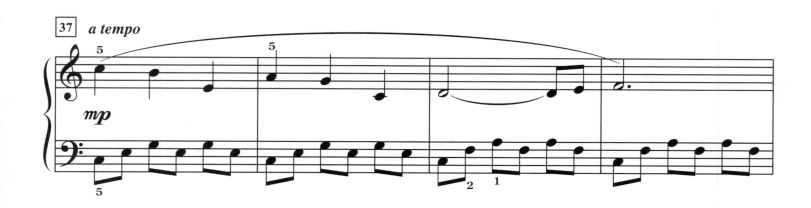

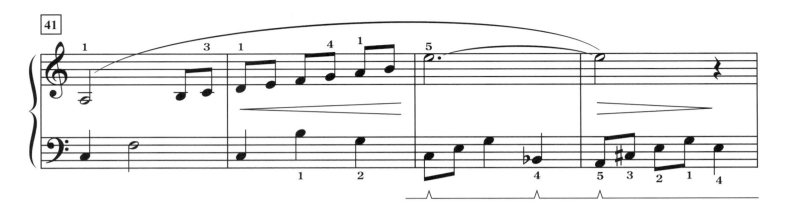

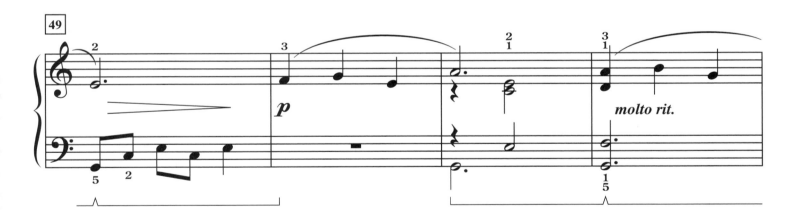

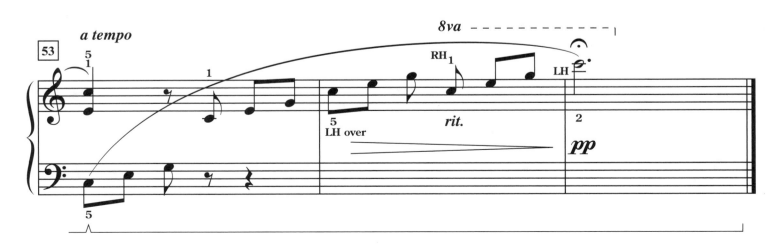

The Blue Danube

Johann Strauss, Jr. (1825–1899)
Op. 314
Arranged by Robert Schultz

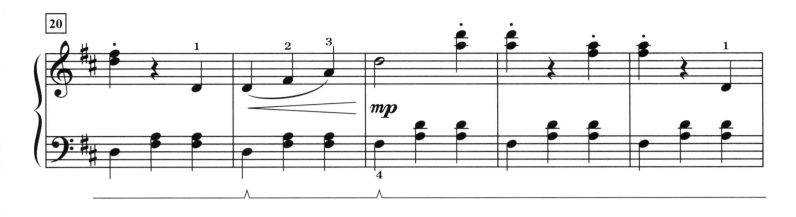

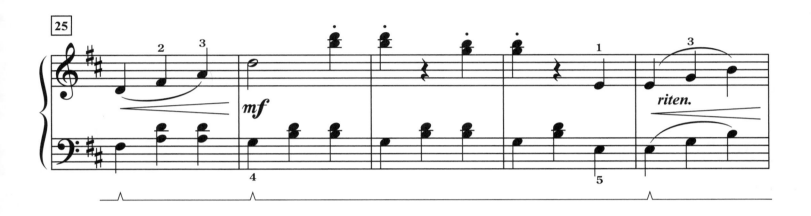

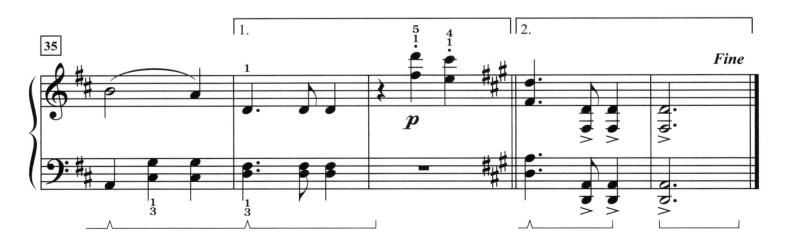

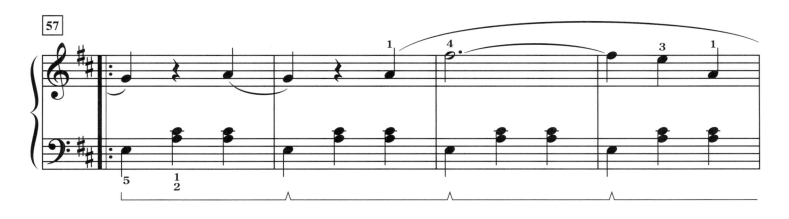

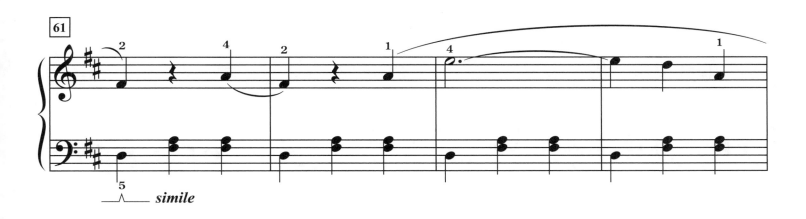

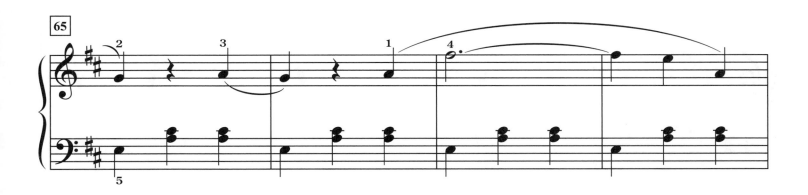

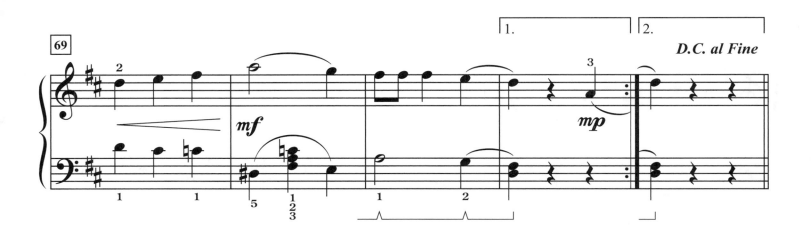

The Moldau (Vltava)

(from *Má vlast*)

Bedřich Smetana
(1824–1884)
Arranged by Robert Schultz

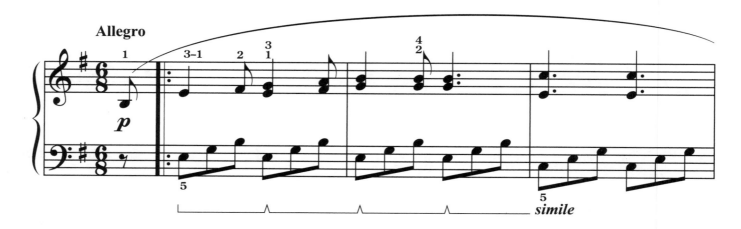

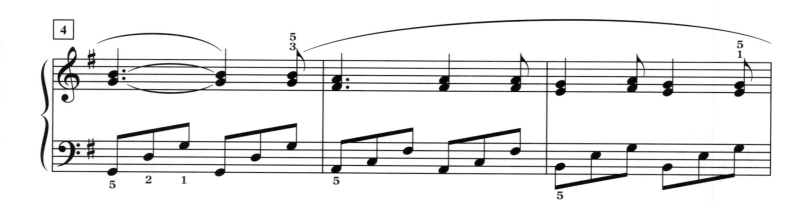

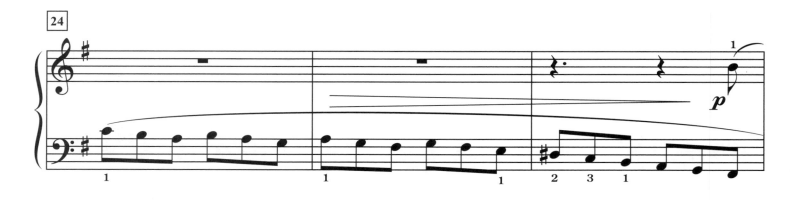

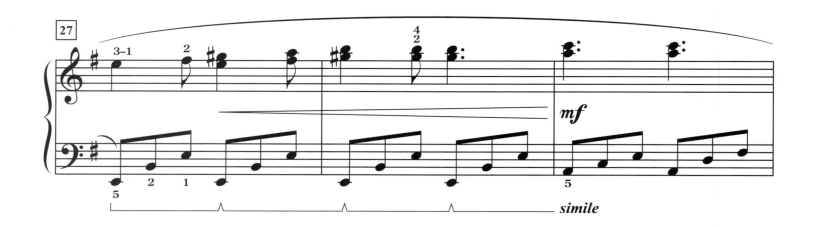

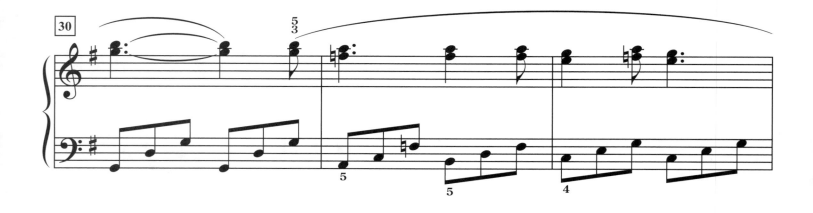

The Garland Waltz

(from *Sleeping Beauty*)

Peter Ilyich Tchaikovsky (1840–1893)
Op. 66
Arranged by Robert Schultz

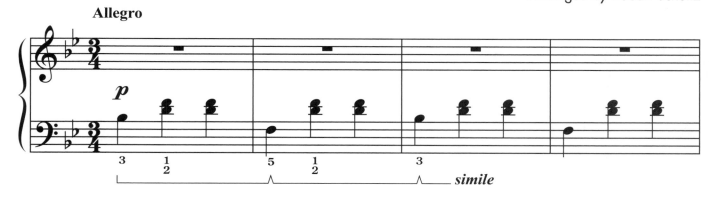

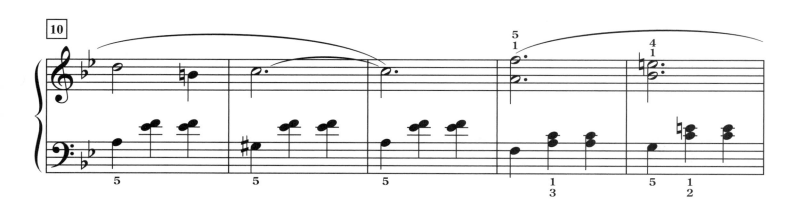

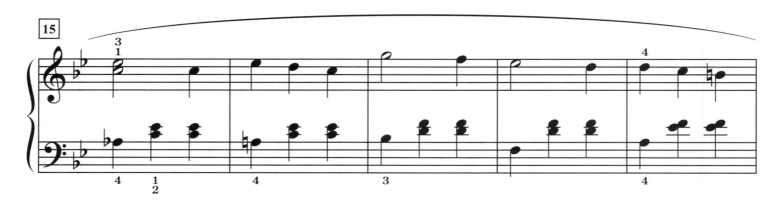

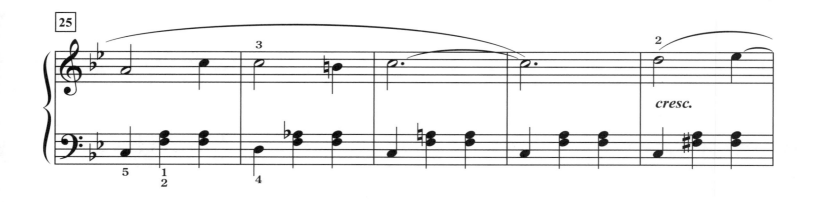

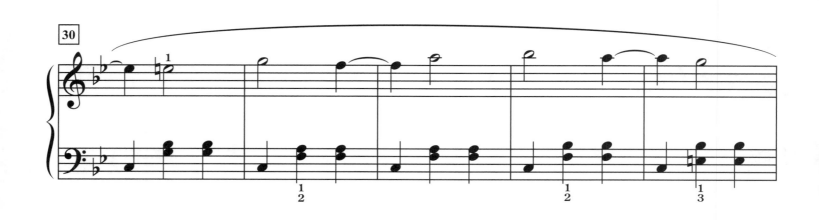

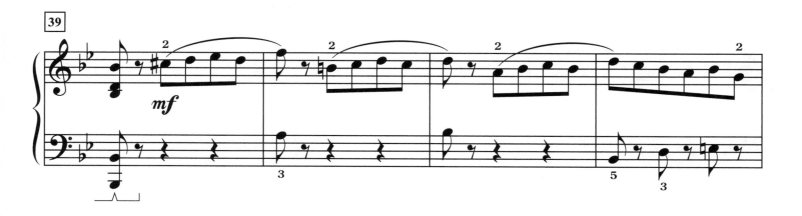

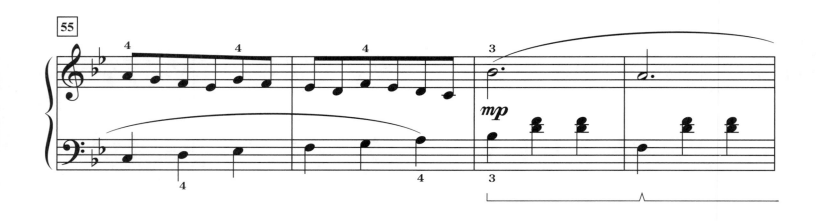

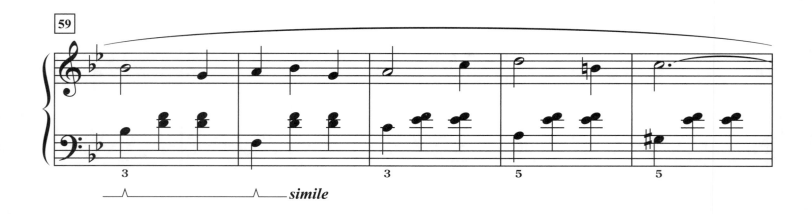

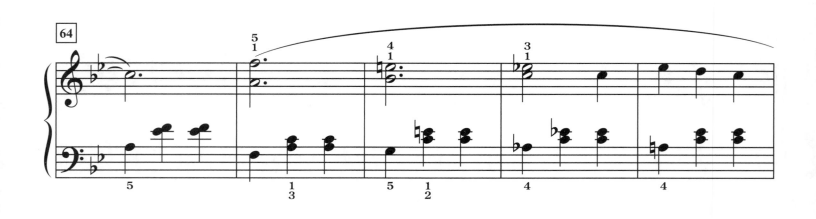

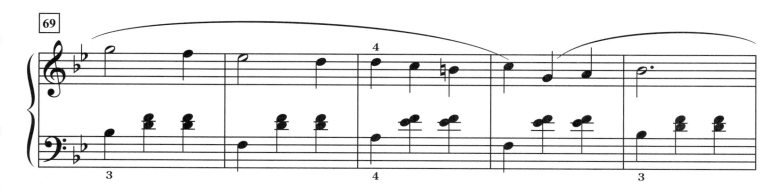

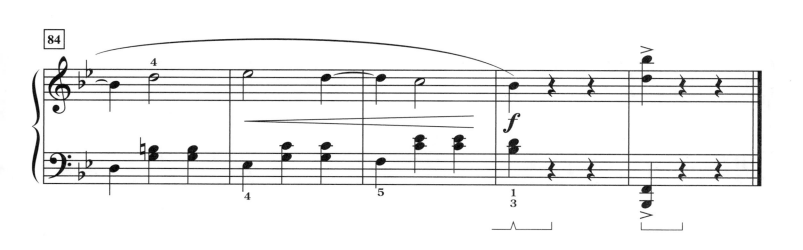

Miniature Overture
(from *The Nutcracker*)

Peter Ilyich Tchaikovsky (1840–1893)
Op. 71
Arranged by Gayle Kowalchyk and E. L. Lancaster

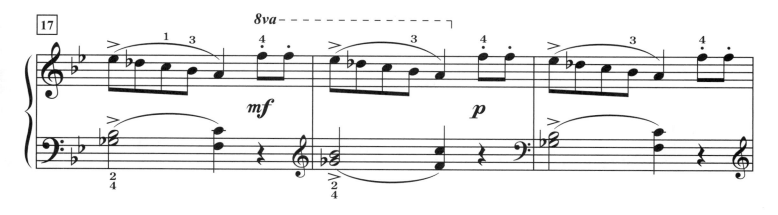

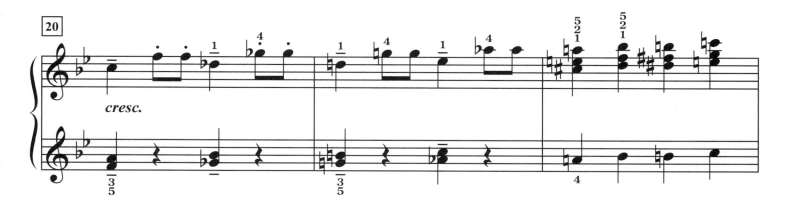

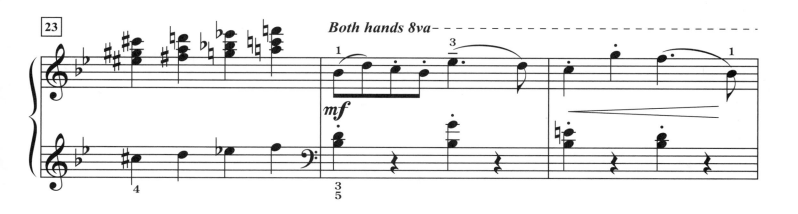

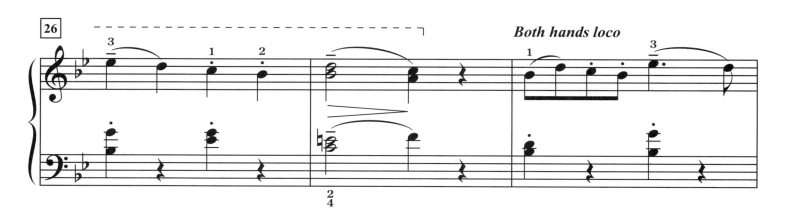

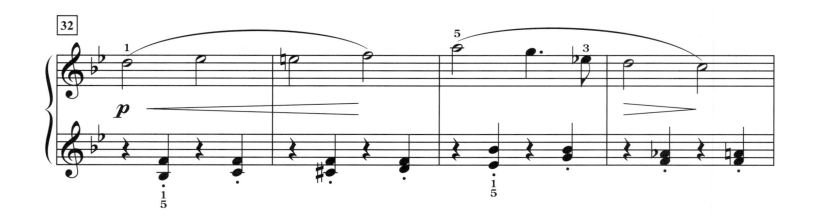

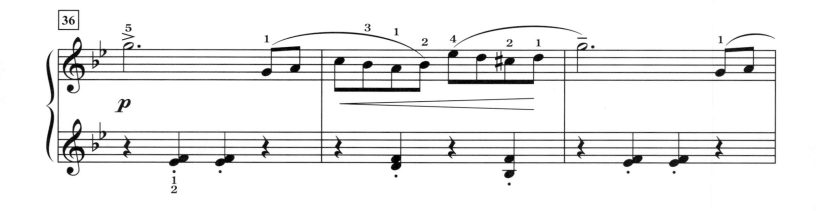

March

(from *The Nutcracker*)

Peter Ilyich Tchaikovsky (1840–1893)
Op. 71
Arranged by Gayle Kowalchyk and E. L. Lancaster

Tempo di marcia vivo

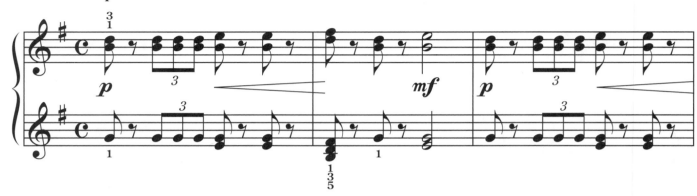

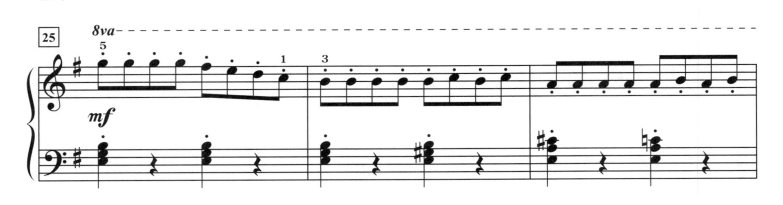

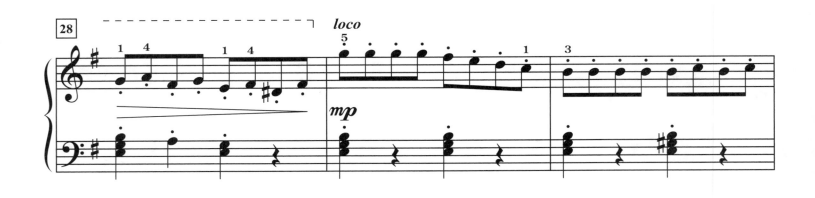

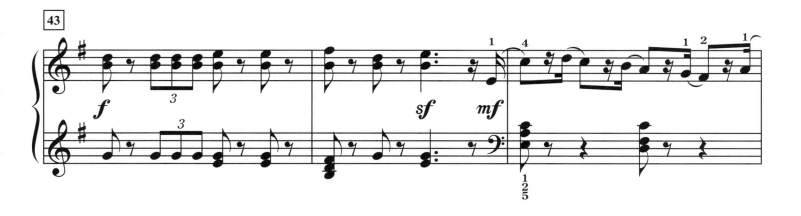

Dance of the Sugarplum Fairy

(from *The Nutcracker*)

Peter Ilyich Tchaikovsky (1840–1893)
Op. 71
Arranged by Gayle Kowalchyk and E. L. Lancaster

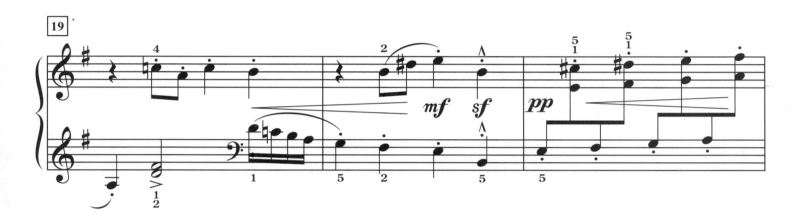

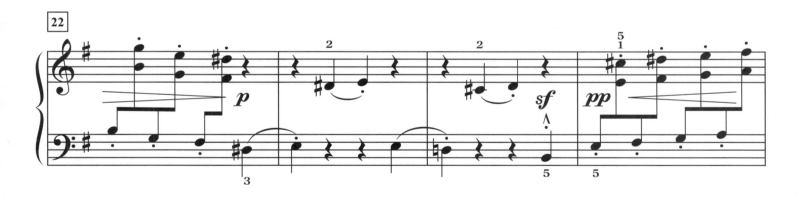

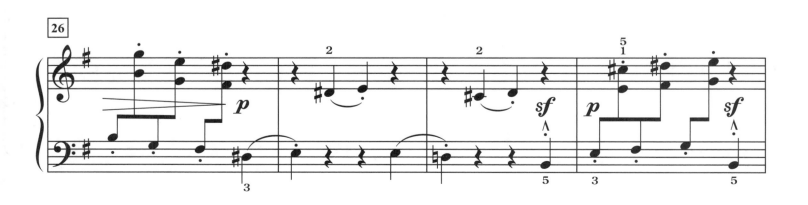

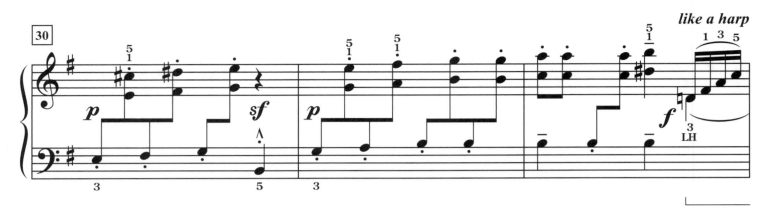

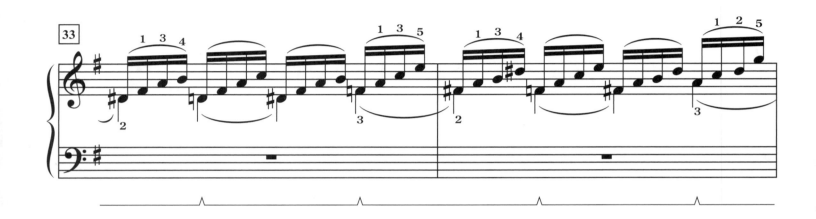

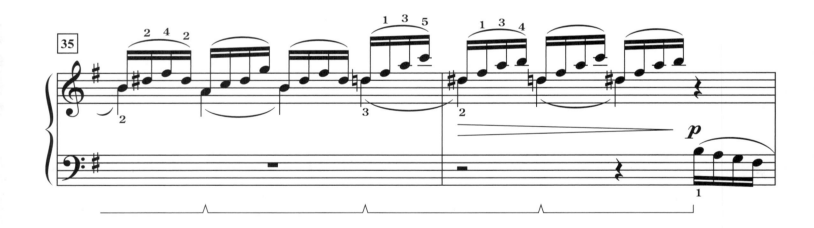

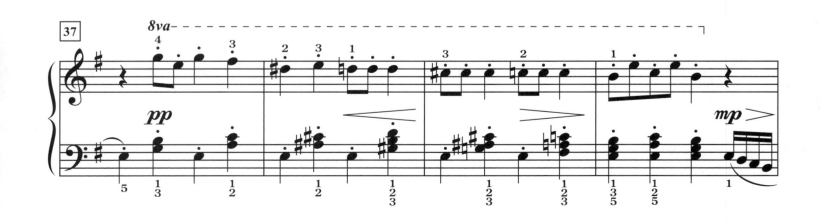

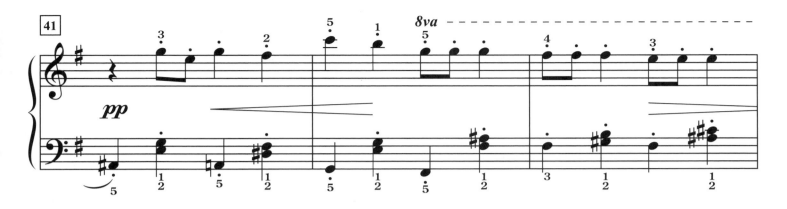

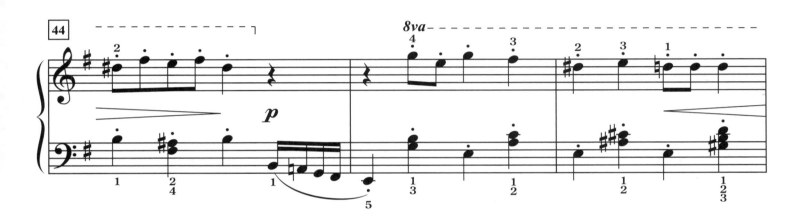

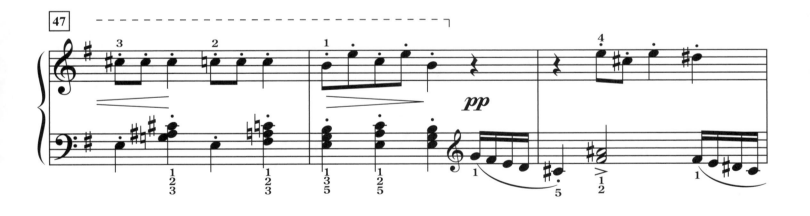

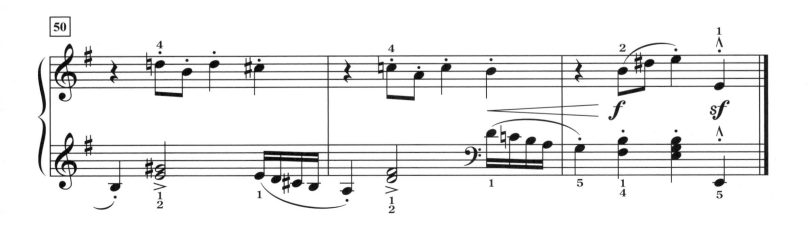

Russian Dance (Trépak)

(from *The Nutcracker*)

Peter Ilyich Tchaikovsky (1840–1893)
Op. 71
Arranged by Gayle Kowalchyk and E. L. Lancaster

Tempo di Trépak, molto vivace

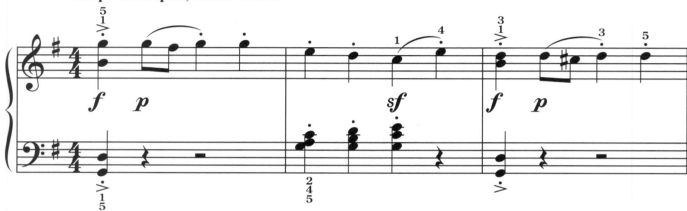

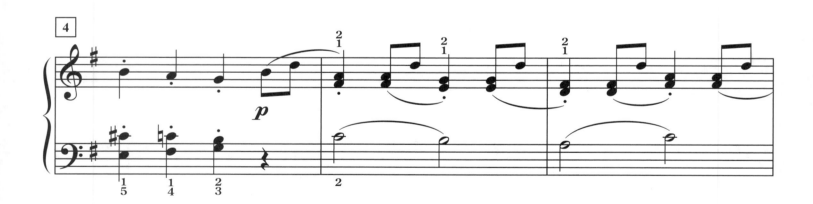

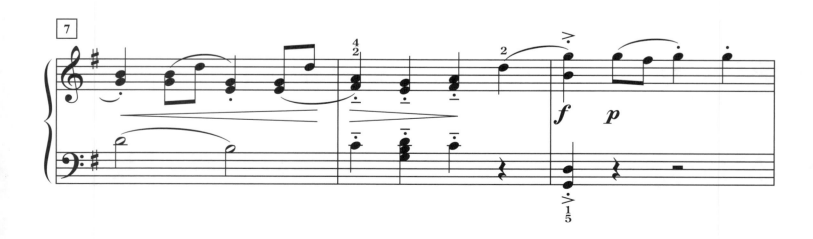

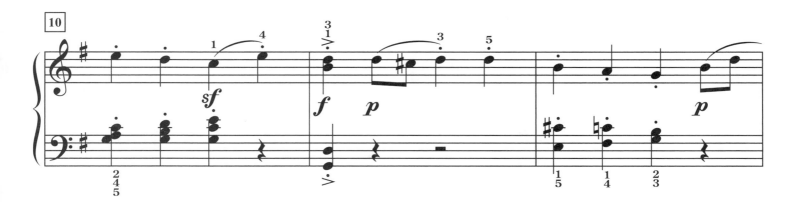

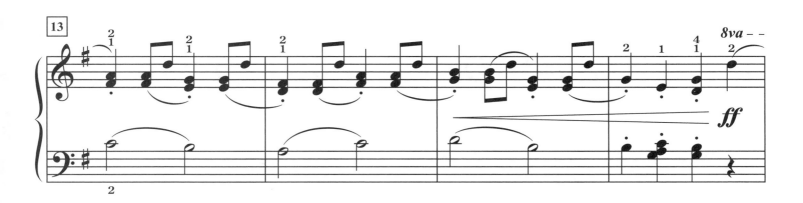

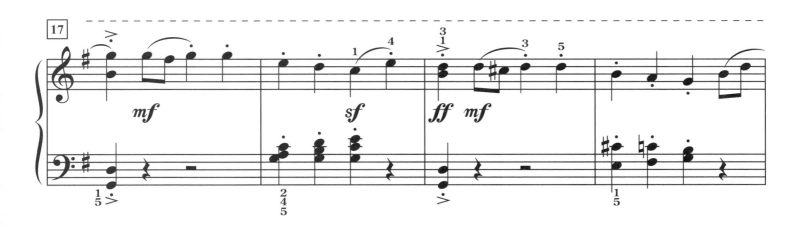

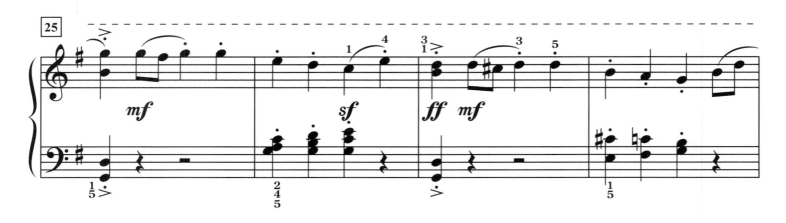

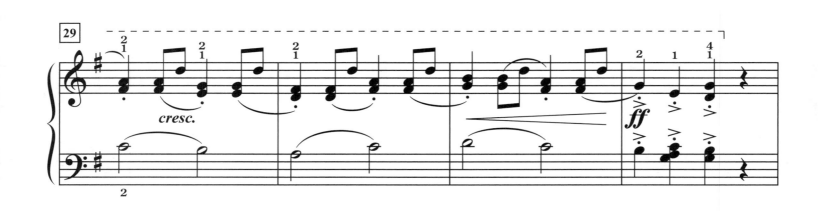

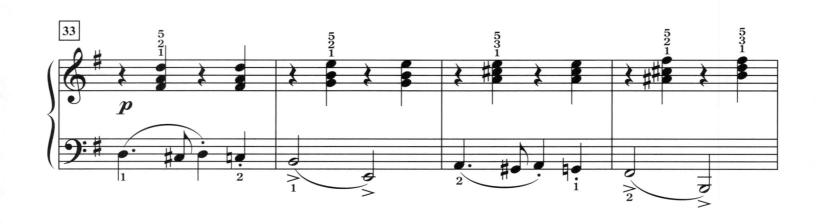

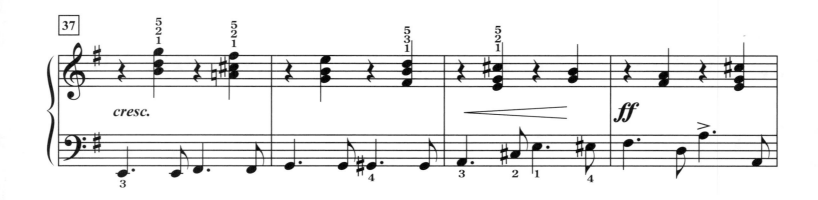

Arabian Dance

(from *The Nutcracker*)

Peter Ilyich Tchaikovsky (1840–1893)
Op. 71
Arranged by Gayle Kowalchyk and E. L. Lancaster

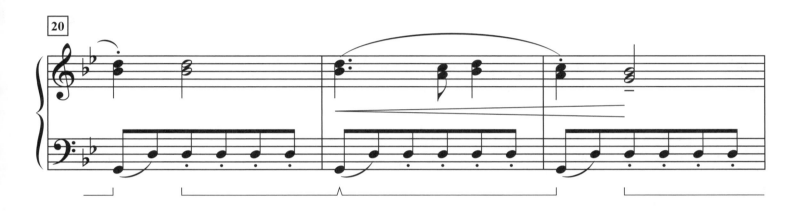

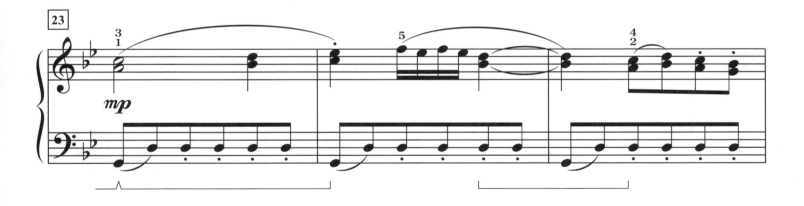

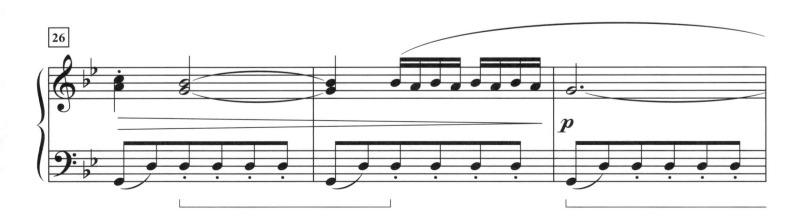

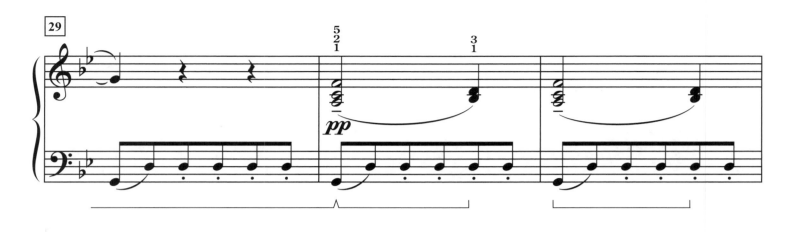

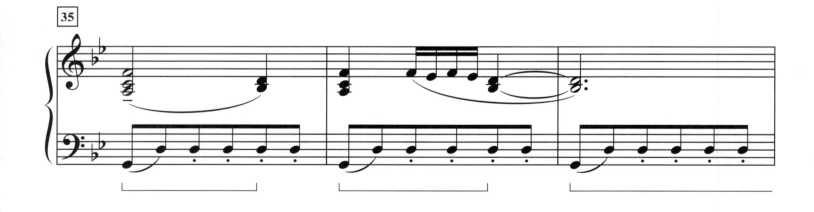

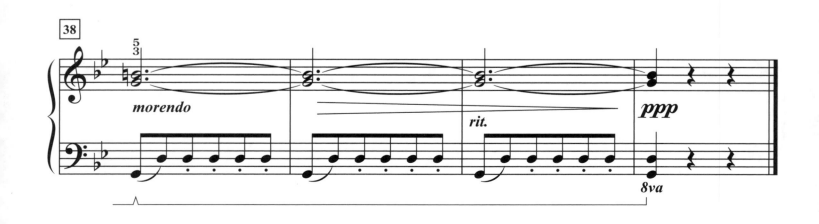

Chinese Dance

(from *The Nutcracker*)

Peter Ilyich Tchaikovsky (1840–1893)
Op. 71
Arranged by Gayle Kowalchyk and E. L. Lancaster

Allegro moderato

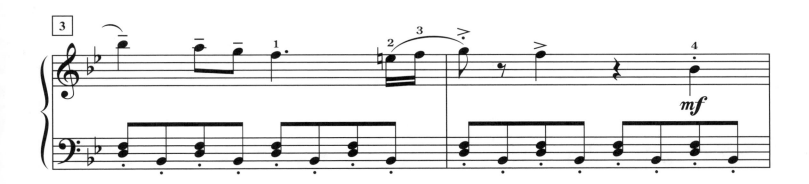

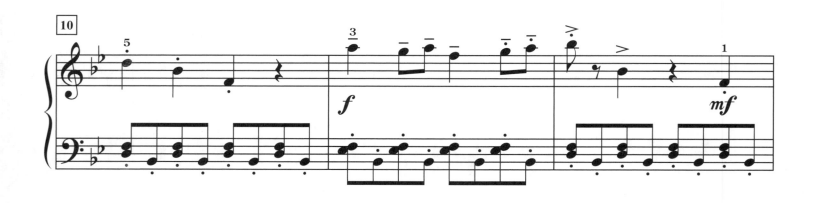

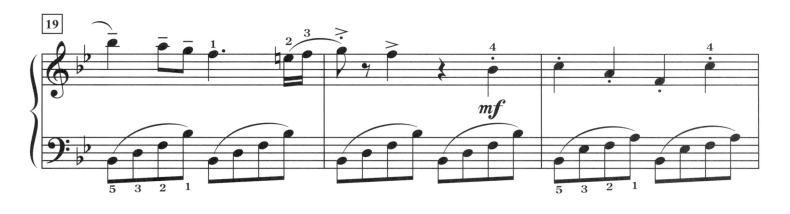

Dance of the Reed Flutes

(from *The Nutcracker*)

Peter Ilyich Tchaikovsky (1840–1893)
Op. 71
Arranged by Gayle Kowalchyk and E. L. Lancaster

Moderato assai

314

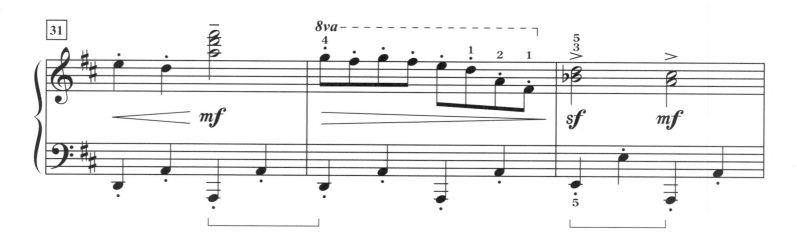

Waltz of the Flowers

(from *The Nutcracker*)

Peter Ilyich Tchaikovsky (1840–1893)
Op. 71
Arranged by Gayle Kowalchyk and E. L. Lancaster

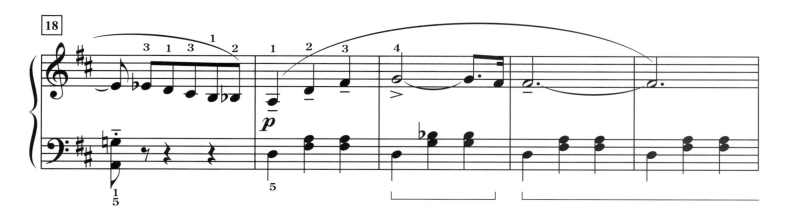

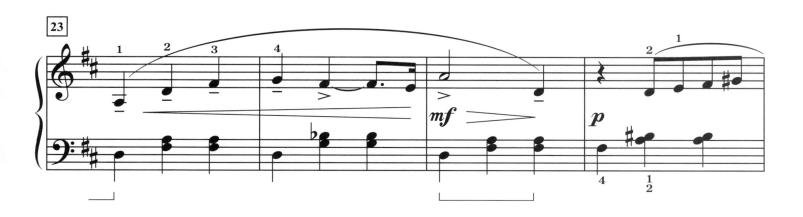

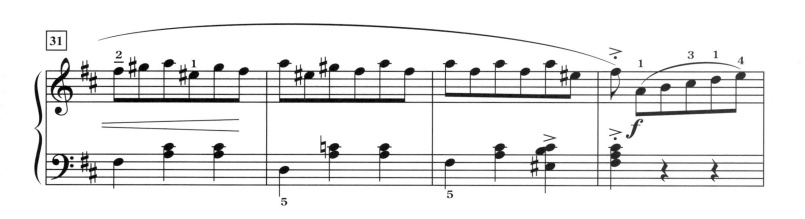

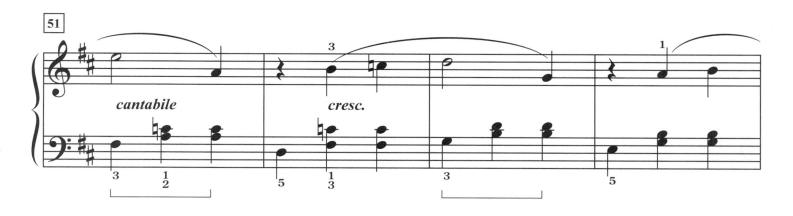

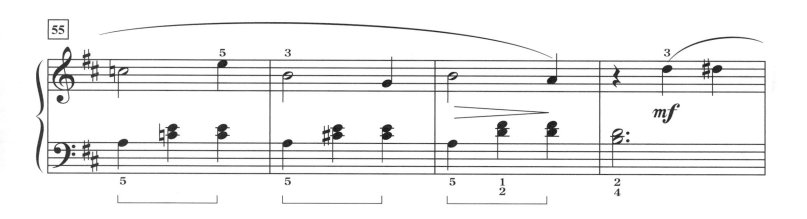

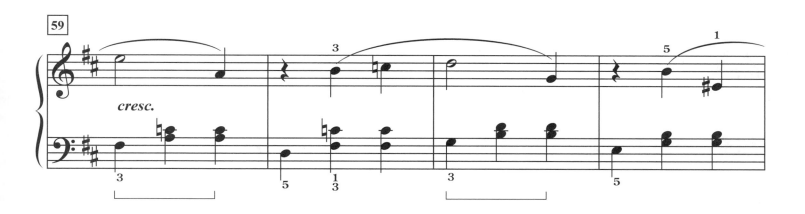

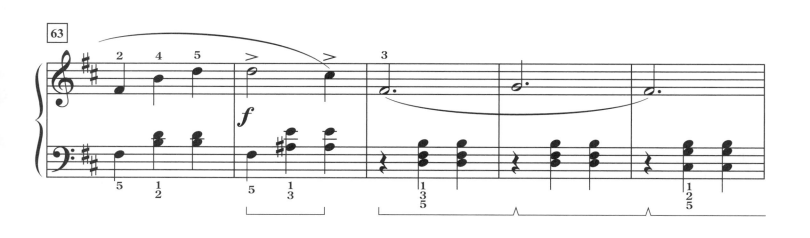

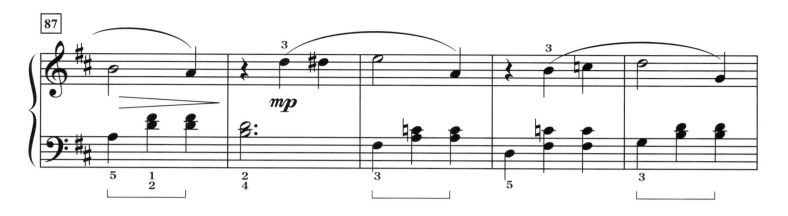

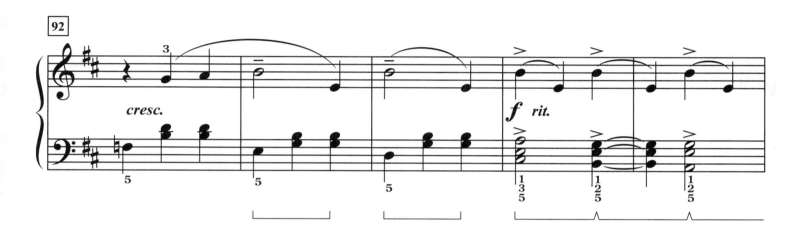

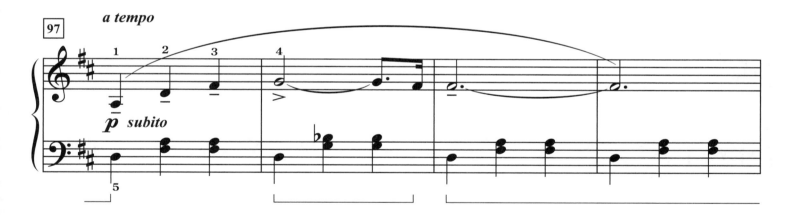

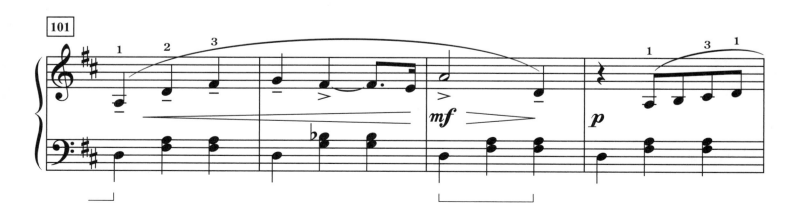

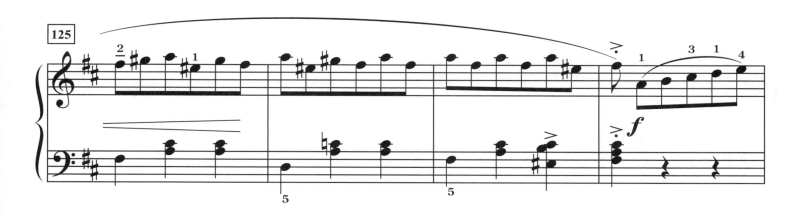

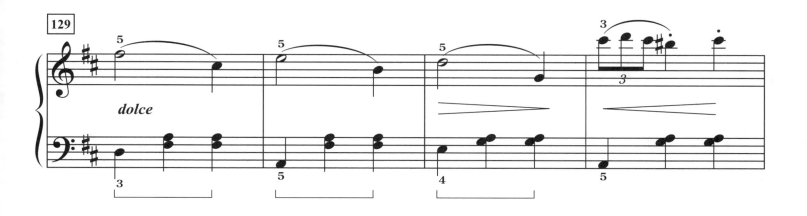

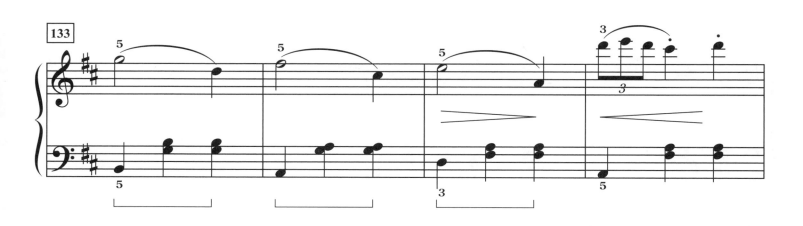

Piano Concerto No. 1 in B-flat Minor

(First Movement)

Peter Ilyich Tchaikovsky (1840–1893)
Op. 23
Arranged by Carol Matz

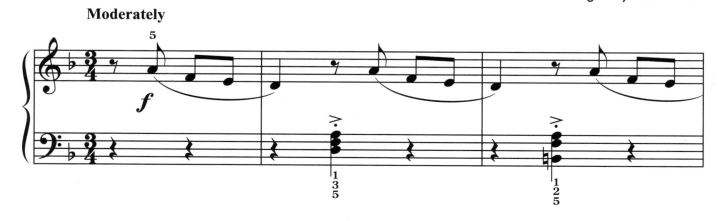

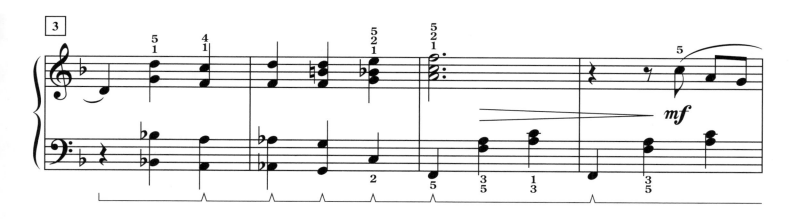

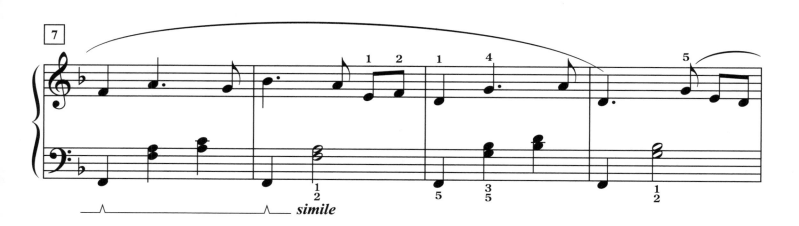

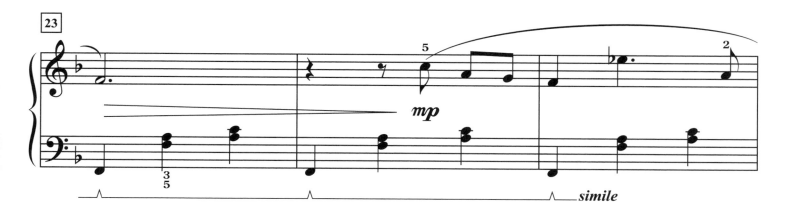

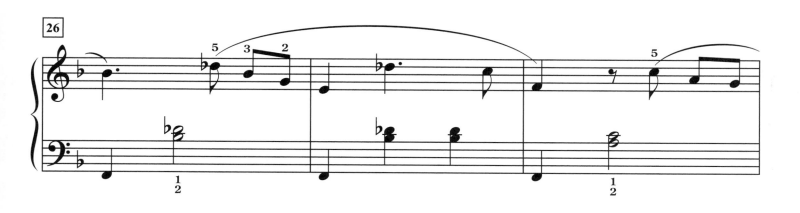

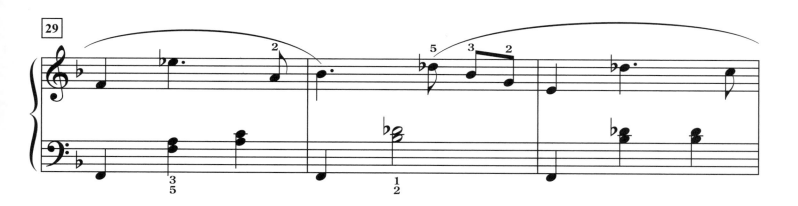

Act I Finale

(from *Swan Lake*)

Peter Ilyich Tchaikovsky (1840–1893)
Op. 20
Arranged by Carol Matz

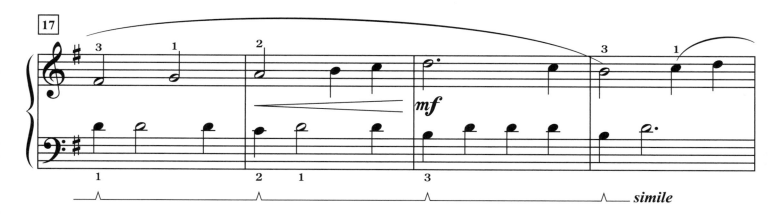

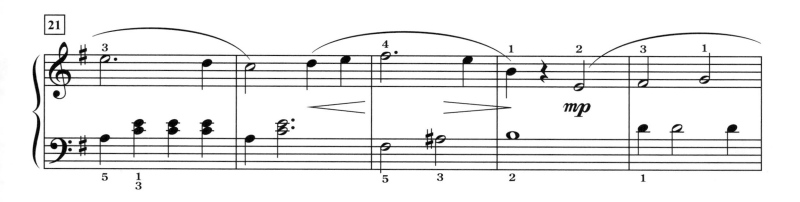

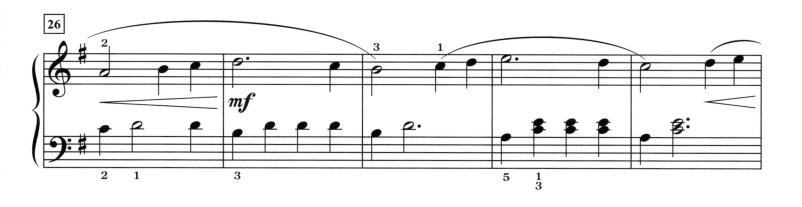

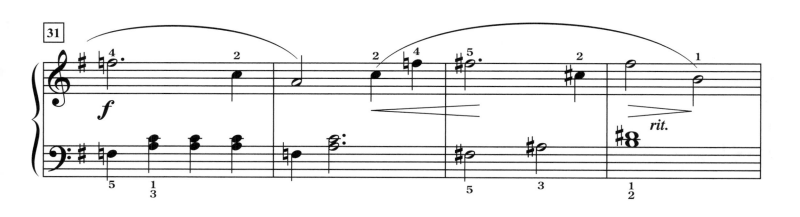

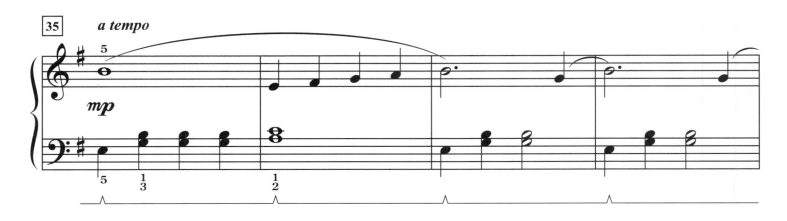

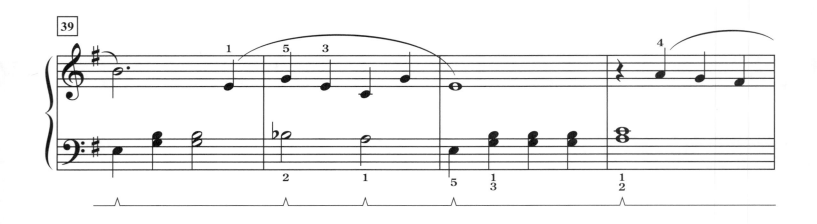

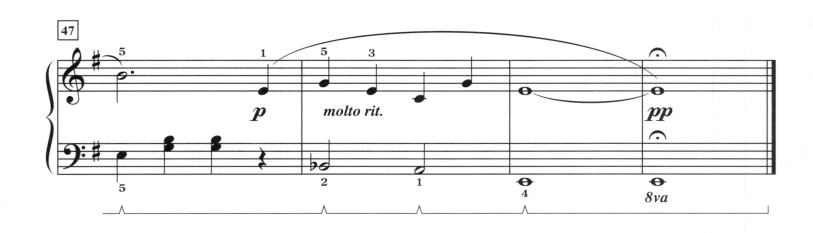

1812 Overture

Peter Ilyich Tchaikovsky (1840–14893)
Op. 49
Arranged by Carol Matz

Moderately fast

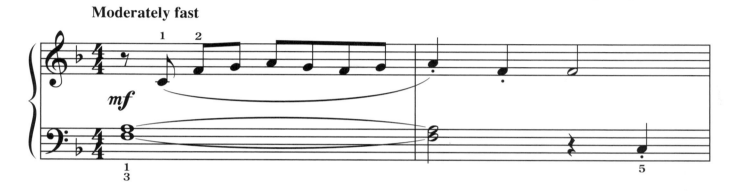

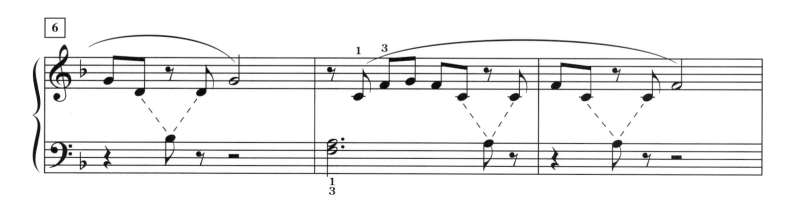

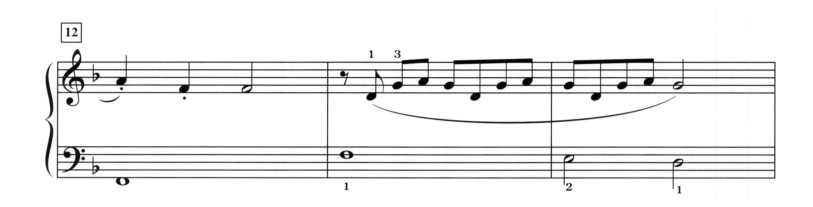

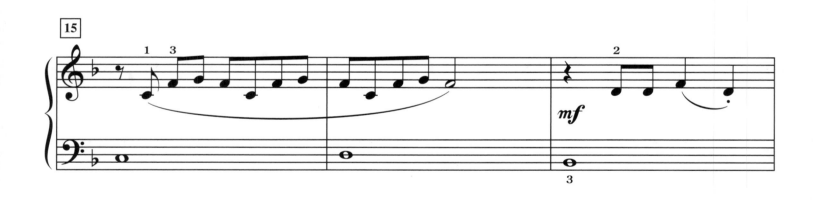

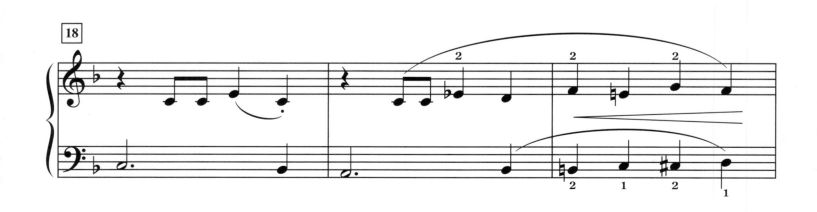

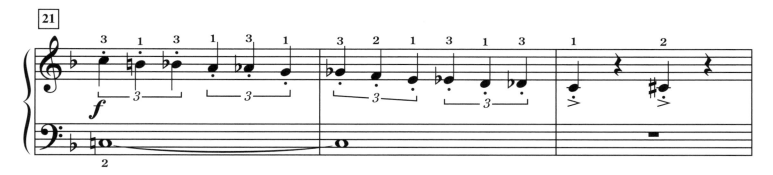

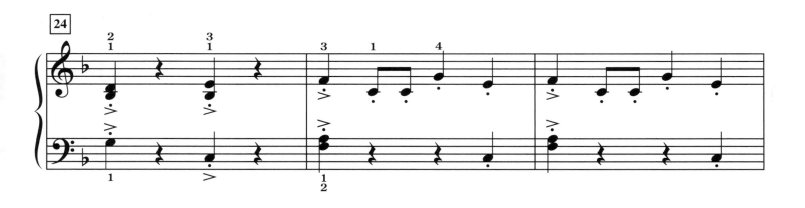

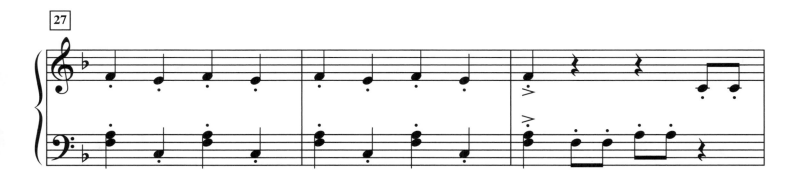

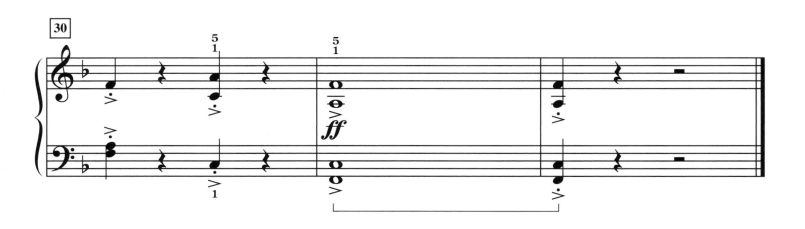

Anvil Chorus

(from *Il trovatore*)

Giuseppe Verdi
(1813–1901)
Arranged by Tom Gerou

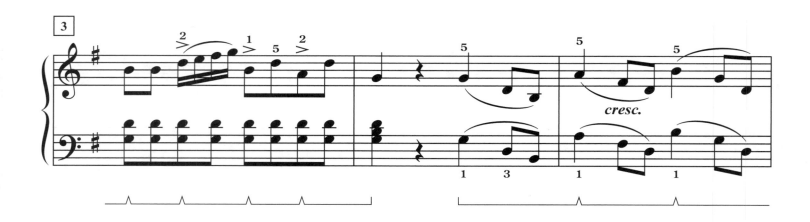

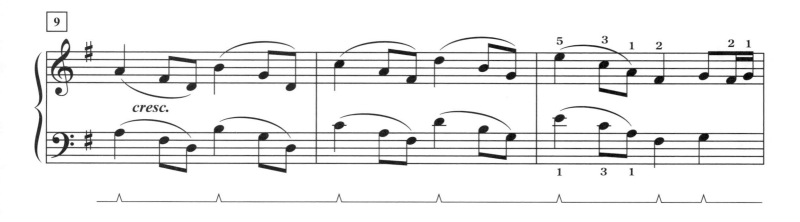

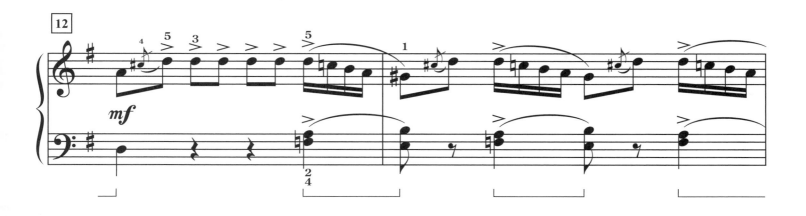

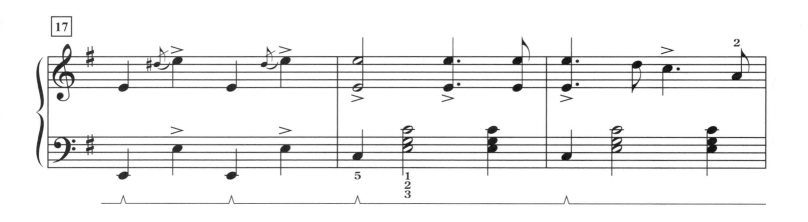

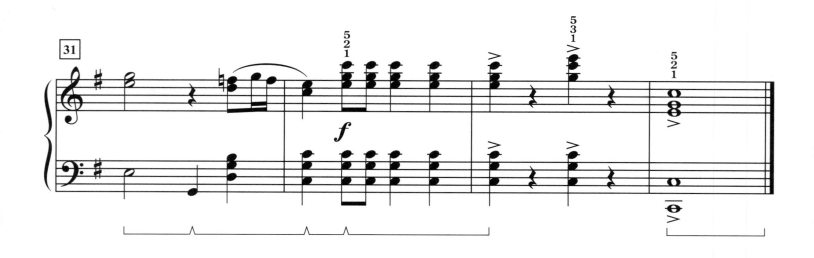

La donna è mobile

(from *Rigoletto*)

Giuseppe Verdi
(1813–1901)
Arranged by Tom Gerou

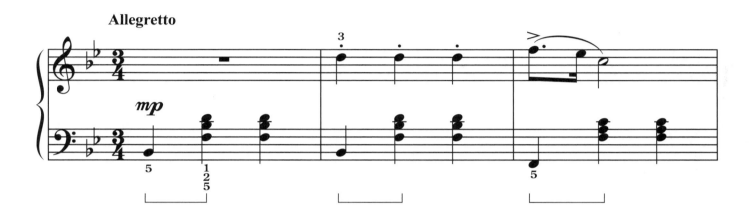

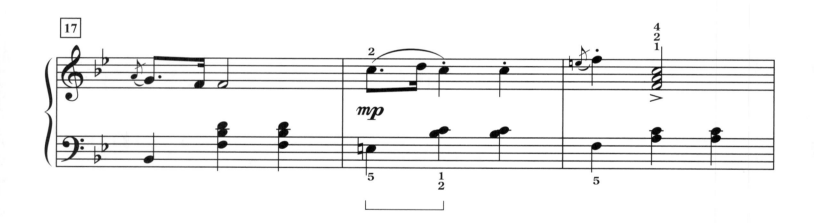

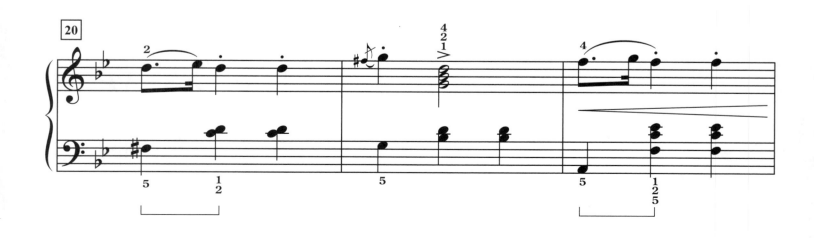

Libiamo

(from *La traviata*)

Giuseppe Verdi
(1813–1901)
Arranged by Tom Gerou

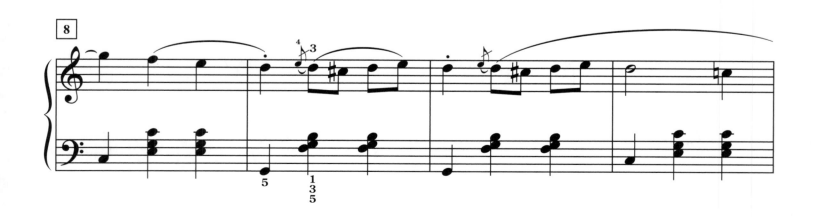

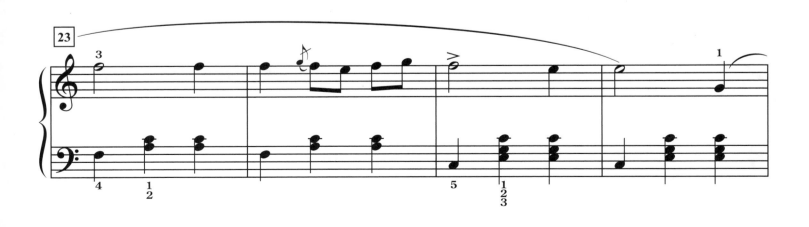

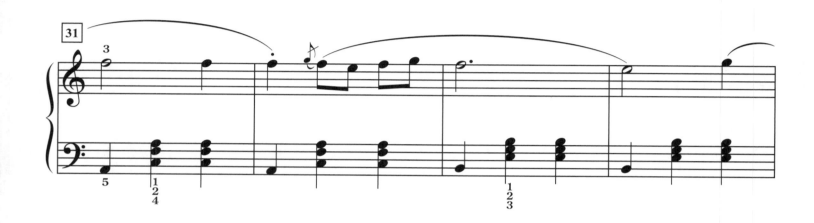

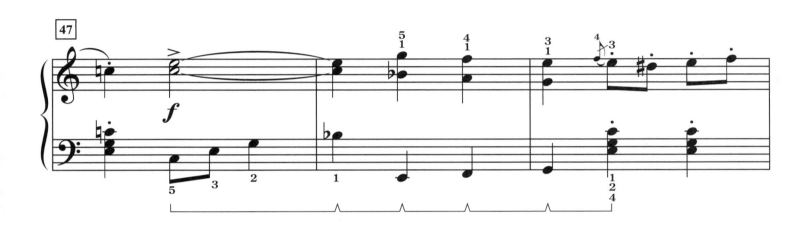

Gloria

Antonio Vivaldi (1678–1741)
RV 589
Arranged by Bruce Nelson

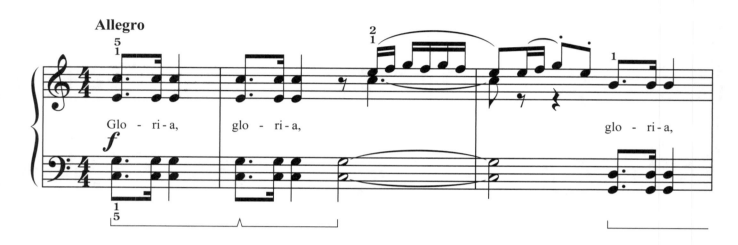

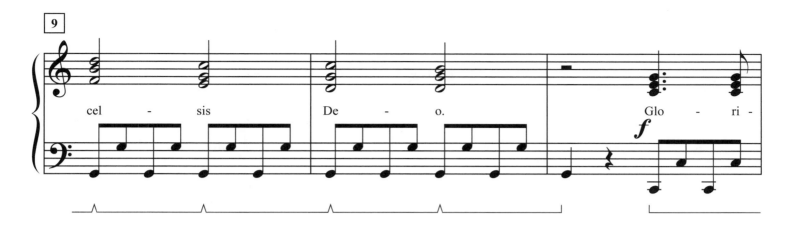

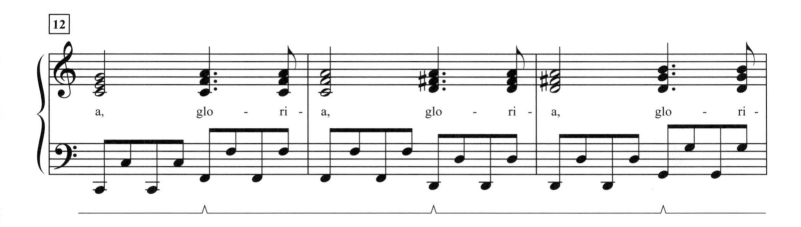

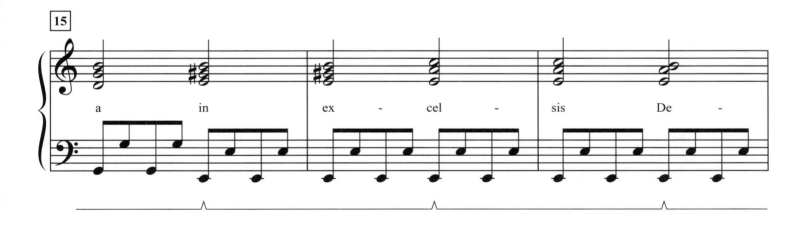

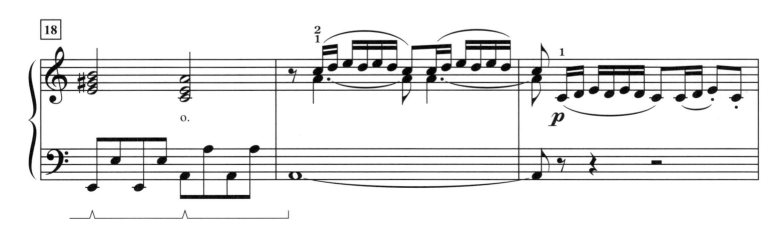

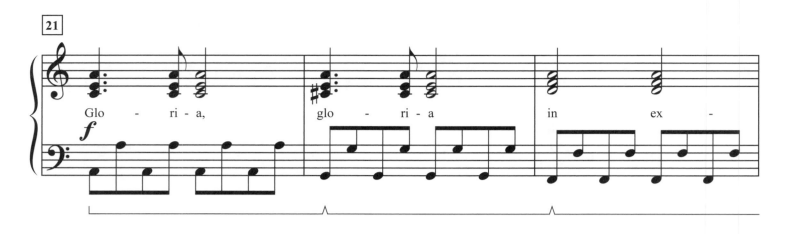

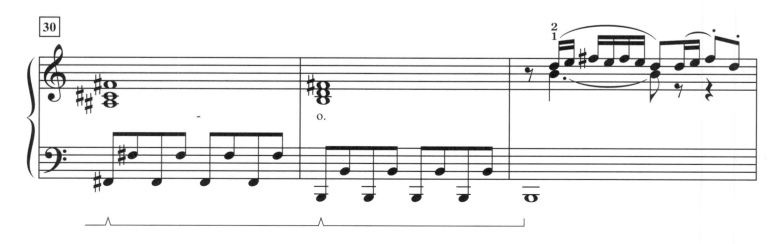

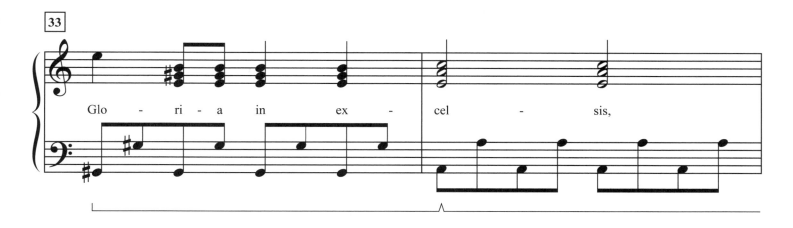

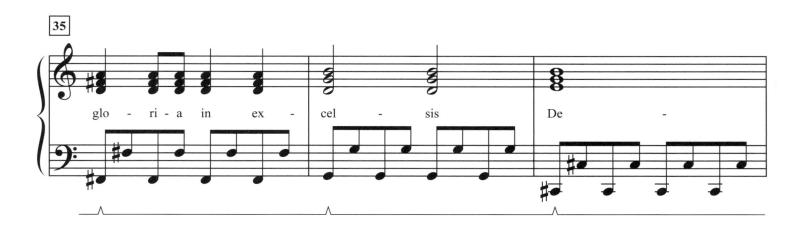

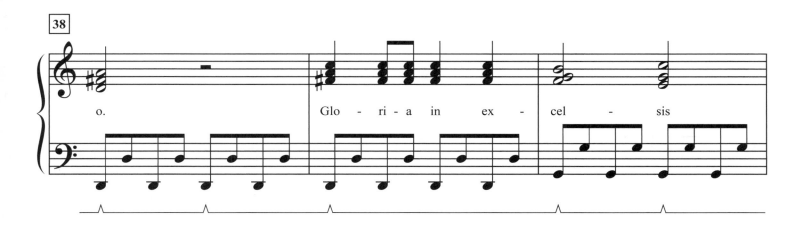

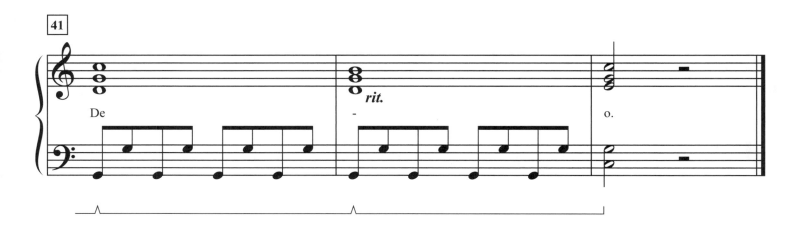

Mandolin Concerto in C Major

(First Movement)

Antonio Vivaldi (1678–1741)
RV 425
Arranged by Bruce Nelson

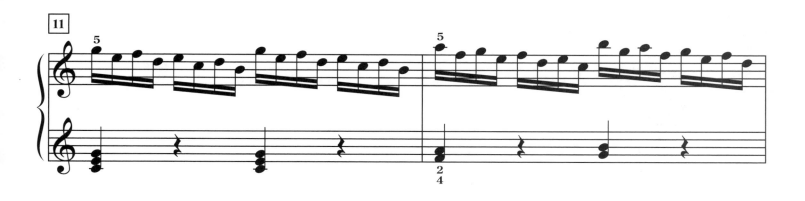

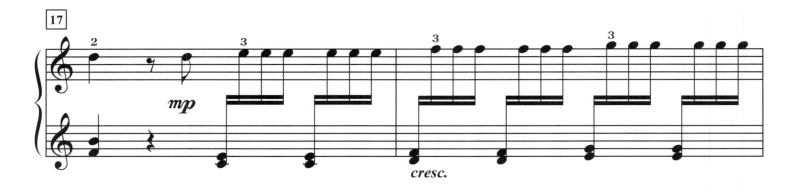

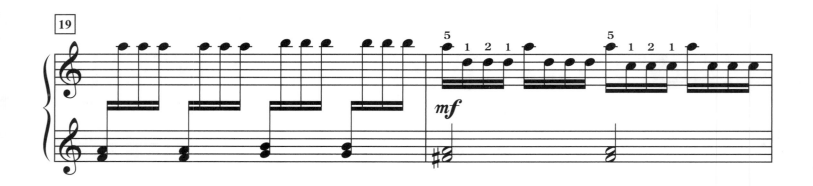

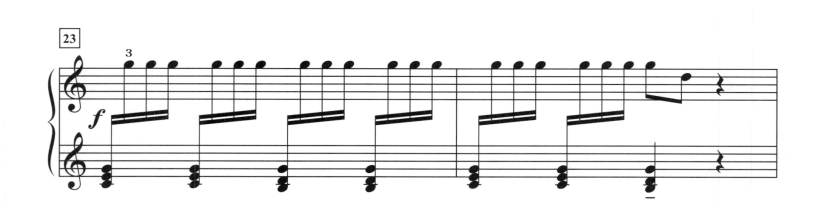

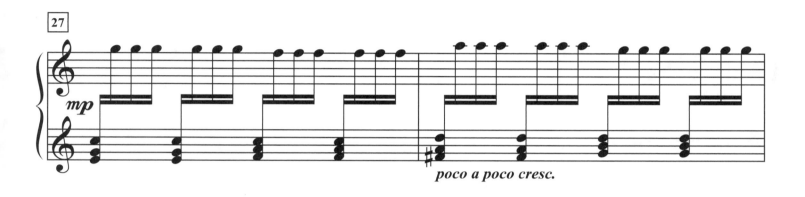

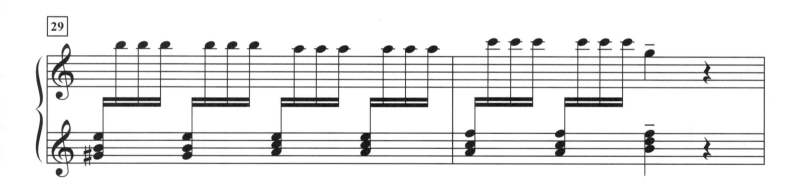

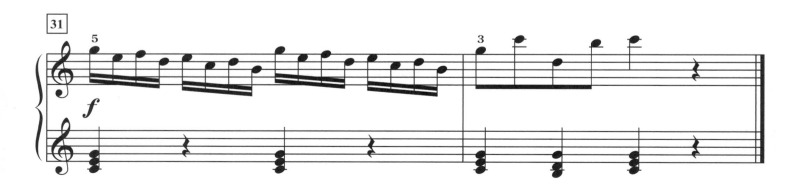

Spring

(from *The Four Seasons*)

Antonio Vivaldi (1678–1741)
Op. 8, No. 1, RV 269
Arranged by Bruce Nelson

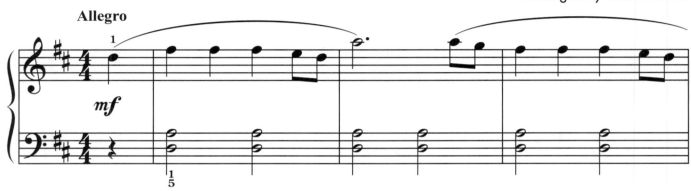

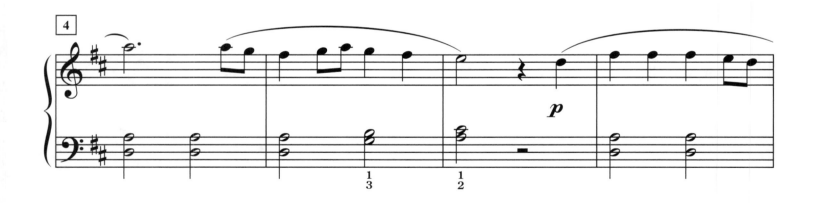

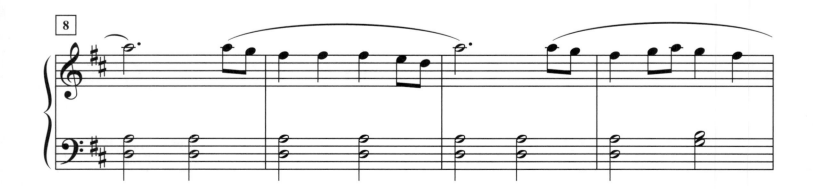

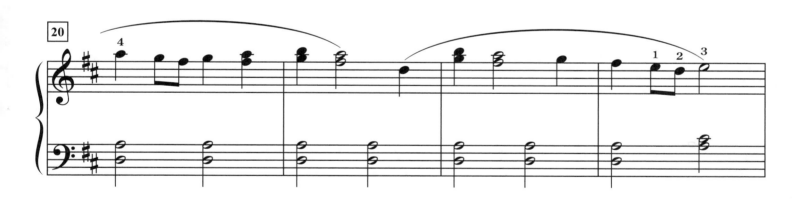

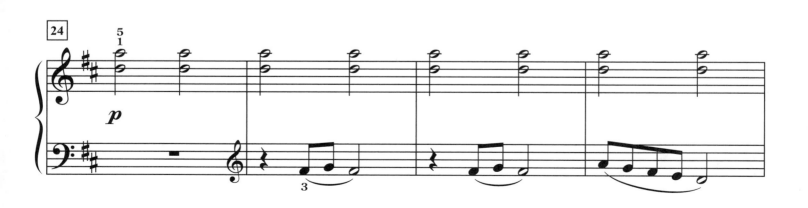

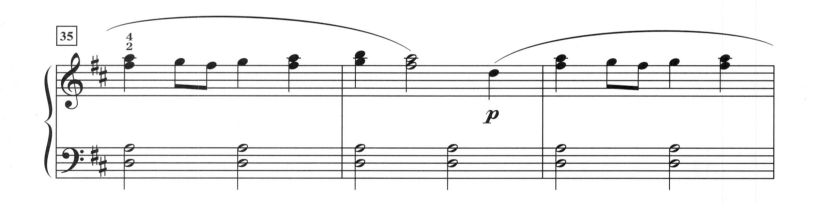